SHE TAKES HER
CHANCES

Janette Williams

Copyright © Janette Williams 2025

The moral right of this author has been asserted.

All rights reserved.

All characters and events in this publication, other than those clearly in the public domain, are fictitious and any resemblance to real persons, living or dead, is purely coincidental.

No part of this publication may be reproduced, stored in a retrieval system, or transmitted, in any form or by any means, without the prior permission in writing of the publisher, nor be otherwise circulated in any form of binding or cover other than that in which it is published and without a similar condition including this condition being imposed on the subsequent purchaser.

Editing, design, typesetting and publishing by UK Book Publishing

www.ukbookpublishing.com

ISBN: 978-1-917329-68-2

SHE TAKES HER
CHANCES

CHAPTER 1

'I don't want to go to Mrs Parson's house. It smells,' I whined, clutching Kip, my floppy, beige rabbit with long ears.

'We must go, Julia. We're too young to go to Daddy's funeral,' my sister Helen retorted.

She was eight, and I was two years younger.

'I'll pick you both up as soon as possible,' Mummy said.

The smell of mothballs reminded me of Mrs Parson's house, where we stayed after my father, Eric, died. She lived nearby and promised to look after us while Mummy attended the funeral. At lunchtime, we sat on straight-backed chairs with hard seats surrounded by dark furniture and heavy curtains. We struggled through plates of chopped meat in a nasty-smelling gravy, with soggy turnips and swede with a small dollop of mashed potato. Her steamed pudding was only half-cooked and sat in lumpy custard, and she insisted we ate everything on our plates, which made Helen and me sick.

Daddy fell ill during the flu epidemic in 1951, was taken to hospital by ambulance and never returned home, leaving a black hole where he should have been. Our mother, Angela, told us that he was with the angels, no longer suffering and at peace, and I imagined him lying on a large white bed, surrounded by wafting sylph-like figures with wings. He taught Maths and Science at a private school, although literature was his first love. I remember him reciting whole chunks of a bedtime story without reading from the book, his bespectacled face looking at me and holding my hand at the scary scenes. After he died, I shall never forget the sadness that permeated every corner of our house.

Unlike Mrs Parson, Mother was a good cook and taught us how to make pies and cakes, although Helen was the budding chef. I would watch them standing together, chopping, mixing or garnishing at the worktop. Helen would measure the flour, carefully pour it into the bowl, and cut the butter into small, neat pieces. She'd wipe up any spilt ingredients before Mummy noticed. On Helen's tenth birthday, two halves of a Victoria sponge, straight from the oven, sat waiting to be made whole by an oozy filling. Helen wanted to colour the icing pink, but when she tipped the bottle of liquid into the bowl, the icing turned dark red. Mummy came to the rescue and helped her blend in the mixture, and we watched the icing dribble down the sides of the cake, a thick, pink avalanche. But when I grabbed the bowl to scoop up the remaining icing into my mouth, Helen snatched the spoon and ate the lot. The finished cake sat in the middle of the table with "HAPY BIRTHDAY HELEN" in chocolate buttons, surrounded by party fare of biscuits, sandwiches, bowls of jelly and ice cream.

'You've spelt "Happy" wrong, Helen,' I said and stuck in another button to make it right. Helen invited her school friend, Anita, always a willing doctor and nurse playmate. After devouring the birthday spread of cakes, biscuits and a few little sandwiches, Helen and Anita dressed in their

CHAPTER 1

toy nurse's uniforms and prepared the hospital ward with bandages, needles, fake medicines and ointments. They lined up the dolls to be the patients, including me, who was always the most seriously ill on the ward.

'Julia, keep still. I must jab you,' Helen said, taking a toy needle and jamming it into my arm.

'Ouch, that hurt,' I shouted.

After getting thoroughly bored with lying on the floor pretending to be ill, I took my chance.

'Helen, could I have a go on your new bike, please? I feel better now,' I asked.

'No, you can't. Wait until your birthday.'

'I'm going outside, then.'

'Don't be long, Julia. It's still a little chilly out there,' Mummy called.

We were having a cold spell although it was mid-April. When I was outside, I saw Mummy and Helen chatting and giggling, before Anita's mother arrived to collect her.

Helen was close to Mum, while I stood on the outside, alone. Or this is what I thought, but I don't remember many occasions when they drew me into their little world. Sometimes, as I grew older, I felt trapped and wanted more space in a different environment away from the four walls of our house. Maybe I was born difficult and rebellious.

We lived in a brick and flintstone cottage on a quiet road opposite a church with a Norman tower. The front garden was small with a squeaky gate, partly obscured by a honeysuckle bush, and a tufted square of grass at the back passed as a lawn bordered by phlox and hollyhocks in flower beds that could do with a spot of weeding. At the end of the garden, we had a small orchard with apple, pear, and plum trees by a stone wall. Each year's crop was too much for us, so we filled boxes with the ripening apples, pears and plums in neat rows, and sold the fruit. I loved to climb the stumpy fruit trees, sit at the junction of two fat branches, and glimpse the two ponies next door at the end of their field. Sometimes, the ponies would wander over and eat our windfall apples, their jaws crunching the fruit.

If Mother saw me, she would call out from the open window to be careful, and when I pretended I hadn't heard, she'd rush out and lift me down, my flaying legs and arms like octopus tentacles.

The farmer who owned the ponies asked if we'd like to ride them, and Betty, his wife, could give us lessons. Helen wasn't interested, but I was keen to try something new. Betty lent me jodhpurs and a riding hat, and when we moved into a trot and then a canter, I felt excited and confident to conquer any obstacle. The pony's name was Plucky, and when Betty was free at the weekend, we would ride out into the country lanes and through woodland. Back home, I tried to persuade Helen to come, but she was more interested in her hospital games. When Betty and the family moved away, my riding experience ended as the new people didn't keep horses and left the field empty. From the tree, it looked neglected, taken over by thistle and stinging nettles, and I missed my rides on Plucky.

Saturday afternoon was hair-wash time. I had to bend my head over the basin and hated the feel of the water trickling down my front. I'd wriggle and scream for the towel to stop the shampoo dripping into my eyes, making them sting. When it was dry, Mummy commented on the

CHAPTER 1

auburn lights and plaited my thick hair, but the plaits hurt, and I couldn't wait to undo them.

'What about Helen's hair? When's it her turn?' I asked.

'I've done Helen's. It's clean and dry and not as thick as yours.'

'It's straggly,' I said.

After the hair wash, I couldn't wait to disappear into the pages of my story books, flying out like Wendy in Peter Pan or finding the magic Psammead in Five Children and It, who became my special friend.

'Who are you talking to, Julia? Why not help Helen with the dishes.'

'I laid the table,' I said.

On Sundays, we sometimes crossed the road, with Mummy holding our hands, to attend the morning service. The congregation was usually sparse, but you could count on the 'faithful ones' and sometimes a few extras. Often, we whined, 'Do we have to,' but she didn't always insist, and we remained at home. But when our grandfather visited, he made sure we were ready in good time and led us to the pews at the front. His tenor voice reverberated around the walls when he sang the hymns while we shrunk into our neat clothes.

When the house started to sag with peeling wallpaper, walls that needed a fresh coat of paint and pockets of ash lying in the empty grates, Mummy looked sad and lost the inclination to light fires that used to burn when my father was alive. 'We must keep stocked up with fuel,' he'd say, and found time from his teaching post to keep them going. But after he died, Mother bought paraffin to fill the oil stove. When she'd lit the wick and closed the lid, I used to watch, mesmerised by the pattern on the ceiling from the flickering light, hoping a genie would fly out. Once, Helen backed into the stove pretending to be a dancer in the Russian ballet and burnt her leg.

'Mummy, it hurts,' she screamed.

'You must be careful, Helen, of the oil stove.'

Mummy inspected the raw wound on the back of her leg and bandaged it with a burn lotion, but when it became red and infected, she called the doctor, who prescribed a special ointment for healing. At night, I heard Helen crying from her sore leg, but when she went into Mummy's bed for comfort, I climbed in and squashed up against them.

'There's no room. Go back to your bed,' Helen would say.

A few times, I went into Mummy's bed after a nightmare, but she said I was a fidget and disturbed her much-needed sleep, making me reluctant to do it again.

When my sister was studying for the grammar school entrance exam, I was told not to interrupt but to help in the house or amuse myself. I sat at the piano in a corner by the fireplace, practising scales and arpeggios, or playing a piece I knew by heart. Daddy used to pay for my lessons, but when he died, the teacher reduced the fees so I could continue, and I passed Grade 6 with distinction, which gave my mother false hopes. Helen wanted to go to dance classes instead of piano lessons, but she preferred tap dancing to classical ballet and used the kitchen floor to practise. Her little feet clattered and flew in all directions, and the drama teacher chose her to be in a school concert. Mummy spent every evening making her dress with a flouncy, yellow and black skirt, which fitted Helen perfectly, and at the concert, we clapped until our hands ached when Helen finished her performance.

CHAPTER 1

Helen failed the grammar school entrance exam and attended the local secondary modern school. Although Mummy was disappointed, my sister was happy because some of her friends at the junior school didn't pass either and went with her to the new school.

Two years later, I took the exam and passed, making our school journeys go in different directions, with Helen on her bicycle and me on a bus for an hour to get to the school surrounded by playing fields and farmland. I made friends with Clare, who wasn't at my junior school, and her quiet resolve helped me feel settled, and we were lifelong friends. We belonged to a group that would fall out and then make up or swap over with best friends. Neither of us was in the school sports teams, but we sang in the school choir and were in a production of Gilbert and Sullivan's Pirates of Penzance. Clare was a pirate, and I was a policeman, and we had fun dressing up in the costumes and daubing our faces with stage makeup, making a moustache, or beard, thick, sticky and black.

During a lunch break, I told the girls about my scary visit to the doctor. I'd discovered a rash on my neck and shoulders, and Mummy suggested we make an appointment to see the local GP. We decided to walk the 20-minute journey, and as the day was fine, I wore a skirt and a short-sleeved blouse without a jacket or cardigan. On the way, the rash started to itch, and I scratched the area, making it red and sore. We passed large houses set back from the road with well-cut lawns and flower beds showing bright colours and trees that formed a shady canopy. In the waiting room, I thought about the houses and jumped when Dr Wainwright, a well-built man in his mid-40s with a high forehead and hooded eyes, called us into the surgery. I wanted to go in alone, but Mummy followed and sat in a chair away from the consultation area.

'You're becoming an attractive young lady, Julia. What's the problem today?'

He asked me to remove my top, but the buttons got caught in the eyelets as I tried to push them through, with the doctor watching me all the time.

'Put your blouse on the chair over there,' he said.

I hadn't reached the stage of wearing a bra at 14 but instead wore a vest. Sometimes, I borrowed Helen's, but that day, I forgot and felt awkward as the doctor inspected the rash with a magnifying glass and prescribed a lotion, saying it was eczema and had I been worried about schoolwork.

'If it's not better in two weeks, you should make another appointment.'

He wrote down the prescription and gave it to Mum to take to the chemist.

I didn't talk much on the way home, and when we opened the front door, the gloom of the house sent me under the fruit trees. I got lost in Gone with the Wind and pretended to be Scarlett O'Hara. After two weeks, we made another appointment as the rash hadn't improved.

'Can I borrow your bra, Helen? It was so embarrassing when I went before.'

'Take this one,' she said, and although it looked too big, I put it on.

But Dr Wainwright was on leave, and a locum saw me who prescribed a different lotion, and the rash went away in a few days. The girls were quiet, eyes wide. One said she was glad he wasn't their doctor, and another said their

CHAPTER 1

doctor would never behave like that. They all said 'gross' and made a face.

One evening, Mummy told us she was looking for a job.

'What for?' I asked.

'We need the money. It should be obvious by the state of the house.'

'None of the girls' mothers at school, work,' I said.

'Some of them do at my school,' Helen replied.

Mummy bought a newspaper and looked at the Situations Vacant pages, ignoring those for a cleaner, shop assistant, or waitress, and focused on office jobs. She highlighted an advertisement for a Secretary Typist position to a Senior Architect.

'Are you going to apply? I didn't know you could type,' I said.

'Yes, Julia, I'll write a letter today. I learned to type at school, believe it or not.'

She raided a savings account and bought a linen dress, heeled shoes and a new handbag in case she was lucky enough to get an interview, and when she did, a woman in a suit with her hair curled into a bun at the back of her neck greeted her and placed a typed sheet on the desk for her to copy. She said her hands were shaking so much they kept slipping off the keys, but when she'd finished typing, the woman took her to meet the boss. She could hardly walk the length of the office to the polished mahogany desk where Ian McClain sat, his dark hair and neat features making her stumble over her words, but when he said, 'When can you start,' she couldn't wait to tell us.

Her face took on a glow with new cosmetics, her slim figure fitted into the dresses, and her eyes shone. She got up at least an hour earlier, clattering down in the kitchen while we slouched over our breakfast cereal, yawning and rubbing our eyes.

'See you this evening. I'm getting a lift with someone from work who has a car.'

'Ladida,' I said.

Helen and I raised an eyebrow when she said she was going to a party with a work friend. She wore a new orange dress she'd bought with her take-home pay and when we saw her, she didn't look like the same person.

'What do we have to eat?' Helen asked.

'There's cold meat and salad and some pudding left over from yesterday. I'll cook a nice Sunday lunch to make up.'

Although she crept up the stairs, we heard the creaks, sighed with relief, turned over and went back to sleep.

The rhythm of our existence changed when Mum started her job.

After school, when she wasn't there, we felt abandoned and had to make our own drinks and afternoon snacks. One afternoon, Helen grabbed me by the arm.

'I've got something to tell you about Mum after the match on Saturday.'

Helen played hockey for the school. The sports teacher told her she had a keen eye for the ball, good coordination, and would be an asset to the team. Often, they won the matches against other schools, but on the Saturday in question, they had lost.

'What about Mum?' I said, intrigued.

'On Saturday, I felt a bit down when we lost the match, and as I was gazing out of the bus window watching the shoppers do their last-minute rush, I thought I saw Mum

CHAPTER 1

walking along with a man. When the bus stopped to let off some passengers, I saw their backs going into the corner cafe, but when we moved off, they'd disappeared.'

'Maybe it wasn't her,' I said.

'Let's watch and wait,' was her reply.

CHAPTER 2

We didn't have to wait long before the mystery of Mummy with a strange man was solved. One evening at supper, Mummy turned to us with a bashful look.

'I've met someone,' she said, looking from Helen to me.

'Who, a man?' said Helen.

'My boss at work.'

'Bit of a cliché,' I said.

'It's serious. We are getting married, and I'd like you to meet Ian. I suggest he comes for Sunday lunch.'

We were silent, and I pushed away my plate.

'Married! A stranger living in our house! No way!'

I couldn't envisage a man we didn't know in Mummy's bed and part of our household, and I hoped it was a flash in the pan, and not serious.

'Are you sure, Mum?"' said Helen.

'I'm very sure. You'll grow up and leave home, and I'll be alone. Ian and I love each other. Give us a chance. He's kind, understanding and good company.'

'So, he'll move in here?' said Helen.

'No, we're moving to his house, which is bigger and much nicer.'

'Supposing we don't want to move,' I said.

'You'll like the house.'

CHAPTER 2

'Not the point,' I replied.

Her boss was an architect called Ian McClain. He looked up from his desk and smiled. 'Angela, I love your new hairstyle, your outfit is stunning, and best of all, I have nothing but praise for your shorthand skills, so down to work.'

His dark eyes brought a flush to her face and made her trip before she sat opposite him, notebook and pencil in hand. She could barely concentrate on his letters about modern architecture, architraves, cornices and mullioned windows, and had to keep stopping herself from gazing at his mouth, which showed a slightly protruding front tooth as he spoke. Her shorthand was always neat, making it easy to type his letters with no mistakes. He usually dictated in the morning when her outfits were crisp and fresh.

The night before, she slowly went through her three dresses and two suits and never wore the same outfit on consecutive days. She pulled her hair back into a knot at the base of her neck and finished the ensemble with a dash of eyeshadow and pink lipstick. Her final touch was a discreet use of the perfume Madame Rochas, rubbed on her neck and wrists. She'd bought a small bottle from a department store in the nearby town and loved breathing in the exotic aroma.

During the lunch break, Ian went out with colleagues to a local pub while the rest of the office bought a sandwich from a local shop or occasionally went to a cafe. If Mum had time, she would make a packed lunch and eat it at her desk, but she often fantasized about spending her lunchtimes with Ian while we complained daily about our school dinners. Her boss was usually away in the afternoon, allowing her to type his letters and organize his diary. Sometimes, Mummy worked late to type an urgent report, and he'd come and stand by her desk to check on her progress as she sat in a cloud of yearning. She wondered what his home life was like and what sort of house he lived in. He talked about Barny, his labrador, and she thought he lived in the country, but they both knew they were single, their spouses dying prematurely.

One Saturday afternoon, when she wanted to buy lamb chops for the weekend, she felt faint and in a cold sweat.

'Sorry, I have to go,' she said to the blood-spattered man behind the counter and went to the library where she sat to recover. She put her head down on a table spread with newspapers and magazines, hoping the spell would pass, but became aware of a slight pressure on her back, which made her look up.

'Hello, Ian. What a surprise seeing you!'

'Angela, are you all right? Let me buy you a cup of tea and something to eat. The teashop is nearby.'

He guided her into the crowded cafe, and they found a recently vacated table with half-eaten scones and a small bowl of jam with a spoon stuck in it. He called the waitress to clear the debris and ordered tea and a plate of cakes.

'I don't know what came over me. I'm probably tired.'

'With two teenagers, I'm not surprised. It's lucky I came into the library and saw you.'

'I must go soon. The girls will wonder where I am.'

'Would you like to come and see me at my house? It would be more relaxed for us to get to know each other better. I don't usually ask staff out on dates, but this is different, Angela.'

CHAPTER 2

She told him she'd give it some thought, and after he'd dropped her near the house, she stood in the kitchen, unable to concentrate on what to cook for our evening meal.

I joined her, standing by the sink.

'You're quiet, Mum. Want any help?'

'Peel some potatoes, please, Julia,' she said.

She accepted Ian's invitation, and he arranged to pick her up at the end of the road by the village school. Helen was out at a hockey match, and I was in my room deep in homework. Ian said Mum looked ravishing in her new dress and jacket, brushed gently by her loose shoulder-length hair. He helped her into his car, and as she concentrated on the fields and patches of woodland, she had a sense of entering another stage of her life. She watched his face, bewitched by his pointed nose with a slight bump, and wondered where the relationship would lead her. They turned into a country lane, bumping over the potholes and stopped outside a long stone house called Thornfield, surrounded by a large garden. The front door opened onto a square hall with several rooms leading off, and when she looked up, she saw a balcony of dark wood and a half-open door. The house was full of original pictures, books, and artefacts, and she looked forward to discovering their history.

'Barny, come here, good boy, you mustn't jump up. Go to your basket, Barny. Sorry, Angela, he isn't usually boisterous like this.'

'I'm not used to dogs, but I will say hello to your cat over there.'

'His name is Cobbles, and he's old.' But the tabby cat ignored her and stayed curled up by the Inglenook, twitching an ear.

'My wife lived in the house until she died two years ago of an inoperable cancer. We were unable to have children, which was a sadness for her.'

'Did you want children?'

'Not particularly, only to please her. And how did you meet your husband?'

She always felt a deep hole whenever she thought of our father and couldn't forget his drawn, grey face in the hospital bed. She hesitated before explaining.

'He was the son of family friends and ten years older than me. I married at 21, and the children were young when he died.'

'Was it sudden?'

'He caught flu in the epidemic and got pneumonia.'

'What about your parents?'

'My mother died before Julia was born, but my father visits us occasionally. He lives over 100 miles away, and it's a long journey for him.'

'So, most of the time, you've been a single mother. That must be hard.'

'Not always easy,' she replied.

As the day had become cloudy with a chilly wind, Ian struck a match to the laid fire, and soon his fireplace became alive with orange leaping flames. They sat together on the deep sofa with a glass of sherry until she jumped up like Cinderella, spilling drops on the carpet.

'I must go now,' she said, straightening her skirt.

'You're always rushing off. You'll have to tell the girls about us. We must stop behaving like teenagers,' he said.

When he kissed her before she got in the car, she felt the frisson again and couldn't wait until Monday morning.

CHAPTER 2

This time, he dropped her at the bus stop near our house, kissed her again before she got out of the car and waited until he saw her enter the house.

If someone saw our kitchen on the Sunday morning of Ian's visit, they would think a bomb had landed. Mummy didn't sleep well the night before and hustled us to assist with the roast beef, vegetables and a choice of pudding. Helen's domestic attributes were more advanced than mine, but without our help, she would have struggled.

'Wear a nice dress today, Julia, and make an effort. You look very pretty when you try.'

But her words were lost as she slipped on something in the kitchen, dropped a bowl and crashed to the floor. She saw her leg bleeding from the broken glass and asked Helen to help her up the stairs, who bathed the gash using a roll of lint from the bathroom cupboard.

Helen pressed the dressing hard on the cut, and when she lifted the lint to check, it had stopped bleeding. Mum reclined in a chair to rest the bandaged leg while I swept up the broken pieces scattered across the kitchen floor; Helen didn't think the cut would need stitches, although she would keep an eye on it. Mummy worried it was a bad omen, but we reassured her that it was because she was nervous, and everything would work out for the best. Mummy knew Ian wouldn't be late, and when she saw him from the window lock the car door, check his watch, and straighten his cravat before lifting the knocker, she made sure everything looked in order, but when we sat down for lunch, we were like statues facing our plates of food.

'Do start, it'll get cold,' she said.

'I'll pour the wine, a special one from my cellar. Do we have a corkscrew?' said Ian.

'I'll get it,' said Helen.

The silence was awkward, waiting for Helen to return with the only corkscrew we had kept at the back of a kitchen drawer.

'How's school, Julia? What are your A-Level subjects?' Ian asked, half-turning towards me.

'Oh, the usual,' I said, as distantly as possible, wondering what he knew about A-level subjects.

'She's doing English, French and History,' Mum said.

'Good subjects that fit together,' he said, smiling at Mum.

'She's a bright girl,' Mummy said, a rare flash of confidence passing over her face.

'I hear you're training to be a nurse, Helen. You've had some good experience today with your mother's leg.'

'She'll probably marry a doctor,' I said.

'Would you like a second helping, Ian?' Mum said, glancing at me.

Mum's choice of either a steamed pudding oozing with syrup to be topped by custard from a jug or a sherry trifle exuded an air of luxury, and we managed a helping of both.

Mummy suggested we play Scrabble to fill the afternoon, and while she went and got the game out of the cupboard, we cleared the table, and Ian helped take out the dirty dishes and piled them neatly in the kitchen.

'We'll do the washing up later on,' Mummy said.

She set up the board and tiles on the table, volunteered to be the scorer and used the pad and pencil kept with the Scrabble game.

'I start,' said Ian, who'd picked an 'A' from the bag.

'I've got masses of vowels,' exclaimed Helen.

'You're not supposed to tell us,' I said.

CHAPTER 2

Ian didn't take long and put down his first word, "Beach".

'You're next, Julia,' Mum said.

I attached "Blazer" to the letter "b".

'Good one. Now you, Helen.'

'Ah, I know, "Zoo",' said Helen.

'Good use of the "Z",' said Ian.

'Now my turn,' said Mother, taking longer than anyone else.

'Come on, Mum. We haven't got all day.'

Her word was "Lover", making her titter and blush. I could see Mum was so in love with Ian and I was sincerely happy for her, but something about him perturbed me. Maybe it was nothing, only a slight personality clash.

'It could mean the lover of anything,' I said.

An hour later, I had used up all my letters except the word "Groak" and put it on the board.

'Is that a word? Don't you mean "Croak"?' said Ian.

'No. Groak is an old Scottish word meaning "longingly watch people eat".'

'Ah, the English A-level student has won,' Ian said after checking in the dictionary.

'I hope there'll be more opportunities like this so we can all take turns being the winner,' he added.

It was dark outside, and when he prepared to leave, Mummy followed him, and they stood on the doorstep talking in low tones for ages. Later on, when we had retired to bed, Helen came into my room, and we talked about the difficulty of moving to a different environment and having a stepfather we hardly knew. I felt apprehensive, unsure I liked him, and could never call him Daddy or Dad. Helen was more optimistic and tried to persuade me it would work out for the best. Mother told me she caught snatches of our conversation that night and worried about us and whether we'd find it stressful to adapt to a new life.

Before we moved to Thornfield, I hugged one of the fruit trees in our garden, reminding Mummy of when I was a young child, and she had to pull me off the branches when I refused to come down. I was heartbroken to leave our cottage, however bigger and better Ian's house was, but sensed Mum's excitement and relief that her life would be more settled and secure.

CHAPTER 3

On Mummy and Ian's wedding day, the scudding clouds hid the sun as if the day wasn't sure what to do, with a cold wind from the north. Mum's cream suit with a dark green trim hung waiting to be slipped over a new bra, pants, petticoat, suspender belt, and stockings, as she didn't like those new-fangled nylon tights. Mummy travelled with Grandpa to the Registry Office, and Ian's brother, Callum, and his wife, Nadine, took Helen and me in their Aston Martin, giving the girls at school a topic of conversation for the rest of the term.

An official ushered us into a formal room with rows of empty chairs, prints of flowers on the walls, and two vases of fresh flowers on the tables. Our small number occupied the first row, with Callum and Nadine as witnesses. Ian had stayed in a hotel in the town and was waiting for his bride, in a dark suit and tie with deep red stripes. Mummy looked radiant, a cream hat framing her face, and we gazed at her when she walked into the room, with her hand on Grandpa's arm as she joined Ian for the ceremony. The couple faced the Celebrant to say their vows, a strong voice from Ian when you could hear every word, in contrast to Mummy's soft voice, the words swallowed and unclear. They exchanged plain gold rings, but I never saw Ian wearing his; instead, he had a family ring on his little finger with a black stone set in gold. Helen and I couldn't believe Mum was married and we had a stepfather in such a short time, but outside the registry office, Nadine looked like the bride in her Mary Quant outfit and cloche hat. The wind chased us to our cars, and we drove to Thornfield.

We were welcomed by Mrs Tidey, Ian's housekeeper, standing at the front door wearing a large navy-blue straw hat that almost hid her whole face. She led us into the hall decked with vases of pink and cream flowers and a variety of cocktail food displayed on a table. Everyone agreed on how elegant Mummy looked and what a perfect couple they were. Callum popped the cork, poured the fizzing liquid into the tall glasses and said, 'to Ian and Angela'. They looked at each other under their eyelids while Callum read out one or two telegrams from guests unable to attend.

'Ian, where are you going for your honeymoon?' Nadine asked, taking a cocktail stick.

'Inner Hebrides to delve into our family's roots.'

'That's interesting, isn't it, Callum?' Nadine said.

'Maybe,' Callum said, and gulped his champagne.

'I hope the weather's good, and the islands aren't shrouded in mist,' Grandpa said with a twinkle.

Helen and I wandered into the dining room to look at the assembly of wedding gifts. Callum and Nadine had given them a complete dinner set in a blue design of country scenes of rabbits and grazing horses. Ian's work colleagues had clubbed together and bought them six cut glass whisky tumblers, and Grandpa had bequeathed a silver teapot, jug, sugar bowl, and tongs. Mrs Parson's gift was a set of china figurines in elaborate Victorian clothes

CHAPTER 3

of blue and white, and we'd pooled our pocket money to buy place mats in a trendy design of blue and green and hoped they'd have lots of dinner parties and use them. One or two packages from people we didn't know lay wrapped in silver wedding paper.

When we joined the others, Ian was anxious to make a move as it looked stormy for the long drive to the ferry.

'We'd better make tracks, darling, we have a ferry to catch. We'll ring when we arrive.'

Mummy looked tearful and hugged us for a long time.

'I'll miss you, girls, but Grandpa will stay for a few days, and Mrs T will look after you. We'll be back before you can say honeymoon.'

Ian hurried her to the car, and she sat in the front seat, looking towards the house, and after Ian had put the cases in the boot, I watched the car turn into the road at the bottom of the drive and hoped Mum was "in safe hands".

While they were on their honeymoon, we wanted to make the most of the warm weather and found four old deck chairs in the shed, put them on the terrace and sat facing the large expanse of lawn with a copse of oaks and horse chestnuts at the far end. Grandpa sat with his long legs stretched out and was always interested in what Helen and I were doing and laughed at our school stories and escapades.

He looked young for a man in his sixties, helped by a head of dark brown hair with a few flecks of grey. Mrs Tidey produced melt-in-the-mouth scones, jam, and cream for tea and brought them out to us as we basked in the sun, listening to the country sounds until the gathering twilight pushed us inside.

We didn't hear a word from the married couple, but when they returned, I was happy to see Mum looking well, her face more rounded with a touch of colour. The weather was hot with no breeze, and one day after school, I took my books into the garden and sat at the wrought-iron table, patchy with peeling paint, and noticed the French window was open, and when I looked in, there was an unfinished landscape resting on an easel. Mum was sorting out paintbrushes with her back to me, her hair tied back with a thin blue scarf. She turned round sharply when I spoke.

'Hello, Mummy, what's all this? I didn't know you were an artist!'

'I used to paint when I was younger, but when your father died, I gave it up and destroyed most of my art.'

'We haven't heard much about the honeymoon. Did you enjoy the Scottish Isles?'

'They were beautiful, and it didn't rain. We had misty days but also sunny ones, but there was one odd incident. We had a view of another island over a stony beach I wanted to paint, and I bought a pad and watercolours and asked Ian if he'd mind my spending a couple of hours sketching. He said he'd go for a walk and discover the area, but over lunch, he was quiet, so I spoke.'

I was intrigued to hear about the "odd" incident and waited to hear what Mummy had to say.

'"Ian, did I show you, my watercolour?"

'"No, you didn't. Show it to me later."

'But when I opened my sketchbook, the painting was missing, and I was sure I hadn't removed it. I looked everywhere; through my sketch book, my suitcase and the chest of drawers, but it was nowhere.'

CHAPTER 3

I was sure Mother wasn't getting forgetful, which left it open to interpretation. I wondered if Ian had taken it for some reason but couldn't think why he would, without asking her.

She joined an art class and bought oils, watercolours, canvases, brushes, and a palette. The room was at the back of the house, with a French window opening onto the garden, and she thought it ideal for a little studio. She moved boxes of photos and letters to make space for her easel and found an old table for her supplies. I was excited to see Mother's creations and liked to watch her standing back from the current project, paintbrush in hand, with a furrow of concentration in the centre of her forehead. Sometimes, she'd arrange fruit and foliage from the garden with a backdrop to create a setting for still life. The rich oils gave them depth and invited you to pick them off the canvas. Once, I noticed a charcoal sketch of the back of a nude man, the bold strokes of his shoulders and buttocks exuding an erotic power.

Not long after their return, Ian planned to have a post-wedding party, and they compiled a guest list in neat columns of acceptances and refusals.

'Will you invite anyone from work, Mum?' Helen asked.

'Yes, there are a couple of women I like, one is married, and the other is engaged. We can invite their partners.'

'What about you, Helen?'

'Dougie.'

'He's a teddy boy,' I said. 'I'll invite my school friend Clare and her brother Colin.'

Mum bought a long yellow chiffon dress with small sleeves, which had Ian's approval, and Mrs Tidey said, 'You look lovely, Mrs McClain. Quite The lady of the Manor.'

I went on a shopping spree to find an outfit to wear that was different from my wedding one. I had three dresses hanging in the changing room at the department store, ready to be tried on. My stomach stuck out with the first one, and it was too tight around my hips. The second one came below my knee and made me look dowdy, and the third was too short, making my legs look fat. Eventually, the assistant found a cream short-sleeved silk dress with a round neckline and a belt, the hem just above the knee.

'Suits you perfectly and brings out the colour in your hair. Is it for a special occasion?'

Helen wore a miniskirt displaying her long, slim legs attracting lustful looks from the men. Mrs T oversaw catering while Ian organised the drinks and was pleased with the opportunity to use his state-of-the-art record player and his extensive collection of records. Fifty guests arrived, cars jostled for parking spots, ladies emerged in the latest fashion, and men looked dapper and ready for fun. I was relieved when Clare and Colin appeared.

'You look super-duper,' Clare said, showing off her blue silk dress that suited her figure.

'And this is Alex,' she said, introducing a fair-haired boy with prominent dark eyebrows.

He smiled and went to get us drinks and some nibbles. We sat and chatted.

'What are you going to do when you leave school, Julia?' Alex asked.

'Ian says I should apply to Oxford or Cambridge, but I've decided to go to London and work. What about you?'

'I've been accepted at Sheffield to do Civil Engineering.'

CHAPTER 3

I was about to ask him to describe civil engineering when Mummy came to say "hello". She looked uncomfortable and said she found it difficult to remember the names of Ian's friends. When she moved to the edge of a group, a woman in a long taffeta dress said, 'Skirts are getting too short, and it's always on the bad legs.'

'I think they're fun,' Mum said.

'And the so-called pop songs are so raucous now,' continued the woman when, without warning, all eyes turned towards the revving of motorbikes outside and the sound of male voices. Dougie had arrived with a mate who had greased hair and winkle-picker shoes. Helen came racing down the stairs, two at a time, as she knew Mother and Ian wouldn't approve, but it was too late as they'd gone over to the record pile looking for Elvis Presley or Jerry Lee Lewis. Dougie found a Bill Haley record and asked Mum to play it for them. She stopped Dean Martin singing Blue Moon and set the disk on the turntable, which encouraged a few guests to start jiving when Ian stormed over.

'Angela, what a racket!' he shouted and put the Blue Moon disk back on the turntable, but when he changed it, he scratched the surface, leaving a nasty groove.

'I was enjoying that,' I said to Alex.

'Is he strict?' he asked.

'We don't get on.'

'Do you fancy seeing a film? I'll find out the programme,' Alex said, but we were interrupted again when three boys in leather jackets burst through the front door.

'Right, mate, get a load of this place. Let's see if there's any booze going.'

Dougie rushed over but was overtaken by Ian and his brother Callum, telling them to buzz off home.

'Snotty bastards,' one of them said as they swaggered off into the night. Ian looked flushed but confident he'd sent the gatecrashers packing. Helen wanted Dougie to stay, but Ian told him to leave with the others, and Mummy told me later she felt like disappearing down the rabbit hole. I wanted to go to my bedroom as Clare and the others had gone, but instead, I sat on the bottom stair and was aware of Dr Wainwright leaning over me and asking if I'd like a drink. His breath smelt of whisky and cigarette smoke, making me gag, and although I told him I didn't want one, he brought me an orange and soda.

'Do you want to dance, Julia?' Dr Wainwright asked.

'I'll sit here and watch,' I replied, hoping he wouldn't insist.

The remaining guests danced slowly to an Ella Fitzgerald song, and I looked around for Helen, but she had probably gone to her bedroom. Later, I saw the doctor draped over a woman, whom I'm sure wasn't his wife, while Ian was standing in a corner, glass in hand, talking to a group of men, laughing at their jokes, and being one of the boys. Mother joined me and asked what the doctor wanted.

'Nothing, Mum. He got me a drink.'

'I wish everyone would go home now. I'm ready for bed,' Mum said, rubbing her forehead.

The next day, she told me she felt dissatisfied, as though her performance wasn't up to scratch, and she was insignificant without purpose.

'You were fine at the party, Mum. You looked gorgeous. Lots of people commented to me how pretty you were.

CHAPTER 3

Don't worry about Ian's choice of guests. They're probably acquaintances and not close friends, invited for their superficiality and who they think they are. You've got your art and a new group of like-minded friends to keep you interested.'

'Thank you, Julia. You're right, I have,' she said.

That night, lying in bed, my head was buzzing, and I couldn't drop off to sleep. I thought of Mum, who lacked self-confidence in the face of Ian's invitees, but she was fine and had enjoyed chatting to her work friends. And then I remembered the lecherous Dr Wainwright, leaning over me, smelling of booze and cigarette smoke, which made me want to gag and get away. But the best thing was the thrill of excitement thinking about going out with Alex, and I imagined all sorts of sexy scenarios. I hoped he would ring and invite me and not forget, or perhaps not mean it, but only said it to make conversation. I thought of him for a long time before I went to sleep.

CHAPTER 4

One evening, I heard from Alex. Luckily, I picked up the phone, and we arranged to see the film 'To Kill a Mockingbird' based on a book we'd both read. We had chatted at Mum and Ian's party, how intimate it was, although all we discussed were school subjects and university. I didn't want to be the first to arrive at the cinema, but when I did, I couldn't see him. I stood on the steps, but not sure which direction he'd come from, instead I studied the posters of forthcoming films, hoping he would come up behind me. But when I turned, I saw him hurrying along, and he apologised for being late although the film hadn't started. There was usually a queue snaking around the corner, but we went straight into the booking office for him to buy the tickets. The usher shone the light on two seats near the back, and as we sat together watching the rest of the trailers, his muskiness sent a tingle through me, and I felt thankful that the film's running time was over two hours.

I turned to watch his profile, hoping he would take my hand in his, but at the end, when we were coming down the cinema stairs, I tripped, and he caught and held me. We both laughed, and he said he liked my hair.

I had arranged to stay at Clare's that night as she was closer to the cinema. Alex had his mother's car, but when

CHAPTER 4

we'd stopped outside Clare's house, I took courage and turned towards him.

'Are you coming in?' I asked, my voice almost too soft to hear.

'No, I'm sorry, Julia, but I have to go.'

'Thanks for the film, Alex. I enjoyed it.'

'Me too.'

I waited a few more seconds before I opened the car door, but I didn't turn to wave and went straight in. Clare offered me a nightcap, but I declined, and we went to her bedroom and lay on the bed to discuss the evening. I was going to talk about Alex when we heard voices downstairs, and Clare's mother appeared in the doorway.

'Ian is here to give you a lift home,' she said, looking surprised.

'Is he? I told Mum I was staying at Clare's. I'd better go down and see him,' I said.

I hoped he wouldn't make a fuss and insisted I go home with him, but he didn't look too pleased and fidgeted with his ring.

'Why are you here, Ian? Mum said I could stay the night.'

'She didn't say anything to me, only you'd gone to see a film with Clare.'

I thought it best not to mention Alex. Either Mum had misunderstood, or he had.

'The car is outside. Go and collect your things. I don't want a wasted journey.'

I hesitated, but he looked so annoyed I thought I'd better comply. I was furious and didn't speak on the journey home even though he asked me several times about the film.

SHE TAKES HER CHANCES

The following Saturday, Mother's art group held an exhibition of members' works of art in the local library, and we were all invited to the opening. I wanted to ask Alex but was embarrassed after he hadn't suggested another date. Helen had two days off from her nursing course, and, for once, Ian left work early and was home on time. There were thirty in the art group, including Mummy, with an equal spread of men and women of all ages. Mummy introduced us to her friend Dorothy, a watercolourist who produced works of nature, plants and flowers and whose husband was a businessman. There was a sizeable gathering as the evening progressed, with three librarians and other members of the public. A woman wearing a purple coat spent the whole time giving a running commentary on each exhibit in such a loud voice we couldn't hear ourselves speak, and when she left, we sighed with relief. Ian was busy talking to one of the men he knew for most of the evening.

A panel of three had chosen a variety of styles and media. They picked two of Mummy's paintings, a still life of a bowl of deep-red cherries, the colour reflected on the glass, and a barn in a field of yellow wheat, both in oils on canvas. She was over the moon when a librarian bought her landscape, and Dorothy's husband had the cherry picture. The rest of the exhibits were a mixture of life drawings, portraits, landscapes, and still life. Helen and I dressed in short skirts and long boots and whizzed around the exhibition before sampling a glass of wine, which was too acidic for us, so we changed to fizzy lemonade and got stuck into sausage rolls, nuts and crisps. Mummy chatted excitedly, her cheeks growing red and flushed, with members of her group and was reluctant to go when the

CHAPTER 4

exhibition finished. We all left in a merry mood, but when we arrived home, everything changed.

Helen picked up a badge lying on the ground outside the front door.

'What's this, Ian?' she said, turning it over.

'No idea. Never seen it before.'

In the hall, there was a strange smell that was hard to place. It didn't feel like our house, but when we heard a shriek from Mum, we saw the door to the cocktail cabinet was open, falling off its hinges, with most of its contents missing. Two broken wine glasses lay by the fireplace, and an empty whisky bottle stood on the small table.

'Oh my God,' said Ian. 'We've been robbed. Where did they get in?'

He stormed around the house, shouting, checking doors and windows until he opened Mum's studio door and saw the French window ajar, causing a draught. He shouted at Mummy, saying it was her fault as she hadn't locked the door and told her to remember to do so without fail. He came towards her, his fist clenched, and I thought he was going to hit her. She backed away and said she must have been distracted as she always locked it. Ian continued his rant.

'The badge is from a biker's jacket. Not one of Helen's bloody friends, I hope.'

'They're not my friends,' said Helen. 'I don't see Dougie anymore.'

'They know where we live. I'm calling the police.'

Although we searched for missing valuables, they had only taken the liquor, and when two constables arrived to take details and items for fingerprints, they went from room to room to see if there were any clues. Helen told them she didn't know the names of Dougie's friends or the unwanted visitors, but explained where Dougie lived on a council estate, the other side of town, although she'd only been once when it was dark and difficult to remember. A younger-looking police constable took a small notebook and a blunt pencil from his pocket and asked Helen to repeat as much as she knew about Dougie and his friends. He wrote slowly, periodically looking up at her as she spoke, and when he'd finished, the police officers got up to leave and said they'd be in touch.

'All the locks will have to be changed immediately. We'll search again tomorrow, but we should go to bed now and get some rest. I'm taking Barny for a walk to cool off and clear my head. You women...' Ian said and grabbed the dog's lead.

The following day, Helen suggested we do some detective work on our own, go over to Dougie's house and see if we could find anything that might be helpful. We caught two buses, and, according to the map, it was a long walk from the bus stop to their address at the end of a row of terraced houses. On the way, we passed children playing, throwing balls against the wall or skipping in the road, and one of them tossed a ball that nearly hit Helen's nose. Dougie's door was green, the paint peeling to expose the wood underneath. When we knocked, a net curtain at the front window moved, and a girl in a black miniskirt opened the door. We asked for Dougie, who came out after she'd called him a few times.

'What yer want, Helen?'

'We had a break-in and checking it wasn't the gatecrashers.'

CHAPTER 4

'How would I know? What did they nick?'

'All the booze.'

'It's not them. They hate booze.'

'Just to warn you, the police may come knocking.'

'We'll be ready,' said Dougie and slammed the door.

We had no idea how true it was but hoped Dougie and his mates were not the culprits. We had to run for the first bus, but the second one took ages to arrive, and we were late back.

'I'm relieved it probably wasn't them, but can't think what I saw in Dougie,' Helen said when we'd settled on the bus.

'Your rebellious stage, Helen.'

When we arrived home after seeing Dougie, we entered through the side door and heard shouting.

'Angela, come here. I've got something to say.'

'Just a minute,' she called.

We stood still, fearful about what he'd say next.

'For God's sake, can't you leave the painting for just two seconds and answer me,' he snarled, striding into the studio.

'Sorry, darling, I was in the middle of a tricky stroke.'

'To hell with your tricky strokes, come here and listen.'

She took off her apron, put down the charcoal, checked she had locked the outside door, and left the room.

'Right. The police have arrested the culprits who took the liquor as they'd done other properties in the neighbourhood. That's the good news.'

'Was it the gatecrashers or to do with Dougie?'

'Neither, but I haven't finished. You should give the art a rest for a while as the house needs attention. Mrs Tidey can't do everything once a week.'

'I do as much as possible and fit in the art.'

'I see piles of ironing not done, dust lying on the surfaces, the house looking generally untidy and messy. Think about what I said.'

Not long afterwards, I began to see an improvement. There were neat piles of laundry in the airing cupboard, shiny surfaces, clean carpets, and the kitchen was tidy. Mum made an effort and cooked a substantial supper of a main course and pudding, but when Ian was away, her cooking skills slipped, and we had an omelette with salad, or she stayed in the studio with a sandwich.

But I missed Helen when she started her nurse training and lived in the nurses' home, and when she came home on her days off, it wasn't the same as before. Although we went to different schools, we would share stories and support each other, but now it was only Mum and me at home until Ian came in after work. One evening over supper, Ian said he'd been to my school to see the headmistress.

'When? Why did you go?' I asked, annoyed.

'To discuss your choice and enrolment at a university. The Headmistress said you were an excellent student and should go to Oxford or Cambridge.'

'Ian, as I said before, I've decided to go to London to live and work. I'll study for a degree later.'

'It may be more difficult when you're older. Now is the time. Anyway, what are you going to do in London? How will you support yourself?'

'There are many employment agencies, and I'll get a good job with my A Levels.'

'You can go to London when you've graduated, and there'd be more opportunities with a degree.'

CHAPTER 4

I understood his reasoning, but I was determined.

'You're being foolish, Julia, and I won't support you. What do you think, Angela?'

'I agree it might be more difficult to go to university when she's older, but I can understand if Julia wants a break from study.'

'Why can't you be sensible like Helen? Her training will prepare her for a worthwhile career in nursing, a choice of hospitals, and overseas if she wants to travel.'

It was lucky Helen wanted to train as a nurse. Nursing wouldn't suit me at all as I'd probably faint at the sight of anything nasty.

One day after school, I came home to see the breakfast dishes untouched and another pile in the sink. Upstairs, I heard sobbing and found Mum lying face down on her bed. In between her tears, she said when she'd gone to finish a landscape, all her art things had disappeared and, instead, were filing cabinets, a desk and an office chair. Mum looked in the bedrooms, downstairs rooms, the scullery and the garage but couldn't find them and said it was like a bad dream. I searched the house and thought I'd try the cellar, although I never went there as it scared me. Luckily, I knew where to find the key. Once, when Ian had asked me to get a bottle of wine, he told me the key was in a pot on his desk. His study smelt musty, and the top of his desk was clear except for a blotting-pad, a pen and the pot. When I tried the drawers, they were locked. I found the cellar key, but it took a while for me to open the door as the key was warped and wouldn't fit into the lock. I pushed it open and shone the torch to pinpoint the stone steps, and after feeling around, I found the light switch, but when I turned it on, the bulb flickered, making uneven shadows over Ian's wine stacked against the wall, a selection of red and white. Beyond the wine racks, all her art equipment was in an untidy heap, with the easel lying across the floor. A small window, streaked with grime, let in some light, but when I tried to open it, dead flies and wasps fell onto the floor and at the back of the cellar was a stone sink, the taps stuck and rusty. I picked up the easel, piled her artwork against the wall, and climbed the steps again, but the door had shut. I twisted the handle to open it, but it had jammed, and all I felt was the dark emptiness behind me. Mummy was in her bedroom and would never have heard me if I'd shouted. I slowly turned the handle one way, then the other, until it finally opened, my heart beating twice as fast as normal. I went into the kitchen, cleared the mess of unwashed dishes, made a pot of tea, and took it upstairs.

'Don't worry, Mummy, we'll sort this out,' I said, sitting on the bed. 'We'll make the most of the cellar space by moving the old crates and cleaning the window to give you some light. You could also fit a lamp down there for more light. Mrs Tidey will help.'

'Oh, don't bother Mrs T.'

'Of course, dear,' Mrs T said. 'I'll do it when I come on my cleaning day. Poor Mrs McClain, she paints some lovely pictures.'

Mrs Tidey kept her word and transformed the cellar, washed the window until it was clean and used her shoulder to push it open. Mum promised to do the housework and would only go in the cellar when Ian was out but must always remember to put away her art things. I hoped our plan would work as I had to put my head down and study

CHAPTER 4

for A Level exams. When I told Clare, she said Colin would always help with stuck windows.

One day, a vase of flowers appeared in the dining room from Ian, who'd bought them to say how clean and neat the house looked. I was suspicious and said she should be careful and hoped the flowers wouldn't soften her into submission. I was relieved she saw a lot of her friend, Dot, and they often painted in the cellar, their contrasting styles of Dot's detailed delicacy and Mummy's bolder brush strokes, a picture of their friendship. For safety, I suggested we took her finished artworks to store in my room and made several journeys transporting canvases and sketchbooks, putting them under my bed or at the back of the wardrobe. I moved the easel to a wall at the far end of the cellar, covered it with a cloth and put the paints and brushes in an old cardboard box.

If Mum was happy painting in the cellar, the atmosphere lifted a little, but for Ian to be so mean and demolish Mummy's little studio was horrible. He already had a comfortable and roomy study, so there was no need to have another one and leave poor Mummy with the cellar, although we'd made it suitable, with enough light and space. What was Ian's problem? Did he feel out of control when Mummy showed some independence? He had control when she was his secretary, but now as his wife, he was trying to kill her individuality. He cannot thwart her artistic talent, her overriding saviour.

CHAPTER 5

Now that the studio storm had abated and Mummy had resigned herself to working in the cellar or, if convenient, in Dot's studio, I had to concentrate on my studies in preparation for A-Level exams. Spring was edging in, but the mornings were still cold with frost on the ground, so getting dressed for school made me shiver. As Helen was living in the Nurses' Home, I didn't have her to urge me on, but once I'd had my toast and marmalade, I was ready to walk the mile to the bus stop, or if Mum were up, she'd give me a lift. When I arrived home in the afternoon, I'd have a hot drink and a piece of homemade cake before I disappeared upstairs to my room to delve into my textbooks and get lost in the Romantic poets or King Lear and his three daughters.

When Ian was away on business, and the house was at peace, Mummy and I ate our meals in the kitchen. We were warm and informal, enjoying Mum's leek and potato soup, shepherd's pie or a light flan. Sometimes, we ate her homemade bread straight from the oven, soft and yeasty. But if Ian was in, the three of us sat at the dining room table for the evening meal, with only the sound of clinking cutlery, until I excused myself to go and study. He couldn't criticise Mum's cooking as she was excellent in

CHAPTER 5

that department, and he would often have a glass of wine with her creations. Sometimes, Mummy joined him, and she began to love it and became quite the connoisseur. On odd occasions, he'd go down to the cellar to get a bottle, but he never commented on Mummy doing her artwork there.

One Saturday, when I was deep in Jane Eyre, there was a knock on my bedroom door.

'Come in,' I said, sick of Mr Rochester, who was blind and couldn't see Jane Eyre.

It was Mummy, who was always considerate and didn't barge in when I was studying.

'How about we take a break and go for a walk with Barny? We'll meet Dot there.'

It was just what I needed. We took Barny to a large area of trees, mainly oak and beech, with different sloping paths and a lake with varied pond life, including butterflies and newts. The trees had burst with new foliage, and the sun shone on the bright green leaves. Barny cavorted around, barking for us to throw the ball, but when we did, it landed near the water, and he bypassed it and ran straight into the lake. We shouted at him to come out, but Barny splashed around until Dot threw the ball in the opposite direction, which did the trick.

But running out of the lake, he sprayed dirty water everywhere, racing towards an elderly couple with a little terrier on a lead. The two dogs rubbed their noses while the friendly couple stood by and smiled, talked about the pleasant weather, patted Barny, and said what a lovely dog he was, all the while unnerved about the muddy water sprayed everywhere. I was invigorated and refreshed after the walk and glad I had gone, but Barny was exhausted and slept in his basket until morning.

The next day, Mum found him panting, whining and foaming at the mouth, looking like a sad, sick dog. Ian said he'd contact his vet friend, who very kindly opened the surgery, although it was Sunday. Ian carefully carried Barny to the car and put him on the back seat while Mummy sat and comforted him. The light was already on in the building, and once he was on the consulting table, the vet examined him thoroughly and said he'd caught a virus from the lake and should avoid it in the future. Mum and Ian kept him in their room that night, and by morning, Barny had improved but needed medication for a week and had to go back for a check-up. We all kept a careful eye on him on Sunday, and on Monday, Barny was in the garden, chasing a ball.

On Wednesday evening of that week, Ian was frantically charging around the house, looking for his passport.

'Have you seen it, Angela? I need it for a business trip to Paris.'

I was curious to know why Paris. Was the company expanding or moving to France? He never told Mummy anything about his work, and I was too scared to ask him.

'I haven't, Ian. Go and have a look in the study.'

'That's the first place I looked.'

'What about in the room that used to be Mum's studio, and you changed it into an office?' I said boldly, wondering if it would have any effect.

Ian didn't reply but went in and shut the door. He seemed to be in there for ages but eventually came out waving the passport. 'I found it behind the filing cabinet. Not sure how it got there,' he said grumpily.

CHAPTER 5

Over the next two months, I had to hunker down and study without too many interruptions. There was a lot of reading for the three subjects I'd chosen, and I didn't have much time for anything else. I was sad to say goodbye to my school friends who were going in different directions. Clare had been accepted at Southampton University to read Psychology, while others were going to teachers' or business colleges. Before they all disappeared, including me, I arranged to celebrate my birthday on August 9th at a nightclub in the nearby town. By then, we had received our results and celebrated our excellent grades.

I asked Helen if she'd like to join us for my birthday, but she declined, saying she wouldn't feel part of the group; however, Maggie, who was Helen's age and not in my class, accepted my invitation. Alex came, although he was with a girl I didn't know. Some weeks before, I had seen him in the town with, I think, the same girl, but it was difficult to identify her as they were in front of me and got lost in the crowd. Strangely, I didn't mind about the girl as I'd got over Alex and looked towards the future and my discovery of the different aspects of London. It was a fun evening without drama, and we danced with gay abandon after two years of serious study. When we were too tired to dance any more, Clare's father picked us up at midnight and dropped me at home en route to theirs. Mummy and Ian were in bed by the time I got in and didn't hear me creep up the stairs, even when I trod on the creaky one.

But not long before I had planned to leave for London, I woke up feeling achy with a slight headache and assumed I'd got tired and rundown.

'You look pale, Julia,' Mum said, concerned, when she entered my room to see if I was getting up.

'I don't feel well. I'm staying in bed.'

Mum suggested I had an aspirin for the headache, and she'd bring me a cold drink, as it was summer. Helen had bought a thermometer, and when Mummy took my temperature, she looked at it in horror.

'You're 102, and you've probably got flu.'

I thought you didn't catch influenza in the summer, but Clare said it was going around. I couldn't do anything all day and lay there stretching my legs, trying to ease the aches. Evening merged into night, and I slept fitfully until dawn, but when I awoke, my throat was on fire, and I felt as if I'd swallowed a razor blade. I lay back on the pillows and felt gruesome; my body was aching, consuming me, the fever giving me lurid dreams of Ian, who had grown horns and had a ghastly leer. I turned the pillow, trying to find a patch to cool my burning face, but whichever side of the pillow I chose, I was still too hot. And then I had an unlikely visitor in my bedroom: Ian brought me the St Hilda's College, Oxford University prospectus for bedtime reading.

'You might like to look at this when you feel better. It's not too late to apply.'

I was too weak to respond, so it stayed on the bedside table, untouched. I stuffed two more aspirin down my throat and gulped a mouthful of water, feeling the tablets struggle before they went down. Several times, I felt his presence by the bed, a shadowy figure staring at me. I thought I was dreaming but didn't have the energy to check if I was hearing things. Was he trying the Chinese torture scenario, the drip-drip of Oxford study versus London life

CHAPTER 5

and trying it on when I was sick and helpless? However, I might never have got into Oxford or Cambridge, which would have been even worse.

I started to worry I wouldn't be well enough to go to London. Clare had told me about a hostel there, something to do with her parents' church, and where I could stay while I looked around for accommodation. I had already booked the first week in September and had spent the time deciding what clothes and personal effects to take, and I had bought a suitcase large enough to accommodate everything and hoped it wouldn't be too heavy. Whenever Ian saw me, he took the opportunity to express his displeasure and my stupidity to be throwing away the chance to study at a prestigious university with my good exam results. Not once did he congratulate me, but uttered negative comments in contrast to Mummy, who said, 'I'm so proud of you, Julia. Your results are brilliant. Hasn't she done well, Ian?'

'She's a foolish girl,' was his response.

I tried not to be affected by his attitude, as I had got used to it over time, but it was still upsetting when he couldn't even acknowledge my achievement, although the rest of the family made up for it. Grandpa had paid for my driving lessons in London, and I passed after a course with a driving school near the flat. Helen gave me a range of expensive toiletries, which was very generous on her nurse's pay, and Mummy also gave me some money without telling Ian.

While I was ill, Clare visited me several times and brought more details of the hostel. It didn't look great from the description and photos, but it was a staging post before I found something more permanent. She brought a bunch of grapes and a bag of tangerines. She peeled a tangerine and gave me a segment.

'Can you smell the aroma?' she asked, sniffing the air.

'I can't smell anything with this cold. I can hardly breathe.'

But I was gradually improving after numerous drinks of lemon and honey, aspirin, Vick rubbed on my chest, and loving care. I began to sleep better at night, and my temperature dropped to normal. After a week or more, I decided to get up and have a warm bath, but not too hot to send my temperature up. I felt weak and unsteady when I got out, gingerly putting my feet on the mat, but I walked carefully down the stairs and sat in the garden to get some fresh air. When Clare visited again, Mummy produced her homemade scones, jam and cream, and a fruity cake, almost like Christmas.

'You look more like yourself, Jule,' Clare said, pouring more tea.

'Thank you, Clare, for visiting so many times, and let's hope you haven't caught it.'

'A lot of girls have it, so you're not the only one. Fingers crossed, I've escaped,' Clare said, giving the thumbs up.

It was just my luck to get the flu before going to London, but in September, I felt strong enough to travel. At least I was over the worst, so I preserved my energy with lots of rest.

That evening, Ian wasn't in at ten o'clock, and I wondered where he was.

'Is Ian away, Mummy?' I said, about to go to bed, feeling tired again.

'Yes, in London, until the weekend.'

'Do you know why he's in London?'

CHAPTER 5

'No dear, he doesn't tell me. Probably a business meeting.'

I asked myself how often he went to London on business. I hoped our paths wouldn't cross, but being in a city like London, I didn't imagine the possibility of our meeting was very likely.

Before I went to bed on my last night, I stood on the landing and took in our portraits.

I was sitting near a window, the light falling on the side of my face, in a dark green blouse. The contrast between my pale skin, the red tones of my hair and the dark green, was outstanding. She had spent a long time working on my face, experiencing the difficulty of my mouth and how to get it right, as the slightest brush stroke changed the expression.

Helen had sat near a window, but her portrait was full-face while mine was three-quarters. The colours were lighter in varying shades, with blue reflected in her fair hair and her prominent eyes and small nose were perfectly reproduced. Mum had hung them together, and the difference between our faces created a perfect duet. She had started a self-portrait, but it lay unfinished somewhere, and I hoped that someday she would finish it. At the other end of the landing hung the Matisse painting of red and orange flowers, but I had no idea where it came from.

I was so nervous the night before my journey to London that I only slept for three hours. I imagined scenes of catching the wrong Tube train, getting lost among hostile crowds and ending up in dark and dismal streets without a clue where I was. But I was also excited about my new experience, and at least I had somewhere to stay, although I had no idea what it would be like.

CHAPTER 6

My hand shook when I powdered the shine off my nose and outlined my lips with a neutral colour, nervous about my first visit to London. Mummy looked tearful but offered me a lift to the station, while Ian said nothing before going to work. My stepfather's displeasure about my refusal to study at university and instead go to live and work in London cast a pall over the whole house.

I found an empty carriage, relieved I had somewhere to stay, a hostel near Caledonian Road Tube station, recommended by Clare's parents and connected to their church. I hoped they weren't too strict and quizzed me about how often I went to Communion, but they assumed I was a regular churchgoer, so I needn't have worried. I caught a slow train and checked the name on the platform whenever we stopped, wondering if the new passengers would choose my carriage, but no one did. I worried about managing the Tube network and apprehensive finding the hostel, but after studying the street map, I was more confident about finding it.

When the train whined to a stop at the terminus, I had to concentrate. I dragged my suitcase onto the platform, carried it to the underground and looked for the Northern Line. I didn't have to wait long, pulled my case onto the train,

CHAPTER 6

and changed to the Piccadilly line for my stop. I walked to the busy road outside, with traffic and people hurrying to and from their business, and found the hostel on a quieter road, a square brick building on three floors. I pushed open the door and entered the foyer, but the sepia walls and two straight-backed chairs by a small table depressed me even more. An effusive woman with a clipboard checked my name, and I followed her up the stairs to a room with a single bed, a bedside table, and a cupboard. She gave me a leaflet of instructions and said the dining room was open for the evening meal, and after she'd gone, I sat on the bed, too tired to unpack, and vowed my stay would be short-lived. The dining room was empty, apart from two women behind the counter, ready to serve, so I collected a plate of cheese flan and a fruit pudding with a glass of water and took the tray to a table near the door. I bolted my food, checking whether anyone else had come into the room, but it was empty.

Back in my room, all I wanted was a warm bath and a night's sleep, but all I got was a freezing bathroom, a brown-stained bath and no hot water. I took my washbag along the dimly lit passage and pushed open the bathroom door. At first, I couldn't find the light switch, but when I located it and pulled the light cord, the bulb was so dim it hardly made a difference. I had to make do with a quick, cold wash, a piece of clinical-smelling soap, hard as stone, and a thin, small towel. I was awake most of the night trying to avoid the lumpy mattress, and turned from one side to the other, praying for a few hours' sleep.

I awoke to a heavy, grey sky, got dressed in a beige suit, the skirt a little above the knee, and without breakfast, left to find the employment agencies Maggie had given me and found a cafe near the hostel. I joined the other occupants, two middle-aged women with headscarves, talking in low voices, and sat by the window and waited for the waitress to take my order. When she finally brought an Eccles cake and a cup of milky coffee, I pushed the skin on my coffee and picked at the cake. I thought about home and Mother struggling with Ian's control and hoped he wouldn't find out about the money she gave me to help with expenses.

At the employment agency, a smartly dressed young woman greeted me.

'Good morning, Miss Langley. Your A Level results will certainly put you on the ladder to getting a good job. I can set up some interviews in advertising, public relations and publishing. You may have to settle for a low-paid job initially, but you can always progress to something better.'

The following day, I went to three interviews, two in the morning and the third in the late afternoon, but the question "Can you type?" was the first one they asked, after my name. Finally, a manager offered me a filing job in a small publishing company, which I accepted, hoping I would get a foothold in the publishing world. On my first day, the Company Secretary, Robert Chandler, shook my hand, welcomed me to Pericles Publishing and showed me a room stacked from floor to ceiling with old files, some of their contents in piles on the floor.

'You can start on this lot and put the contents in date order,' he said, giving me an untidy pile. The print was faded and difficult to see, and at the end of the day, dust from the files had covered me from head to foot. I got ready to leave on the dot of 5.30 and was just about to open the

CHAPTER 6

door when Mr Chandler poked his head in. 'You're doing an excellent job, Miss Langley, and I'm looking forward to more progress from you tomorrow,' he said.

Every morning, I dreaded going into the dusty office, and as the day progressed, my neck and shoulders ached, struggling with the heavy files. Some pages were so faint it was impossible to see the date, while others were creased or folded and falling apart. At the end of the first month, I wanted to leave and called the agency to see if there were any suitable vacancies, and the manager set up an interview for me at an advertising agency. But after I had arrived at the agency, early, and had waited for an hour without being called, I walked out, exasperated.

It was a trek back to the hostel in the evening, and on the way, I bought an evening paper and ringed flat-share agencies to investigate further. After the dreary days with the dusty files, the evenings at the hostel did nothing to cheer me up. There was a sitting room off the hall where we could chat, read or play board games, and on the second evening, after supper, I plucked up courage and went in, but it was empty, apart from two women concentrating on a game of draughts. They glanced at me but continued with their game, and when I tried to introduce myself, they ignored me. I looked at the books on the shelf, but most were Dickens or Thackeray and a few about different church denominations. I returned to my room, lay on the bed and read my book, The Lonely Girl by Edna O'Brien, about two girls living in Dublin, not dissimilar to my situation in London. I wondered if I'd made a mistake and should have followed Ian's advice and applied to one of the women's colleges at Oxford. I looked around at my dismal room and started sobbing until someone knocked on my door. I didn't answer and continued to spill the tears until the person gave up and walked away. One evening, the Hostel Manager invited me into her office and told me I wasn't fitting in, hiding in my room and not joining the others in activities, but I longed to leave and find somewhere else to live.

The following evening, I saw an advertisement for a garden flat in Chiswick, near the river, which looked promising. The accommodation was a single occupancy but living in my own flat was certainly preferable to the dreary hostel. I imagined a large, airy room with white walls and sand-coloured furnishings, leading into a cosy bedroom and modern bathroom. Through an open French window, the secluded garden would be paved and surrounded by shrubs and trees. I didn't mind if the kitchen was small as cooking wasn't my forte, and at the weekend, I saw myself walking to the shops to get the paper and fresh rolls for breakfast.

I made an appointment for Saturday afternoon. But the flat wasn't near the river, and I found myself in the centre of Chiswick and had to ask someone. 'Second road on the right down there,' said a woman. It didn't look how I'd imagined it, and when a thin man with a wispy beard answered the door, I knew it wasn't right for me.

'Excuse the mess. I haven't had the chance to clear it up,' Wispy Beard said.

I thought he might have made the effort. The main room looked like a storage unit filled with boxes and piles of newspapers, covering a worn and stained carpet. The bedroom was an alcove, with a single bed pushed against the wall covered by a grey bedspread. A smell of fried food

CHAPTER 6

permeated the room, and instead of a kitchen, there was a two-ringed gas oven in the corner. I'd seen enough, and as for the garden – a tiny concrete space with dandelions poking through, overlooked on all sides by blocks of flats.

'There's potential here,' the man said, pointing, 'with fast-growing plants to create a screen and space for a lawn.'

'Thank you, but I'm not interested.' I picked up my bag ready to leave.

'You're lucky to have a garden,' he fumed and slammed the door in my face.

What a cheek to call it a garden flat near the river, I thought, when it most certainly wasn't worthy of that description. I wandered around the Chiswick shops feeling very low, and began to see that London life for me was not meant to be. I thought of the comfort of home, Mummy's warmth and our affectionate Barny. I pushed Ian to the back of my mind and hoped he wouldn't answer the phone when I called in the evening but fortunately, it was Mum.

'It's not working out here, Mummy. I'll have to come home. The hostel is awful and I've just seen a depressing flat that is not for me.'

'Of course you can, darling. Your room is waiting, and we miss you so much.'

'I will let you know when I can come home after I've sorted things out here.'

A few days later, there was a call for me on the lobby telephone and I thought it was Mummy checking when I'd be home. But a chirpy voice said, 'Hello Julia, it's Maggie. I've some news about a flat in Holland Park and you'd have your own room. The other girl there is Babs who is great fun, and I think you'd get on.'

I couldn't let this opportunity slip by, so I made an appointment to see the flat before I rang home.

With the address scribbled on a scrap of paper and a map, I found the ground floor flat half-way down a crescent and climbed the steps to a freshly painted front door with a gold knocker. Babs opened the door and said in a faint Essex twang, 'You must be Julia. Please call me Babs.'

She ushered me into a comfortable-sized sitting room, with a sofa and two easy chairs in the same fabric, a deep blue that contrasted with a light brown carpet. It had a small garden at the back with flower beds and a paved area. In the corner of the sitting room was an upright piano and I sat on the stool and played a few notes, mostly out of tune.

'Fraid the piano needs tuning but do play something. I'm all ears,' Babs said with encouragement.

I felt shy but tapped into my memory and found a Prelude by Chopin, and when I'd finished, she clapped and said, 'Gosh, you're a good pianist.'

The flat was quite spacious for two people and infinitely better than the hostel. Babs showed me my room, tidy and ready for me to occupy. The bed was made with a blue eiderdown and a cream bedspread, and the wardrobe was empty, ready for my clothes but devoid of coat hangers. Babs's room was like a jumble sale. The dressing table was spread with hairbrushes, face powder, perfumes, lipsticks, eye make-up and several china jewel boxes, each sitting on a layer of dust. Her bed was unmade and strewn with magazines, more make-up and items of clothing.

'Who lives in the flat above, Babs?'

CHAPTER 6

'Two hippy girls who have some odd visitors, but I don't often see them. I think they smoke pot as you can smell it sometimes.'

'Where is the entrance to their flat?'

'They go through another door at the side, but it doesn't bother me. They're alright, quite pleasant and friendly.'

I wasn't sure what pot smelt like, but I liked Babs, and it was so much better than the hostel.

'So, is everything to your liking and you'll share the flat with me?' Babs asked, with a big smile.

'It looks just right, especially after the hostel, and I'll see you in a week's time.'

I had to give a week's notice and chose that evening to tell the manager. Fortunately, she was in her office at her desk.

'Ah, Miss Langley, come right in. How can I help?'

'I have the offer to share a flat so will no longer be a resident here,' I said, sounding a bit too formal.

'That will probably suit you better, so I'll terminate your residency.'

I rang home that evening hoping Ian wouldn't answer but as fate played its hand, he did.

'Have you come to your senses now, Julia,' he said immediately.

'Yes, and I'm staying in London. I have found a nice flat to share with another girl and will move in a week's time. Is Mum there?'

She sounded disappointed when I explained, but said she had a feeling I wouldn't be coming home.

Babs worked late at a theatre as an administrator and often came in at midnight, although having separate rooms,

I didn't always hear her. When I did, lights would go on, she'd loudly open and shut her drawers for at least thirty minutes, and falling asleep again was not always easy. On my walk from the Tube station, I found a small supermarket where I bought bread, milk, cheese, eggs and other basics and carried them into the kitchen. I found an old frying pan at the back of a cupboard and fried an egg and a rasher of bacon, thinking I'd have to get creative about meals for one as we hardly ever ate together.

Babs introduced me to the social side of London, to theatre parties crammed full of stage people where I shrunk into a corner with an unknown "bit part" actor, trying to make myself heard above the babble. Or Maggie would drag me to bottle parties, everyone bringing a bottle of cheap plonk that we'd drink out of paper cups and stuff ourselves with cheese or nuts. The parties were in shabby flats hidden under low lights from lamps with chianti bottle bases and a red bulb giving everything a dingy red glow. There'd be frantic dancing to sounds of the times, The Platters, Cliff Richard, twisting to Chubby Checker or slow dancing to Adam Faith. But those parties at different flats merged into one inebriated experience.

One day, Babs asked me if I had heard of a therapy called reflexology, which involved pressure on different parts of the foot. She had been once and said it was relaxing and suggested we booked a session. The therapist lived in a ground floor flat in Swiss Cottage and had set up a room at the front of the house for treatment. Babs said I could have the first booking, while she waited in another room and read magazines that were left on a table. The therapist told me to remove my footwear, and I lay on the treatment bed

CHAPTER 6

with bare feet, and she explained that certain parts of the foot were connected to organs in our body. She rubbed my feet with an antiseptic cream and then massaged the right foot first, putting pressure on different parts of the foot. Sometimes, when she pressed, it felt sore, but overall, it was a relaxing experience. I loved having my feet massaged and could put up with a little discomfort, but after she had finished the right foot, I was almost asleep. She repeated the treatment on my left foot and at the end, I had dozed off. She gently nudged me, and suggested I stay on the bed for five minutes, to rest.

'The treatment can affect you in different ways. You could feel energised, tired, thirsty or just relaxed,' she said, giving me a glass of water. I was glad I had gone and made another appointment and thought this could be an ongoing therapy.

I settled into my London life, sharing the flat with Babs and working at the publishing company, but this is when I met Russell, who changed my life considerably.

CHAPTER 7

I'd noticed Russell about the office with a charming smile, and when he left some files with my boss, he stopped and looked at me.

'It suits you,' he remarked, out of the blue.

'What does?' I asked, puzzled.

'Your necklace. You don't often wear jewellery.'

I tried not to feel irritated, although his accent intrigued me; was he Irish or American?

'Not usually to work, but today I fancied wearing one of my favourite necklaces with green stones.'

'What are the stones called?' he asked, looking at them.

'I'm not sure.'

We managed a brief exchange most days until he asked if I'd like to have a drink after work. We chose a Friday and wandered along the Bayswater Road to a club where Russell was a member and sat outside in a little courtyard at the back with our gin and tonics. He said he was an American from Boston and had been in London for about a year.

'And how do you find it?'

'Varied and so much to see and do. Do you like music, Julia?'

'Yes, and I play the piano.'

CHAPTER 7

'I play guitar. How about we go to a Prom concert at the Albert Hall?'

He booked seats for the following week, and the days couldn't pass quickly enough. Each evening, I went through my wardrobe to decide what to wear, but finally, I bought a sleeveless black and orange patterned dress, and Babs commented on how stunning I looked.

We met outside South Kensington Tube station and walked the ten minutes to the Albert Hall.

'I love the circular structure. When was it built?' Russell asked as we climbed the steps to look for our entrance door.

'About 1870 and opened by Queen Victoria in honour of her late husband, Albert.'

'I'm glad I bought tickets,' said Russell, pointing to a long queue winding around the building.

'They are the prommers who queue for cheap tickets to stand in the central arena, as there are no seats. It's a tradition.'

Our seats were on an upper level, and we felt suspended looking down on the orchestra. The programme was a guitar concerto by Rodrigo and other works by Vivaldi and Mozart. We watched the auditorium fill up. Some searched for their seats, tickets in hand, settled, read the programme notes, or contributed to the noise level. One or two orchestra members wandered onto the stage carrying their instruments, followed by the first and second violins at the front and percussion at the back. The sound of tuning up was a mishmash, the notes clashing and sparring until the real thing, but when the conductor strode to the podium, all was quiet. At last, the exquisite sounds had found their place.

In the interval, we went to a bar and stood with the crowd among the excited chatter of music enthusiasts. The guitar concerto was in the second half, and the hush over the auditorium was heavy and expectant, waiting for the soloist. It seemed to last forever until the rapturous applause when he walked on, tall and smiling. Russell was intent throughout, leaning forward to see the finger movements of the soloist and when the performance finished, the applause was rapturous. The applause went on and on, but the soloist didn't oblige with an encore.

'That was unreal,' Russell said, 'and I'm inspired to practise more.'

I found the lilt of his voice sexy and when he took my hand, I felt as if we were the only ones on the crowded Tube as we sat together, squashed up against the other travellers.

'Do you want to come in for a drink or coffee?' I said, but Russell was at the doorway before I finished the sentence. He went straight to the sofa, draped his arm over the back and said whisky would be great. I hated whisky, so I mixed a Bloody Mary with vodka and the last can of tomato juice in the bottom of the fridge. I found the only tray, brought the drinks in with a bowl of peanuts, dragged over a small table and sat beside Russell. He turned my head and looked towards my eyes, scanning them both.

'Your eyes are an unusual mix of green and blue.'

I looked at his in return.

'And yours are just green,' I commented, beginning to feel embarrassed. I thought it was time to have some music.

I found a record of jazz guitar in the collection, put it on the turntable and watched Russell's face as he tapped his feet to the rhythm.

CHAPTER 7

'How about giving me a tune on the piano over there?' Russell said, sipping his drink.

'I have a book of duets if you'd like to have a go.'

'I only play guitar, but I'll have a bash.'

He brought in a chair from the kitchen, and I found an easy piece, but sitting next to Russell made me play the wrong notes, and so did he. When it all got raggedy and out of sync, we started laughing and couldn't stop until I heard the key in the door.

'That must be Babs,' I said.

'I could hear you playing from the street,' she said, looking flushed. 'Ah, you must be Russell. I've heard so much about you.'

I hate it when people said that, as though I'd spent all my time talking about him. Russell flashed his smile at her.

'I'm getting a drink. Anyone for anymore?' said Babs.

'I'd best be off,' Russell said when Babs settled herself down.

'Why not stay for another drink?' Babs said, putting on a wheedling voice.

Russell hesitated but said he had to get back. I saw him to the door and watched him walk down the road to catch his train to Ealing, and I looked forward to our next meeting when he planned to cook for us at his flat.

I studied the map and found the road where Russell lived, not far from the Tube station, and walked up the shaded front garden of No. 5 Argyle Avenue, a detached house belonging to friends of his parents from Boston. I laughed when Russell appeared at the front door in a green and black apron, and as he led me up the three flights to his attic flat, my mouth watered from the aroma wafting down the stairs.

'I'll give you a three-second tour,' he said.

He pointed to the kitchen where everything was in place, a round table set for two in the sitting area, next to a tower of books in the corner.

'The bathroom is here, and next to it is my bedroom.'

He had large cushions on a russet bedspread, and a black dressing gown lay draped across the bed.

'What room is this?' I said, pointing at a tightly shut door.

'That's another bedroom. Handy for visitors.'

'Do you get many?'

'I expect you'd like a drink,' he said, taking down a glass, putting in some ice and mixing a dry martini. I leant back on the sofa, crossed my legs and felt like Sophia Loren while he carried shrimp cocktails to the table.

'Where are the friends who live here? Are they out for the evening?'

'They've gone back to Boston to see the family. They have loaned me their Austin which will be useful.'

I hoped that he'd take me to places by car instead of catching public transport. Not many people had a car in London, so it would be fun.

He lowered the piece of steak into the pan, turning it at the right time for medium rare, checked the vegetables and poured two glasses of red wine. The liquid flowed through my channels, and the candle's flicker transported me into another world. I looked at Russell, who watched me cut my piece of steak.

'I hope it's done to your liking, Madam.' He smiled.

'Perfect. Neither overdone nor too rare. You're an excellent cook. Much better than me.'

'Do you like cooking, Julia?'

CHAPTER 7

'Only if I'm in the mood.'

I asked him about his mother and if she was a good cook, but he said she only produced traditional American food. When I steered the conversation towards home and family, he looked uneasy, as if he didn't want the topic pursued.

'I hope you like pecan pie for dessert.'

'I've never had it, so I'll let you know. Is it a traditional American pudding?'

'The story goes that French settlers in New Orleans made the first pecan pie from pecans given to them by Native American tribes. So yes, it's traditional.'

I looked at the expertly made pie, the pecans in a circle nestling in the pie crust and a large bowl of whipped cream beside it. Russell cut a neat slice and passed it to me with a spoon for the cream.

'I call this the homesick course.'

'Are you homesick?' I asked him.

He didn't reply but cut himself a slice of the pie.

'Are you?' he asked instead.

'I thought I'd be at first, but now I'm enjoying my life too much, meeting new people and having new experiences, so there isn't time to be homesick.'

'I expect your family miss you.'

'I'm sure my mother does but certainly not my stepfather.'

Russell didn't ask any more questions about family and switched to work.

'I hear you got the junior copywriter job. Well done,' Russell said and gave me the thumbs up.

'It's better than the dusty files, and I like Susan. She's a good boss and thanks, Russell, for telling me about it.'

The smell of Russell grinding coffee beans was evocative, and after we'd had a couple of sips from small bone china cups, he took my hand, pushed me gently down onto the sofa, and leaned over to kiss me when we were interrupted by a loud knocking on the front door. We froze as it sounded urgent, and I hoped it was nothing serious. Russell muttered and went downstairs to investigate while I looked closely at the portrait of a man with a high forehead who looked like Russell and wondered if it was his father. My thoughts were disturbed by a high-pitched voice, on the edge of hysteria, and Russell's low tones. I wanted to investigate, and looking over the bannisters at the empty hall, I went down the stairs into the kitchen. Russell was looking in one of the drawers while a thin, tall woman with long hair was pulling the contents out and flinging them on the floor.

'Just stop, Sylvia, and calm down,' he said.

'I've got to find them.'

'Sylvia's locked herself out. We're looking for her spare key.'

'Let me help. Where is it kept?'

'Pardon! No idea, that's why we're looking,' Russell replied.

'It's urgent. My husband walked out, but he might be trying to call,' Sylvia said.

I wandered into a study and felt like a trespasser or a police detective searching a house after a murder. I opened the top drawer, full of pens and notepads, but in the next drawer were bundles of keys.

'I've found them,' I called out.

'This is mine,' she said, picking up her key from the others.

CHAPTER 7

I wondered how well Russell knew Sylvia and if he might invite her for a drink. They must be friendly to have her key, although Russell hadn't known where they kept it. Sylvia looked calmer holding her key, fluttered her fingers and crossed the road to her house, but when we went back upstairs, it wasn't the same. I sat on the sofa, had another drink, and leant against Russell's arm on the back of the sofa. Suddenly we heard more knocking at the front door.

'I bet Sylvia's forgotten something, or her husband's thrown her out,' Russell said, infuriated, and went downstairs again.

'I must go,' I said, looking for my coat.

But I felt rooted to the spot, mesmerised with no energy to leave. It wasn't long before they returned, Sylvia in floods of tears, saying her husband wasn't coming back and for her to get on with her life. Russell put his arms round her and immediately, I felt the odd one out, and wanted to leave and let them get on with it. Without looking at them, I walked to the bedroom, got my coat and bag, and made for the door.

'Where are you going, Julia? Join us for another drink,' Russell called out, but I ran down the stairs, through the gate and into the street. I looked across the road at Sylvia's house, with its overgrown garden hiding the entrance and wondered if her husband had left for good. I tried not to imagine Russell and Sylvia together, but when I saw them at the theatre not long afterwards, I was suspicious about their relationship.

CHAPTER 8

I wasn't prepared for another shock when I got to work on Monday. I went in early to finish a piece for Susan, and was surprised she was already in, wearing her grey suit, her large blue eyes with a touch of eyeshadow. Annie was sitting at her desk, taking dictation.

'Good morning, Julia,' Susan said, giving me an intense look. 'We're going to miss Russell when he leaves.'

'What do you mean leave?' I said, hearing my heartbeats.

'Hasn't he told you? He's got a job at another publishing company. I thought you knew.'

I went to the cloakroom, sat on the lavatory seat and thought about how he'd been instrumental in my copywriter job and was upset he hadn't told me. I washed my hands, over and over, until Annie came in.

'Did you know Russell was leaving?' I asked her.

'I didn't know until today.'

I went to his desk, but he wasn't there. Russell's colleague said he'd popped out for lunch, which meant I had to wait until I finished work to confront him. It was hard to concentrate throughout the afternoon, with imaginary conversations circling my head. At 5.30, I tidied my desk, earlier than usual, and made my way to his office. I quickened my pace, hoping to catch him before he left, but

CHAPTER 8

as I turned the corner, I saw him walking briskly down the corridor, his suit jacket flapping behind him. I knew I had to walk fast to speak to him before he was gone.

'Russell, thanks for telling me you're leaving,' I said, breathless.

He turned around and grabbed my arm. 'Julia, I was going to tell you, but in a special way.'

'A special way? I suppose the whole office knows except me. When did this happen?'

'I've only recently been offered the job. I didn't want to say in case it fell through.'

'Excuses, Russell. You might have told me earlier.'

'If you're free, we could go for a drink. Give me fifteen minutes, and I'll meet you in the foyer.'

The room was almost empty, but we sat in a corner with a gin and tonic for me and for Russell, a whisky sour.

'Julia, I'm sorry I didn't tell you earlier. I wanted to do it somewhere away from the office. It's a more senior job, with better money and a promotion. And it's easier for us, too. Office romances are tricky.'

We sat there, not saying much, and watched the room fill up, raising the noise level.

'Are you free to come back to Holland Park with me?' I asked, taking the plunge.

'I'd love to, but I can't this evening. I have a meeting with someone at my Club. I'll call you, and we'll have dinner one evening.'

I didn't think he'd be able to, but there was no harm in trying.

'Which Club is that?' I asked, intrigued.

'The Arts Club, Soho, for men only.'

I wondered if he was meeting someone well-known, but I could wonder forever and never find out. I took the Tube to Holland Park and spent the evening mulling over recent events. I wondered about his relationship with Sylvia and whether she was just a neighbour opposite or there was more to it. Strangely, I saw him in Kensington, shopping with a woman and a young child, so perhaps he has lots of female friends who are not girlfriends. I was too nervous to go and say 'Hello' so I pretended I hadn't seen them and walked the other way, but they were busy explaining something to the child and were preoccupied. However, there was no call from him. I was chained to the phone and would often lift the receiver to check the dial tone, but perhaps I'd been silly to hassle him about his new job.

I decided to pay him a surprise visit in Ealing. The journey seemed unreal, like a dream, my face glued to the window, watching the station signs, walking down his road and up to the front door. I glanced over at Sylvia's and wondered about her, took a deep breath and lifted the knocker. A woman with short brown hair flecked with grey stood in the doorway.

'Hi, can I help?' She had an American accent, so it must be Gloria back from Boston.

'Is Russell in? I'm Julia, a friend of his.'

'Hi, Julia. Russell is with Sammy today, but come in.'

'Sammy?'

'His little boy. It's his day for him. He's four now.'

I looked at Gloria, finding it difficult to form any words and remembered seeing him with the woman and young child. Was that Sammy? Were they alike, father and son, or was he more like his mother – but it had been difficult

CHAPTER 8

to see. All I saw then was the doorway and the desire to escape.

'Would you like a coffee?' she said, opening the door wider.

'I must go,' I said.

I had to escape, hoping he wouldn't see me from the window. Feeling faint, I searched for somewhere to sit and found a small park with swings and a roundabout at the end of the road. I sat on a bench and put my head on the armrest until the spell passed. So, he's got a child. Was that the mother? She must live in London. Are they married, separated, or divorced? How little I knew about him. Everything he's told me could be a lie. I watched a mother push her child higher and higher on the swing while another sat with hers on the roundabout, going round and round. One of them came over and asked if I was alright and if she could help, but I thanked her and said I'd recovered. I watched the children for a while longer, thinking about Russell with a child, putting him in a different perspective. He can't think much of me not to say anything and Gloria would be sure to mention my visit, but he didn't call.

About a week later, though, he was standing by my desk when I returned after a lunch break. I stopped and stared.

'Did anyone see you walk in, Russell? You don't work here now.'

'Julia, please come for a drink so I can explain about Sammy.'

'No more drinks. You tell me now.'

I wanted him to tell me, not arrange some future date which he might never keep.

'Just sit down, Russell. Why didn't you tell me about Sammy?'

I was all fired up and confident as it didn't matter, as there had been so many secrets.

'I'm sorry. I should've done. I was nervous about how you'd react.'

'Tell me now.'

'I knew Alice at College, and we started dating in our third year. My degree was in Fine Arts, and hers was in History. A year after we graduated, we married, and at first, it was a good marriage, although we were young. We bought a house on the outskirts of Boston, and both worked; Alice was a history teacher, and I was in marketing. After three years, Alice was pregnant and gave birth to Sammy without complications, but afterwards, she was depressed and tearful. We had screaming arguments, which weren't good for Sammy and talked about splitting up. Then, tragically, Alice's father died. Her English mother decided to live in London again with Alice and Sammy, and we divorced, but I missed Sammy and decided to apply for a job in London.'

'How often do you see your son?'

'The arrangement is every other weekend unless something else crops up.'

I thought about those weekends when he wasn't around or unavailable, but I never imagined he was with his son. We make up our version of events, often miles from the truth.

'What attracted you to Alice at first?' I asked.

'She was fun. Lively, we both liked art and music.'

'Do you see much of her now?'

'Only when I have Sammy. He's our only link.'

CHAPTER 8

'I understand why you'd want to be close to your son. So, you're older than I thought.'

He didn't reply but asked me if I'd like to meet Sammy and go with them to an amusement park outside London. I was intrigued to see his ex-wife when she dropped off Sammy, but all she said was 'Hi', and drove away, a slight figure with shoulder-length, mousy hair. The journey took an hour, with Sammy fidgeting in the back.

'Sam, stop pushing your legs into my seat,' said Russell.

'Stop the car somewhere, and I'll sit with him in the back and help with his colouring-in book.'

Russell found a side road, and I got out and sat with Sammy while he picked out the different crayons. I asked him if he could name the colours, and he was spot on. The motion made it difficult for him to keep between the lines, but I persevered so Sam didn't trouble Russell. When we arrived, Sammy was very excited, wanting to try all the rides at the park and jumped up and down when he saw the children's train.

'Would you like to go on the bumper cars first or the roller coaster?' asked Russell.

Sammy opted for the bumper cars, and we found ones for children with two seats so Sammy could sit on Russell's lap. We zoomed around the track, Russell weaving in and out, Sammy shouting with delight when we collided with another car. The roller coaster was next on our list, and we walked to the other side of the ground and waited in a queue after paying for our tickets. We watched the previous ride finish its journey and waited for the passengers to get off. Sam sat next to Russell in the carriage, talking all the time while I sat in the seat behind, feeling nervous. Then we started, with Sam clinging to Russell as we went down and then up, leaving my stomach behind. Sam said it was "groovy" and wanted to go on it again, but Russell said they'd go on the train next. He lifted him into one of the small open carriages, but I stayed behind, leaving them to spend time together.

I sat there for a while, but feeling bored, I wandered around the stalls and tried my luck at a coconut shy. You would have lost count of the times I threw the ball to knock off the coconut, but when I had succeeded and collected my prize, I couldn't see Russell or Sammy anywhere.

'Has the train returned?' I asked the attendant.

'About ten minutes ago,' he said.

I looked around and caught sight of Russell's head through the crowd.

'I can't find Sammy. He must have run ahead wanting to find you,' he said.

'Oh no! I'll go to the office and ask them to make an announcement.'

The rides and stalls were closing for the evening, people were leaving, and officials switching off the lights around the ground, but the office was open.

'Sammy, Sammy,' Russell shouted. 'If you hadn't wandered off, Julia, this wouldn't have happened.'

The loudspeaker crackled, 'Please look out for a four-year-old boy who is lost and separated from his father. If you see him, report to the office.'

The ground emptied except for one or two stragglers walking towards the exit.

'We'll have to go to the police,' I said.

'Let's wait a bit longer and ask again at the office,' Russell said without hesitating.

CHAPTER 8

Inside, a man and a woman were packing up, tidying the desk and putting scattered papers into neat piles.

'I'm Sammy's father. Have any sightings been reported?' Russell said to the man.

'No one has been in,' he said, adjusting his glasses.

'Some while ago, I did see a young woman leave the ground with a small boy,' said a woman with a jowly face, who came into the office from a room at the back.

'What did she look like?' Russell asked.

'Slim, fairish and walked quickly with a small boy towards the exit.'

'Sounds suspiciously like Alice. I told her we were going to a fairground.'

'Did you say which one?' I asked.

'I can't remember, but she could've followed us. Funny, I didn't notice.'

'She may not have been directly behind us but with one or two cars in between.'

Russell asked to use the phone in the office and dialled her home number three times without success, but on the fourth attempt, someone answered.

'Hello,' a husky voice spoke loud enough for me to hear.

'Elizabeth, it's Russell. Is Alice at home with Sam? We've lost him at the fairground, and we're frantic.'

'She went out ages ago and isn't back yet,' replied Elizabeth.

'When she comes in, ask her to call the office number here. It's urgent.'

He repeated the number several times to Elizabeth before he rang off.

When the phone rang a few minutes later, Russell and I jumped and stood up, but it wasn't for us. The man and woman were anxious to close but stayed open while we waited to hear. They filed away more paperwork while Russell paced the floor. After another fifteen minutes, the phone rang again. Russell grabbed the phone.

'Alice, we've been worried sick about Sammy. You've got no right to go off with him like that. We've been going crazy wondering where he is. How did you know we were here? Did you follow us?'

I didn't hear her reply, but Russell said,

'Julia is responsible and not an empty-headed floozie. You had nothing to worry about. You've caused us a lot of angst. Don't do that again. We'll drop Sammy's bag off later.'

Russell thanked the office staff for staying open and asked them to direct us to the nearest cafe, and we relaxed with a coffee and something to eat. I was more at ease now that Sammy was safe, although I felt guilty.

'I expect Sammy ran to see his mother, so it wasn't your fault,' Russell said after a while.

We walked back to the car, but he didn't take my hand, and I was too shy to make any advances. I felt sad to see Sammy's crayons and colouring-in-book lying on the back seat and missed sitting with him on our return. I thought about having a child, a boy, to do things with and take to places, but that was a future event.

When we approached Hampton Wick, it looked villagey, the water giving it a romantic feel, as though it was a holiday advertisement. We turned into a quiet, leafy road and stopped outside a Georgian house converted into flats. I sat in the car while Russell took Sammy's bag of toys to give

CHAPTER 8

to Alice at the door, and I could see they were arguing, their voices muted. Elizabeth joined them at one stage, a slim, elegant woman with dark hair and the same husky voice I had heard on the phone. We were silent in the car on the way to Holland Park, but when we arrived at the flat, he gave me a brief kiss and was gone.

CHAPTER 9

I hadn't heard from Russell for three or four weeks, but when he called me out of the blue one evening, I was taken aback. I must have sounded nervous, as I had given up on receiving any communication from him. He wanted me to cook for him, and we chose a Saturday when Babs was out. It would be a learning curve for me and a surprise for him as I hadn't a clue what culinary wonder to produce. It's just as well we can't see into the future! I found a cookery book at the flat and chose coq au vin, followed by a fruit tart, although I was anxious cooking for a proficient chef like Russell and remembered his expertise in the early days. I made a list of ingredients from the recipe and went shopping on Saturday morning. I spent the afternoon preparing the dish. I pulled apart a chicken into manageable pieces and timed it to when we would start eating. My eyes streamed when I cut the onions, and I had to take out my lenses and wear glasses. Finally, the whole kitchen worktop was a mess with flour, herbs, and mushroom stalks mixed up with unwanted bits of chicken. The pastry attempt was no better. I rolled it out, but it crumbled into sections, looking like a jigsaw puzzle in the tin. But I managed to have the supper ready before Russell arrived, and waiting for him was like a visit

CHAPTER 9

to the dentist. I was shaking. When I heard his footsteps outside the door, my stomach went into a knot. I looked in the mirror to check, ran a comb through my hair, and opened the door.

He kissed my lips gently and held out a bottle of Chateauneuf. I found an old corkscrew in a kitchen drawer, and Russell had no trouble uncorking the bottle. I had set the table with two candles from a gift shop and a vase of flowers picked from our garden at the back.

'I like the marble mantelpiece,' Russell said, looking around the room, 'but the ornaments there don't fit.'

He referred to a brightly coloured ceramic bird and a graphite elephant that didn't match, but I'd never thought to ask Babs where they came from, although they'd been there since I moved in. He filled two wine glasses, and we drank the burgundy liquid while Russell said, 'To us,' and raised his glass. I felt his green eyes watching me.

'Bon appetit,' I said.

''It's good to see you again, Julia. Long time no see.'

'Have you been busy lately?' I hoped for an explanation, but I would probably get an excuse.

'Work has been frenetic, and I've had Sammy for the last three weekends as his mother was not well, and Elizabeth was away.'

We started with a small dish of tabouleh and some fresh bread from a nearby bakery owned by a jolly husband and wife who tempted you with cakes, buns, pies and all types of bread. The wholesome smell of baking wafted down the street, enticing customers to come and buy.

I looked at him across the table.

'How is Sammy getting on at nursery school?'

'He goes twice a week while Alice works, but I took him when Alice was ill.'

'I was sorry the fun fair trip turned out as it did.'

'Sammy and I enjoyed it despite the drama. I hope you did as well.'

I cleared away our dirty plates, took the chicken dish out of the oven and carried everything to the table. I carefully spooned a portion onto his plate, praying it would taste delicious. I passed him the mashed potatoes and carrots, and he took a generous helping and waited for me to start. He took a mouthful.

'What have you put in this dish, Julia? It tastes disgusting.' He spluttered and almost spat it out.

'It doesn't taste too bad,' I said, taking a small mouthful.

'It's horrible. We'll go out and find a restaurant. There are plenty in this part of London.'

'Why don't we eat the vegetables? The pudding is in the oven and nearly done.'

'No, I'm starving. You can stay here, but I'm going out. I was looking forward to this evening.'

I was shocked at his sudden change of mood. It was so unlike him to look so angry, and I wondered what the problem was. I felt a failure and hardly had any energy to protest.

'What's wrong with you, Russell? Why are you so angry?'

'I was looking forward to a nice dinner.'

'Why didn't you tell me you were leaving the company?' I said, with a final glimmer of protest.

'You knew before I left,' he retorted.

'Because Susan told me. And then there's Sammy. I had to find out from a stranger. It was so embarrassing.'

CHAPTER 9

'Oh, for God's sake. That's very personal information.'

I took the opportunity to bring up the theatre episode and wondered how he'd react.

'And I saw you at the theatre with Sylvia. What's going on there?'

'At the theatre? When was that?'

'I'd booked tickets for The Homecoming by Pinter and went with an old school friend who was spending the weekend in London. When we found our seats, I saw you in the front stalls chatting with Sylvia. Clare suggested we go and say "hello", but when we got to the stalls, you had left the theatre, and when we came out at the end, the street was crowded, with people spilling onto the road, blocking the way, making it impossible to spot you.'

I had been shocked to see Russell with Sylvia and thought they were involved in a clandestine relationship. At first, I wasn't sure it was them as heads kept blocking my view but when I stood, I knew.

'Sylvia had a spare ticket because, as you know, her husband had left her and asked me to go with her. Naturally, she didn't want to waste the ticket. Why would you object? She's a friend but not a girlfriend. It wasn't a date. You're being childish, Julia.'

After the tirade, I felt embarrassed and wished I'd never said anything about Sylvia at the theatre. I had wanted to discuss Ruth's sexual dominance in the play, with Russell, but it wasn't the right time.

He pushed his plate away, spilling sauce, chicken, and vegetables over the white tablecloth, and stood up.

'I'm going to find a restaurant to have dinner. Are you coming with me, Julia?'

'No, Russell, I'm going to finish eating what I have cooked.'

'It's not edible.'

He strode out of the flat and slammed the front door. I sat at the table, horrified. I couldn't understand what was wrong with him and why he'd overreacted in that way. I finished the helping, emptied my glass of wine, and poured another. When Babs came in, we drank the whole bottle and had the fruit tart and custard.

'Despite everything, the tart is delicious,' said Babs. 'I wonder if he'll return like a forlorn dog, his tail between his legs.' Babs scraped up the last morsel on her plate.

'I don't want him to. It's all too upsetting. He's a good cook, but my offering wasn't too bad.'

'Maybe it's not to do with you or your cooking, but something else,' suggested Babs.

She advised me not to contact Russell but to let him cool off. He would probably apologise and be as charming as ever, but there was no contact from him for over a week, and I began to feel desperate. I didn't want the relationship to end on such a sour note. I tried his number in Ealing several times, but no one answered. Finally, I gave up and went to the house.

Walking down his road gave me an odd feeling as though I'd gone back in time, but when I reached the house, it looked deserted, as though no one lived there. I knocked on the door, peered through the stained-glass window, and saw a pile of mail on the mat. Through a window at the side of the house, the room looked too neat and untouched, and his attic flat glared back at me, blank and cold. I crossed the road to Sylvia's to find out if she knew of Russell's whereabouts and hoped she was in. The path

CHAPTER 9

to the front door was overgrown with brambles and one of them scratched my leg, making it sore. Sylvia opened the door in an old jumper and torn trousers, her hair scraped back with a scarf, looking puzzled.

'Hello, I'm Julia, a friend of Russell's. I'm trying to contact him, but no one is home.'

'I remember you. Come in. Please excuse my scruffy clothes, but I'm clearing the garden, weeding and stuff.'

I followed her into a small sitting room at the front of the house crammed full of furniture and ornaments, looking like a junk shop. She told me Russell had gone back to Boston to be with his mother after his father died suddenly after a short illness. Gloria and Egbert had also gone, as they were close friends of the family.

'I'm very sorry to hear this,' I said, upset that Russell hadn't told me.

'It was a great shock for all of them,' Sylvia said.

Perhaps his father's death explained why he was so disgruntled, and it wasn't me or my cooking after all. Although I was a young child, I thought about my father's death and the memories of him that were like snapshots. I could have sympathised with Russell if he had let me.

Sylvia poured me a cup of tea, but it was black and bitter and tasted like medicine, making me shudder. She offered me a piece of sponge cake, but I wasn't hungry. I took a deep breath.

'I saw you and Russell at the theatre recently when I went with a friend,' I said, my voice sounding too loud.

'Russell said he'd seen you but felt embarrassed. I had a spare ticket booked ages ago when my husband was living here and asked Russell if he'd like to go with me.'

'Do you have his address in Boston?' I asked, hopefully.

She flicked through an old address book and scribbled it on the back of an envelope. When she handed it to me, I felt empty, like the house, and further away from Russell than ever before.

'Come and visit me any time you're in this area,' Sylvia said as I left her house, but I didn't think I would ever return to Ealing, whatever the circumstances.

Armed with his address, I wrote a letter.

Holland Park
6th July

Dear Russell

I was very sorry to hear your father had died, which must have been a terrible shock for you and the family. I tried to call you at the flat, but there was no reply. I was reluctant to contact your office and went to the house in Ealing on the off chance. I knocked several times, but no one was there, so I crossed the road to Sylvia's to ask if she knew your whereabouts.

I was upset you didn't let me know you were returning to Boston, and I'm sorry you felt the need to storm out during our last supper. I apologise again for the unpalatable dish. We've had some lovely times together as a couple, but there seems to be so much secrecy. Please write and let me know how you are.

Love Julia.

CHAPTER 9

Predictably, there was no reply to my letter, so months later, I tried the Ealing number again on the slim chance he could be there.

A woman's high voice said, 'Hello.'

'I'd like to speak to Russell, please.'

'Russell? I think you've got the wrong number.'

'He was a tenant about a year ago and a friend I've lost touch with,' I said, puzzled.

'The previous tenant was a woman called Celia.'

It sounded like Russell had never existed and was a figment of my imagination.

'Are your landlords an American couple, Egbert and Gloria?' I asked, puzzled.

'No, my landlady is Margaret Pritchard. I can give you her number. She might know something.'

I hesitated to call the landlady, but as I was keen to find out about Russell, I picked up the receiver and dialled. But when Margaret Pritchard answered, she said that Egbert and Gloria weren't the owners but had leased the property from her. I was sure Russell said they were the owners. She didn't know anything about Russell. I tried the publishers where he worked, but the switchboard girl said he didn't work there anymore, and she had no idea where he went.

My last hope was to look up the name Bankes in the telephone directory, and I might get through to his ex-wife. It wasn't a common name, and I might have struck lucky. I found three Bankes in the Hampton Wick area, although Elizabeth's name wouldn't be Bankes. My first attempt answered abruptly and said he didn't know Russell Bankes.

The second call rang out unanswered, and the third was equally unhelpful.

I had come to a dead end and probably would never know what happened to him.

CHAPTER 10

I first saw Jim standing in the club where I played the piano for an hour on Friday evenings. His face was in profile, talking to another man, and the movement of his hand caught my eye, but I didn't think any more about him. But when I saw him again, he came over, stood by the piano and asked me to play 'This is my song', a popular number by Petula Clark. One of his friends had requested it, and I wondered if Jim had drawn the short straw. He was tall and slim with crinkly eyes and said he was an air force pilot. I asked him to describe the aircraft, and Jim said they were pointy and fast. He introduced himself as Jim Maddox and asked if he could buy me a drink when I'd finished my performance. After playing for an hour, my eyes felt sore, and when I looked in the mirror, I saw they were bloodshot and hoped Jim wouldn't notice. We sat at a small table away from the others with my order, a dry martini.

'How did you get the piano job here?' he asked.

When I had come with a friend and heard the honky-tonk piano, I went over to Jo, the pianist, a middle-aged man with shoulder-length hair. When he had finished the piece, he looked up and smiled.

'Do you play?' he said.

'Sort of,' I said.

'They're looking for someone else for Friday nights. Interested?'

'I don't know. I might not be good enough.'

'You don't have to be a brilliant pianist. Nobody listens. We need someone from eight to nine in the evening before I take over. Can you come in for an audition, say tomorrow, midday?'

'What sort of music do you play?' I asked.

'Light and cheerful,' he replied.

I felt a rush of daring and bought a book of easy popular music to practise and hoped I could play from memory. Jo welcomed me at the audition and introduced me to the manager. My hands were shaking, my legs jigging, but when I sat on the piano stool, I calmed down and played a medley of tunes from musicals and popular bands, and when I'd finished, they said 'bravo' and 'you'll do'. On the first night, I wore a dark red dress, tied my hair back in a knot and wore shoes with small heels to work the pedals.

When I arrived, the club was only half full. Jo met me and showed me the cloakroom to get ready before my performance. I sat at the piano and tried out a few notes before starting on my repertoire. My choice was a mixture of slow, dreamy pieces and bright, jolly ones, and because I had practised, I managed them all from memory, making the hour seem like five minutes. At a quiet time, I was too self-conscious and played a few wrong notes, but when the chatter started, it improved, and I felt more confident. After the hour, as I was getting ready to leave, I heard 'encore' several times from the audience. I chose Moon River from Breakfast at Tiffany's, because I knew it was popular, and some of the crowd started singing along and clapped when I'd finished.

CHAPTER 10

'You're very talented. Do you ever get propositioned?' Jim said with a twinkle.

'I get the odd cheeky comment or an invitation, but I wave my hand and laugh it off. It makes a change from work.'

'My young brother plays drums in a band. He's pretty good, and they perform locally.'

'Do you have any more siblings?' I asked.

'I had a twin brother, but he died.'

'That is sad, especially a twin you were close to.'

'He was ten and died of scarlet fever, which left a tragic gap. I missed him terribly as he was my playmate. My little brother was only three.'

'When my father died, there was a black hole. I was six.'

'Do you want children, Julia?'

'One day, I will. Certainly not yet. What about you?'

'I love kids,' he said.

We stayed quiet and listened to Jo playing a sad and lyrical piece.

'Do you like or play any sport, Julia?' Jim said.

'I played tennis at school and sometimes with friends. My serve isn't brilliant, but passable. My backhand is better. What about you?'

'I like sport, but rugby is my passion. I'm in the squadron team and played at school. Would you fancy coming to Twickenham for the England versus France game?'

On a cold February day, I dressed in a jumper, coat, scarf, woolly hat and boots, and travelled with Jim to the Twickenham Rugby Stadium. The crowd carried us along until my feet barely touched the ground. Jim looked tweedy in his brown jacket as he guided me through the mob, a collective sound of voices high and low, and when we climbed up to our seats, I stared at the pitch, watching some of the players exercising, doing press-ups and throwing the ball in preparation for the game. Jim said he was expecting a couple, Rich from his squadron and Poppy, his girlfriend, and said their seats were behind us.

While we waited, he explained the basics, which seemed complicated, but I couldn't wait for it to start.

'I'm afraid the seats will be uncomfortable, but you won't notice after a while.'

'I'm covered well in the seating department,' I said, making Jim laugh.

He was right, I didn't notice. I was only aware of his presence beside me at the end of the row, the brief brush of his arm and the shift of his legs during the game. I sensed him looking at me, and once I turned and caught his eye, we smiled.

'Hi Jim,' an American voice spoke behind us. My heart fluttered.

When I turned around, a tall man with lean features stood beside a blonde girl with high cheekbones who must have been Poppy. Jim explained that Rich was from the United States Air Force but was posted to his squadron for about two and a half years. We watched the teams coming onto the pitch, and the national anthem of the two countries echoed, making us feel proud. The whistle blew, and the crowd quietened, watching intently, then shouting encouragement or cheering when they scored a try. I stood up and clapped with the rest of them, joining the ripple of waving flags, the stadium in moving colour. I was excited to see a player running the field with the

CHAPTER 10

ball, dodging the threatening players and reaching the finish line. I loved the oval ball sailing through the posts when England scored. Sometimes, Jim leaned forward to see a lineout or scrum, and I noticed the strength of his shoulders and the way his hair shaped at the back of his head. The man next to me was on the large side, so part of him occupied the edge of my seat. I tried to push him away, but being an enthusiastic England supporter, he was up and down like a jack-in-the-box. France won, but we all enjoyed the game. We moved with the crowd to leave the stadium for a drink in a nearby pub and found seats by a log fire, while Jim and Rich went to the bar to order our drinks.

Poppy told me she lived with her family at the air force station as her stepfather was a group captain, but she was thinking about moving to Lincoln to be nearer her part-time job in a book shop tucked away in a small street near the cathedral.

She said it was easy being at home, although her mother and stepfather weren't sure about her relationship with Rich.

'Why is that? Don't they like him?' I asked, curious to know why.

'They don't want me to be serious about someone from another country and then marry him and disappear.'

'Do you want to marry him?' I asked, putting her on the spot.

'I haven't thought about marriage. Rich hasn't asked me or talked about it.'

Poppy and I were only in our early twenties and marriage for me seemed a long way off.

When Rich gave me a shandy, I asked what part of America he was from, although I didn't know one place from another.

'My father is British, and my mother is American. She came here as an au pair and met my father. I was born here, but my father was transferred to the United States with the company when I was five. We lived in California.

'I understand it has a lovely climate,' I said.

'Mediterranean style.'

I pictured a vast, warm place, in contrast to the cold February day we had braved to watch the game.

'Do you play rugby in America?' I asked.

'It's not one of our main sports like baseball or basketball. I've become anglicised and love the game, although I'm not in the squadron team like Jim.'

Poppy looked pale, clutched her stomach and said she felt sick and needed the cloakroom, and I went with her. She was a long time in the cubicle, and I was about to knock when she emerged.

'How are you feeling?' I asked.

'Not too good. The curry I had at a friend's last night had a strange taste.'

'You're welcome to stay in the flat tonight if you don't want to drive back,' I suggested.

'We'll sleep anywhere,' replied Rich.

Walking away from the pub I wanted to know the time, but when I looked at my wrist, I realised I had lost my watch. I stopped in horror. It was an unusual watch with an oval face, and a linked chain for the wristband. It had belonged to a great-aunt and was bequeathed to me when she died. I knew the catch was faulty but, stupidly, hadn't done anything about it.

CHAPTER 10

'I must have left it in the Ladies cloakroom. I'll have to go back.' I said, when I told Jim.

'We'll catch you up,' Jim called to Rich.

Jim and I pushed our way through the crowd back to the pub. I looked everywhere in the cloakroom, on the basins, the floor, and in the empty cubicles. One of them was engaged so I waited for the person come out, but when she did, the watch wasn't there or anywhere, and I hoped it hadn't been stolen. I joined Jim at the bar and described it to the barman. A woman serving said she thought someone had handed it in and would look in lost property. She was away for ages, and I began to worry that it had gone for good.

'Is this your watch?' she said, holding it up and putting it on the counter.

Because it was different and old-looking, it had become a topic of conversation among the bar staff, each trying to guess the date it was made, and some debated whether the linked chain was solid gold.

'It's a lovely watch. I suggest you get the faulty catch repaired,' the bar lady advised.

As soon as we got into the flat, Poppy rushed into the bathroom and vomited. I said she must sleep in my bed for the night and suggested she keep a bucket beside her. She lay down under the covers in her underwear. Rich decided on the sofa, and Jim slept on an old rubber Lilo on the floor.

'One of you could have Babs's bed, but it'd be awkward if she returned in the early hours,' I said, with a chuckle.

'That could be fun,' Jim said, winking at me.

I made up a folding bed we had for visitors, put it in the sitting room, and found a sleeping bag in one of the cupboards to use for extra warmth. The three of us left Poppy resting in bed and went out to a bistro not far from the flat, but Saturday night was busy, and we had to wait for a table and then for our order. After plates of steaming spaghetti and a glass of red wine, we returned to the flat and prepared for bed.

Fortunately, Poppy was asleep when I looked in the bedroom, but I spent the night trying to block out Jim and Rich's loud snores, and when one stopped, the other started. I drifted into a light sleep, and when I awoke, I thought I'd fallen out of bed. I looked up at the ceiling with its ornate pattern and four ceiling roses, realising I'd never studied it before. It was impressive but would look even better with a coat of paint. I checked on Poppy, but the gentle rise and fall under the blankets assured me she was sleeping peacefully. I rinsed out the bucket and went into the kitchen to prepare breakfast.

The chaps looked zombie-like, and Poppy appeared pale and fragile, dressed in her jeans and beige jumper. She had a few bites of toast, honey, and a weak cup of tea.

'How are you feeling now, Poppy?'

'I don't feel sick anymore, and my tummy ache's gone, and thank you so much for giving me your bed, Julia. I wouldn't have coped with the drive back yesterday.'

After breakfast, they gathered their belongings, and I hoped she wouldn't be car-sick on the journey. I looked forward to seeing Jim again and enjoyed the ease I felt with him, unlike the tension with Russell, who wasn't like a proper boyfriend, but someone who contacted you when he felt like it. Maybe I saw something in the relationship that wasn't there but for Jim to invite me to watch his favourite sport was a compliment, and I would be happy to do it again.

CHAPTER 11

'Are you ready?' Poppy called out to me, anxious to be on our way to the shops.

Poppy was staying with me in London and had offered to be my shopping buddy to find an outfit for the summer ball. Jim had invited me to be his partner, and I didn't hesitate to accept. Our first port of call was Bond Street, and she stopped outside a shop with a silk dress displayed on a stand. It looked expensive.

'Try it on,' said Poppy.

The assistant found my size and led me into a changing room, which was more like a sitting room, with easy chairs and a couch. She said she'd return in five minutes to give me time, but after I'd struggled to zip up the back, I knew the dress wasn't right. I was relieved to put my clothes back on before the assistant entered the room with two similar dresses.

'They don't fit properly,' I said, and we quickly left the shop.

Our next stop was the King's Road, Chelsea. We passed busy boutiques and cafes until we saw the entrance to a large undercover market full of clothes. At the far end, Poppy picked out a pale burgundy ballgown with thin shoulder straps for me to try on. We went to the changing room, and she said it flattered my figure and suited me perfectly. It was easy to wear, and when I looked in the long mirror, it said, 'Buy me'. At the shoe shop next door, I had the whole floor covered, but I found a pair of evening shoes in a similar colour to the dress and hoped I could manage the heels. I packed the dress in layers of tissue paper and the shoes in their bag.

We caught the train to Lincoln and found a non-smoking carriage with plenty of space on the rack to put our cases. The carriage was empty, apart from a man with a briefcase who stared at us until we arrived at our stop. I was glad to get out, and when we walked towards the exit, we saw Jim hurrying to meet us, and he helped us with our cases, fitting them in the boot. It wasn't long before we left the city behind and were in the countryside, the roads narrow and twisty.

We passed the RAF base on our way to Poppy's house, and I looked in awe at the line of aircraft. When I heard the engines roar, I turned and saw two take off, their swept-back wings and noses pointing to the sky. The flat land stretched for miles, surrounded by red brick buildings, and further away, groups of married quarters, homogenous, with no outstanding features to tell them apart. Areas of grass and trees in the distance softened the starkness, but any desire to live away from the station was not allowed. Poppy's stepfather, being a higher rank, lived in a bigger house set apart from the others, double-fronted with a Georgian appearance. I wondered what it was like inside. The house was spacious and formally laid out, with a square hall and two equally sized reception rooms. The married quarters were furnished, although you were allowed to

CHAPTER 11

add your furniture if there was room. There were several pictures of aircraft, one of a spitfire doing aerobatics and a large portrait, in oils, of a man in uniform, Poppy's stepfather. I was shown the guest room, left my overnight bag on the bed, and joined Jim and Rich downstairs in the sitting room, sipping sherry. There were groups of framed photos on a sideboard, one of Poppy and her older sister in Switzerland, but they didn't look like sisters. She had short dark hair with a round face, the opposite of Poppy's blonde hair and prominent cheekbones. She showed me another of her mother and stepfather at a formal dinner, he is looking ahead, and her mother is talking to the guest next to her.

'What about your father, Poppy? Where does he live?'

'In Sydney. He married Sasha, an Australian, when she was here on an overseas tour, and they went to live there, her hometown.'

'Have you ever visited them?'

'Yes, and I'm due to go again within the next two years. Perhaps you'd like to come with me, Julia.'

That sounded like an enticing invitation, but it depended on what else was happening in my life.

'I may take you up on that, Poppy,' I said.

We all separated to dress for the ball; I dropped in a bottle of bubbles for a long soak in the bath before dressing in my new matching underwear and the ball gown. Poppy and I sat in the back of the car on our way to the Officer's Mess, careful not to spoil our dresses or ladder our stockings. As we drove, I sensed an air of discipline beneath the superficial bonhomie. We could hear the dance music and followed the sound of a live band to the ballroom, a kaleidoscope of colour, the gowns in contrast to the dark suits, white shirts, and bowties. The buffet choices were extensive, with hot and cold food and sumptuous desserts accompanied by champagne, wine, Pimm's or anything else you fancied. It all looked grand, and when Jim pulled me to the dance floor, we merged with the swaying mass.

Poppy looked beautiful in a pale blue figure-hugging silk dress matching her long blonde hair, and Rich couldn't stop staring at her. I wanted to discover more about Jim and his family, and sitting out one of the dances, he said his father was a businessman, and his younger brother was at Durham University. They were happy their older son was a pilot and doing something he liked, the opposite to my stepfather, who was very scathing about my going to London to live instead of reading for a degree at Oxford University.

'Do you regret going to London?' Jim asked.

'Not at all. I enjoy it, and my job is going well at the publishing company. I may study for a degree later.'

'Where would you study? Are you thinking of somewhere in London?' he asked, puzzled.

I hadn't thought seriously of where I would study, but it had made an impression on him. Maybe he didn't approve of women studying later in life.

'Do you ever feel homesick?' he asked, wrinkling his brow.

'Sometimes I miss Mum and worry about her and my controlling stepfather, but I wouldn't go back and live at home.'

'I wouldn't have met you if you'd gone to Oxford,' he said.

'How do you like living in an Officer's Mess? Is it a little like boarding school?'

CHAPTER 11

Jim laughed. 'Not quite,' he said. 'We have more freedom, but it's only temporary before we settle down. Some of the chaps on the squadron are married and live in married quarters.'

'Would you prefer that?' I said, thinking of the rows of identical brick houses we passed to the ball.

Jim hesitated. 'With the right person, yes, I would.'

When Jim was away, Poppy sat beside me, out of breath, her face flushed. She had met Rich at a party not long after he'd joined the squadron, and they had hit it off almost immediately.

'You'll miss him when he leaves unless...' I ventured.

'Hmm. Not sure at this stage. I like Rich, but air force life as a wife has restrictions.'

'What do you mean?'

'The usual tour of duty is two and a half years. At the end of that period, the officers get a posting to another RAF base. You can't feel settled anywhere, and most families send their children to boarding schools for consistency. Also, you must entertain and attend functions even if you don't feel like it. There's a protocol to follow. Occasions like this can be fun, but life isn't all balls and parties, and it's always the same people, making the conversation stale and repetitive.'

'I suppose you could try and meet non-service people,' I suggested.

'Yes, that's possible, but you have to make an effort and like them anyway.'

'Is there much bitchiness or competition?'

'You get that in any closed society. Then there are sherry mornings when you have to invite all the wives on the squadron, not just the ones you like.'

I wondered how I would fit into air force life but didn't think it was my scene. I would be jumping ahead if I thought of Jim in the context of marriage, but Poppy's words shone a new light on service life. Alternatively, you could make the most of seeing new places and enjoy the change.

'The accommodation is nice, judging by your parents' house.'

'A higher-ranking officer has a larger house. The ones for the lower ranks are more basic. The walls are magnolia, but if you paint any wall a different colour, you must change it back to its original colour before you leave.'

'That sounds boring and bossy.'

'There's lots of bossiness,' Poppy replied. 'And you don't leave a married quarter, you "march out".'

'What, literally?' We laughed and did marching movements.

Jim and I joined the jiving dancers, making up our steps, and Jim twirling me until I felt dizzy. He was a good dancer and had rhythm, unlike most men. We stayed on the floor for a slow smooch, and as Jim held me close, I could feel his muscular chest and strong fingers on my back. After the music stopped, we stayed apart and held our hands out to each other, and then Jim hugged me like a strong bear. But back at our table, Poppy was frantic. Rich was on the other side of the dance floor with a busty blonde having a good time, and she was going over to sort them out. I offered to assist by diverting his attention, but Poppy told me not to and strode over to where they were in a clinch. There was much gesticulation while the busty blonde stood on the sidelines until Poppy returned and said she was leaving and nothing could change her mind.

CHAPTER 11

Poppy retrieved her wrap from the back of her chair and disappeared into the night, her cheekbones taut and angry. I worried I'd have to spend the night in her garden if she was too far gone to let me in. Jim stood and took control, got Rich away from Busty, fetched the car and drove us across the airfield towards her house, but it wasn't long before we saw a slim figure holding her shoes, her feet squelching in the dawn-soaked grass. Jim stopped the car and wound the window down.

'Get in, Poppy,' he said.

She pretended not to hear and went straight to the house, unlocked the door and disappeared inside. When we arrived, Rich found her collapsed in a chair, holding her broken stiletto heel. He stood behind her, put his hands on her shoulders and kissed the top of her head, but she remained motionless.

After Jim and Rich returned to the Mess, we had a nightcap. Poppy had a whisky, and I opted for a brandy.

'Do you see your sister much?' I asked.

'Not often, but I like seeing my nephews when I do. What about you?'

'Only when I go home. Helen is always busy being a nurse and is usually on duty.'

'Do your parents worry when you'll marry?' I asked.

'Periodically, they bring up the topic, but I'll marry when it's right.'

'Me too,' I said.

That night, I had a vivid dream of a plane crash. The details were vague, but I saw the aircraft twisting out of control, and the sight of charred wings and fuselage among the scattered debris stayed with me for a long time.

On Sunday morning, I awoke late and remembered that Jim had suggested we go to the beach before I returned to London. I saw Jim standing in the hall, spruce and ready to go out, but I must have looked bleary-eyed and half asleep when I came down the stairs.

'Are you ready, Julia?' he asked, sounding efficient.

'Just give me a few minutes, Jim.'

I went to the bathroom, splashed cold water on my face, applied skin cream and pale lipstick and felt more able to face the day. We headed for the beach, and I longed to breathe the sea air and perhaps paddle at the water's edge. The morning was warm and still, with a slight breeze from the sea, and a few people were sitting or lying on the sand, watching children build sandcastles with turrets or similar structures. Some were digging holes to sit in or were covering each other so only their heads showed, the rest of them a lumpy mound.

We removed our shoes, and the salt water tickled our bare feet as we walked together.

'I love being by the sea,' I said, breathing deeply.

'Yes, it gives you a boost and makes you feel healthy,' Jim agreed.

We walked along the beach, but I could hear my tummy rumbling as I hadn't eaten breakfast.

'Shall we have a bite to eat?' Jim suggested, reading my thoughts or perhaps hearing rumbling noises.

We found a busy cafe and ordered plates of fish and chips and glasses of beer.

'How long have you got at the station here?' I asked, wondering where he would go next.

'I'm due to be posted soon.'

CHAPTER 11

'Do you have any idea where they'll send you?'

'No idea at all. It could be abroad.' He looked at me intently, waiting for a reaction. We were getting closer as a couple, so being sent overseas would be disappointing.

'Where could you go abroad?'

'Cyprus, Aden, or several places in Germany. But it will probably be somewhere more local.'

I hoped I would see Jim again soon and was tempted to invite him for a weekend in London but was too shy to ask. He took me to catch my train and said he'd call me one day in the week. I sat on the train with a warm feeling as I gazed at the passing scenery, but as we approached London, I felt melancholy, and thought of home comforts like Mum's tasty Sunday suppers that Helen would enjoy instead of me. It was not as if I wanted to go back and live at home, it was just the lonely feeling you get in London sometimes. But when I opened my front door, there was a note from Babs: *Julia, I won't be in Sunday night. See you tomorrow evening. Love Babs."*

CHAPTER 12

After I had been to the summer ball with Jim, Babs said we had an invitation to a party in the flat upstairs. I had never been to their flat but didn't want to be at a drug party and surrounded by a haze of cannabis smoke. I didn't like ordinary cigarettes, so no one could tempt me to smoke pot. I tried to think of an excuse not to go, but Babs was insistent and said Miriam, one of the girls in the flat, would be disappointed if we didn't. Unfortunately, I couldn't see Jim that weekend, as he was on a survival course, and Babs knew I had nothing else to do.

'We don't have to stay long, only show ourselves for an hour or so and then leave. No one will notice, as everyone will be "out of it",' Babs said, trying to convince me.

I was still enjoying the memory of the RAF ball, but I said I'd go if only for a short time as I had a headache and didn't feel like partying until the small hours.

I found a necklace of dark red beads Helen had given me one Christmas and wore it to fit in with the hippies. I dabbed on a smear of lipstick, finished off a glass of wine Babs was drinking, and we climbed the stairs. By the time we had stopped faffing around and decided to go to the party, we were late, and everyone had been there for ages. You could see the haze wafting outside their door, and when I entered,

CHAPTER 12

I tripped over someone stretched out on the floor. Comatose bodies sprawled everywhere, some slumped in chairs or lying across the sofa. Miriam said how pleased she was to see us and offered us a drink. I had a glass of red wine while Babs had a gin and tonic. Babs wandered over to speak to a group of boys she knew, and I met a few of Miriam's friends, who were all smoking pot and giggling, but I had no idea what was funny. I sat on the sofa beside a girl who wore a skimpy top and numerous rows of beads around her neck. She asked me where I worked, and when I told her, she said she knew someone who used to work there.

'Who was that?' I asked.

'Russell, someone.'

Hearing his name out of the blue made me gasp visibly. I hadn't thought about him for a long time since meeting Jim and was catapulted to a previous life.

'You knew Russell Bankes?' I said, amazed.

'Yes, vaguely, but not very well. He went out with a friend of mine.'

'Really! When was that?' I asked, astounded.

'Oh, ages ago. I only met Russell a few times.'

'Did you like him?' I asked, curious.

'Yes, he was a dish,' she replied.

'I also went out with him for a while,' I said, hoping to surprise her.

The girl studied me and looked perplexed. Perhaps she thought I wasn't Russell's type.

I wondered how many different women he had been out with, but he must have been a "ladies' man".

'Do you know where he is now?' I asked, not confident I would find out.

'No, I've lost touch with the friend who went out with him. She has moved abroad somewhere.'

I was so surprised to bump into someone who knew Russell that I went and poured myself another glass of red wine and saw Babs still talking to the group and smoking. I knew she smoked, but there was a "no smoking rule" in the flat. I wondered if she was smoking pot and checked to see if she was laughing hysterically. Babs wasn't, but was listening to a young hippy type who may have been telling her a joke. I started to feel peckish and looked around for something to eat. I saw a plate of homemade shortbread biscuits and took two from the plate on a side table. The red wine had made me feel woozy, so I went to ask Miriam if I could get a cup of coffee with the biscuits. She said they only had Nescafe but showed me the kitchen and where the mugs were. I made a cup with a drop of milk from the fridge and ate the two biscuits. I went back to talk to the beaded girl on the sofa, but her face was starting to look distorted and kept changing as if it were liquid. I stared at her, trying to make it out, but attributed it to fatigue and vowed I wouldn't stay at the party for more than an hour.

The Who were playing on a record player with separate speakers, making me sleepy, but the liquid face beside me multiplied. I blinked, trying to erase what I saw, but a dark tunnel opened, the walls decorated with wide, laughing mouths, the ground moving with swarms of insects. I think I was shouting and trying to push the mouths away, but they came through the narrow tunnel, enclosing me in a tiny space. I felt like Alice in Wonderland, but as hard as I tried to push the walls away, I couldn't move them until I began

CHAPTER 12

to feel suffocated. I heard someone say, 'Julia, are you okay?' but I screamed and blacked out.

When I woke up, I was in a bed with a ceiling light shining on my face, and the room looked too white and bright. I had no recollection or memory of anything since the party. I must have vomited as there was a receptacle by the bed, and I felt as though I wanted to be sick again and tried to sit up but was too weak and fell back on the pillows. I didn't recognise where I was, but the faint smell of disinfectant suggested I was in a hospital. The sound of squelching shoes in the corridor outside gave me a clue and a nurse appeared and stood by my bed. She gave me a glass of water, and I drank the welcome liquid through a straw until I had drunk the last drop.

'Julia, two friends brought you here after you collapsed at a party. It's very likely you ingested LSD from cakes or biscuits, and as you had drunk alcohol, you had a bad trip. What did you have to eat?' the nurse asked.

'I had two biscuits, that's all.'

'That would be enough. Now you must rest. Your friend Babs will be here during visiting hours this afternoon.'

'Did she bring me here?'

'Two of them came in the ambulance. They were very concerned.'

I longed to see Babs's familiar face and escape the hospital ward that wasn't helping my condition. I thought about Mummy and what she'd think about my experience, but I wouldn't tell her about it. She would be shocked and worried. Ian would say I was stupid and shouldn't be at parties like that.

'I'd like to use the bathroom, please,' I said to a replacement nurse, desperate.

The nurse took my arm, and I gingerly walked along the ward.

The nurse stayed with me as I sponged my face and washed my hands. I longed to clean my teeth to eliminate the sour taste in my mouth and hoped Babs would bring my sponge bag when she visited. I felt wobbly on the way back to the ward and flopped onto the bed, exhausted. When I awoke again, Babs and Miriam had arrived with a bouquet of summer flowers, and the sweet scent wafted around my bed. They looked worried and said I was having a fit, screaming and clawing at something, and they didn't know what to do with me, but when I fainted, they called an ambulance. Babs handed me my sponge bag and a clean skirt and blouse and put the dirty ones in a bag to wash when she got home.

'We won't stay long, Julia, but we'll come and visit you tomorrow. It was frightening. A few others ate the biscuits, but luckily, they weren't affected,' Babs said.

'I am very sorry, Julia, that this has happened. We have no idea who laced the biscuits with LSD, but I can assure you it wasn't us. We will attempt to find out who it was,' Miriam said, frowning.

'Thanks for the lovely flowers and visiting me,' I said, exhausted.

Although I was exhausted, I was too scared to go to sleep in case I had nightmares. The nurse gave me a light sedative, which I pretended to swallow, keeping it under my tongue. I don't think I slept at all because a group of nurses talked in raised voices for most of the night, which was very thoughtless of them, and in the morning, I struggled with a cup of tea and a bowl of cardboard-tasting cornflakes.

CHAPTER 12

When the nurse came to remove the tray, she said Mr Maddox had called to enquire how I was.

'Thank you. That was Jim, a close friend of mine. He must have rung the flat, and Babs told him what happened. Did he leave a message?'

'He asked me to pass on his love and good wishes.'

I was chuffed that he took the trouble to ring the hospital and presumed he had survived the course. I couldn't wait to see him again, and I bathed in a warm glow like a warm bath.

Most of the beds in the ward were empty, but a woman in one further down had her leg and arm in plaster resting on a pulley, and I presumed she was an accident case. When the nurse returned to take my blood pressure and temperature, she said I had to stay another night because both were too high. I slept a little, and when I awoke, I looked down the empty ward where the accident woman lay and found the strength to put on my slippers, to visit her. She smiled, pleased to see me. She had been hit by a speeding car at night when she was crossing the road to her flat and had a badly fractured arm and leg and several broken ribs. The groceries she'd bought from the shop opposite lay scattered across the road, but as it was a hit-and-run, it was a while before someone called an ambulance. Recovery was slow and frustrating, and she had weeks as a patient in the hospital before she could leave.

'I hope the police catch the driver,' I said, shocked.

'I doubt it,' she said.

Early the next morning, a doctor came with a bunch of students who gathered around my bed, but they all looked too young to be trainee doctors. He explained my condition and threw questions at them, and it turned into a morality lesson, which made me feel like a drug addict, as though I had purposely taken LSD. He said he would discharge me that day but to be careful, 'young lady', of innocent-looking cakes. The students sniggered and moved on to the next patient.

When I said goodbye to the accident patient, she wished me good luck and said her 18-year-old daughter had had a similar experience to mine and was wary about eating anything at parties.

Back at the flat, a large pot of pink and white camellias sat on the doorstep, accompanied by a card that read: *'We are so sorry, Julia and hope you feel better soon. With love from Miriam."*

When I thanked Miriam for the flowers, she said they had found the LSD culprit who laced the biscuits. He was the chap talking to Babs at the party, and he and some friends did it as a joke. But when they knew about my reaction and hospital stay, they were shamefaced and apologetic. Babs assured me he didn't say anything to her about the LSD during their conversation. It was a learning curve for me to be more careful.

CHAPTER 13

I was nervous the day I was meeting Jim for lunch after his interview at the Ministry of Defence. I told Susan I wouldn't have more than an hour out of the office, and she said she'd keep me to that.

Whitehall was bleak the day Jim had his interview, the wind lifting fragments of paper around his feet as if they were autumn leaves. His appointment was at eleven-thirty, and to be on time, he hailed a taxicab to drop him outside the Ministry of Defence. He went into the dimly lit foyer, climbed two flights of stairs, found the interview room and knocked on the heavy door. A Squadron Leader, a man in his thirties, shook his hand, showed him a seat, and sat behind a large desk. Sitting opposite, Jim felt nervous and excited, waiting to hear about his future.

'A post has become available with the Sultan of Oman's Air Force,' said the Squadron Leader, studying a file of papers on his desk. Jim waited to hear more.

'It's a voluntary unaccompanied eighteen-month tour with a break of six weeks after nine months. I assume you are single?' the officer said.

'I am, sir,' Jim replied.

'If you take my advice, I'd accept it, or it could jeopardise your career advancement,' the officer said, looking directly at him. 'A large percentage of the job is supporting the army, and flying is often in a stifling cockpit over mountainous terrain,' he continued.

'That won't be a problem,' Jim replied.

They discussed conditions and pay, and Jim agreed to accept and made a mental note to pop into the library and read up about the history of Muscat and Oman. When he left the Ministry, he felt nervous and wondered how I would react to him being away for nine months. He walked briskly to the restaurant near Trafalgar Square and pictured my silhouette through the window, praying I would understand why he had accepted the posting.

'Your cheeks are cold. Did you walk?' I said when he kissed me.

The tension hung in the air, and to compensate, Jim ordered a bottle of good red wine, a martini each, and our entrees.

'Well, what's the verdict?' I said, not wanting to waste any time, but all I heard was Muscat, eighteen months, and a lot of flying.

'Eighteen months!' I exclaimed. 'That's ages. And I suppose I can't visit you there as it's so remote?'

'No, I'm afraid not. But it will pass quickly, and we can do lots together during my six-week break.'

I drank more wine and picked at the breaded mushrooms. I couldn't believe this was happening. I hadn't known Jim long, and now I wouldn't see him for nine months. I knew it wouldn't be fair to persuade him to turn down the posting, so I would find a way of dealing with it.

'I understand how you feel, Julia, but it's a step up for me, and I can't turn it down.'

CHAPTER 13

'No, you mustn't. It's how it is. I'll deal with it.'

'I have four weeks before I go and thought we could spend a few days together in France.'

'France would be wonderful.'

He sighed with relief, and we began to make plans.

After lunch, Jim walked to the St James's Square library and read more about the country and surrounding area. The librarian directed him to the history section, and browsing the shelves, he found a couple of books and took them to an empty table to read about his next port of call. Jim read about its ancient history and how the Portuguese had dominated the area in the 16th and 17th Century. He found a short piece about Muscat and Oman in one of the library books: "Tucked away on the edge of Saudi Arabia and facing the Indian Ocean and Persian Gulf lie the states of Muscat and Oman. Unlike other countries of Eastern Arabia, Oman is the oldest independent state in the Arab world. On the immense expanse of the desert beyond the Hajar mountain ranges lived the Bedouin tribes, carrying out their daily lives under the trees. Here, they tended their goats and camels, and it was not unusual to see a man riding a donkey with the woman walking a few paces behind. It was to this part of the world in 1958 that members of the Royal Air Force were attached to the Sultan of Muscat and Oman's Armed Forces. There had been an internal conflict between the people of Muscat and Oman for many years due to strong differences. Muscat rests on the coastal lowland, and its people are cosmopolitan and seafaring, with a mixture of nationalities, including Persian, Arab, Indian, and Baluch. On the other hand, Oman is in the interior mountains, and the area is agricultural and pastoral. The people are strictly

Arab, and the religion is the puritanical Ibadhi Moslem sect. A treaty was signed in 1920 at the small coastal town of Seet between the Sultan of Muscat and the Imam of Oman to help control the many internal rebellions. This treaty also gave the Omanis the right to administer their local affairs."

Jim arranged the trip to France, and we decided to take the ferry mid-week and stay with his parents, Hilary and Francis, the night before. He was anxious about his mother's reaction to me as she could be critical, but he was sure his father would like me.

We arrived at six, and the aroma of a three-course dinner wafted around the house. After I'd presented Hilary with a bouquet of warm-coloured autumnal flowers, she found a cut-glass vase and arranged the flowers, putting them in the vase, one by one, until she was satisfied. She showed me the guest room upstairs at the end of a passage and the bathroom next door. I looked at the other bedroom doors and wondered which one was Jim's, but not wanting to linger, I followed her down the stairs. It was warm for late September, although the cool evenings reminded us that summer was almost over.

'I love this soup. Gazpacho, isn't it?' said Jim, taking a spoonful of Hilary's soup, the green liquid lying in shallow white soup bowls.

'Jim tells us you live in London, Julia. Which area?' said Hilary, breaking a piece of bread.

'Holland Park,' I said, hoping she'd approve.

'Where did you meet Jim?'

'In a club where I play the piano on Friday evenings.'

'That's different! Is that your job?' Hilary said with a little snort.

CHAPTER 13

It was like walking on eggshells with Hilary who looked at me critically whenever I spoke. She probably doesn't approve of me after Jim's previous girlfriend.

'No, I'm in publishing.'

'You must be a good pianist. How enterprising to do a little moonlighting,' said Francis.

Jim laughed, and Francis gave a wry smile.

The next course was a paella, and Francis produced a different wine to go with the course.

'Mum and Dad often go to Spain and love it there, although we'll be sampling French food for the next few days.'

'I'm not so keen on France,' said Hilary.

'This is where we disagree,' Francis said.

After a sweet souffle for dessert, we sat together in the sitting room, and Jim showed me photos of his brothers, his twin who died, and his younger brother.

'Which twin are you, Jim? You look so alike.'

'I'm on the right. Our eyebrows are different if you look closely.'

'Philip's got a rounder face than you and different eyes.'

'Ah, looking at my boys. We have albums of them,' said Hilary.

'Losing Jim's twin brother must have been hard,' I said, thinking of my father. My memory of Daddy is like photos in an album, with no definite beginning or end, like holding my hand when we went for a walk, his hand, large, compared to mine.

'It was hard for all of us, Julia. They are always with you. It must've been difficult for your widowed mother and two young children, but I hear she's married again. I am pleased she has found someone special to share her life with,' Hilary said.

'I often think of Mummy on her own and us two young girls, sometimes a bit of a handful.'

I didn't want to elaborate on Mummy and Ian's relationship with Jim's parents, especially his mother. She came across as inflexible and eager to indulge in adversity in a gossipy way. I had mentioned my difficulty with Ian to Jim, but I hadn't gone into detail, particularly Ian's visit to London.

After Francis poured Jim a whisky, Hilary went to the kitchen, and I went upstairs to leave Jim and his father together.

'I hope you'll adapt to the heat and terrain in Oman,' Francis said to Jim.

'I'll be fine, Dad.'

'Congratulations, Jim. It's a good posting. I'm proud of you.'

Jim popped his head around my door to wish me sweet dreams, and when I asked him, he said his room was down a passage off the main one.

'We have an early start tomorrow, so lots of sleep tonight, darling. It'll be a long day tomorrow, and we'll have to find somewhere to stay on the way. You have good French, so that's your job to do the talking.' Jim smiled and closed the door.

I woke up in the night, hearing footsteps stop outside my door, but when they receded, all was quiet, although I didn't sleep for the rest of the night.

Hilary and Francis looked tired but were up to give us breakfast of boiled eggs, toast and coffee to wish us a bon voyage. It was early, and the traffic was light, so we had plenty of time.

CHAPTER 13

'Do you think your mother liked me?' I asked.

'I'm sure she did, although she hasn't said one way or the other. She probably sensed your strong character, but there's nothing wrong with that.'

'Have you brought many girlfriends, home, Jim?'

'Only one other serious one. Marta was Argentinian, but it didn't work out, and she returned home.'

I imagined a passionate, hot-blooded Spanish type.

'What did she look like?'

'She had oval brown eyes and spoke good English, but with an accent.'

'Did your parents like her?'

'Yes, especially Mum. Anyway, it's you now.'

His parents were very relaxed about us going on holiday together. I knew many parents who wouldn't approve of anything like that before marriage.

'I'm excited we can be together,' said Jim, taking my hand.

As we drove down to the ferry port at Dover, the September early morning sun shone in our faces, making it difficult to see. I had Jim's directions and a map on my lap that kept falling to the floor.

'Let's see your passport photo, Jule,' Jim said when we stopped in the queue to board the ferry. He studied my face, staring into the lens with a fixed look like a waxwork.

'Why do passport photos always make us look like criminals?'

'What about yours,' I said and remarked how photogenic he was, even a passport photo.

After Jim positioned the car on the lower deck, we went up to watch the receding cliffs and to listen to the cry of the circling seagulls leading us out of the port. We stood close together by the rail, looking ahead to get our sea legs, feeling the gentle swell of the calm sea, and neither of us spoke, alone in our thoughts, thinking about our separation.

Once off the ferry, we had to be alert to find the correct road from Calais to our destination. We followed the signposts, and after driving for nearly seven hours, we needed a break. As we approached Lyon, the heavens opened, and through the wet, a deep-red glow from a restaurant window looked inviting. When we opened the door, the warmth, chatter and flicker of candles in red glass jars persuaded us to stay, and when the proprietor approached us, I asked if we could have a table for dinner and whether there was accommodation for one night.

After we'd feasted on steak, chips, and the house red, the proprietor took us to a flight of stone steps outside, flanked by peeling walls, and showed us a room with orange wallpaper and black bed linen. We looked at each other but didn't have the energy to find somewhere else. We undressed and immediately fell into a dreamless sleep, but I woke early, feeling lumps on my leg and scratching.

'Jim, I'm covered in red bites.'

'So am I. The bites are on my arms, legs and back. It looks like the bed bugs have been busy.'

Jim pulled off the sheets and blankets to try and find evidence of the nasty beasts, but they had vanished, so we dressed and settled the bill. When we were leaving, a woman asked if we'd stayed the night there and said, 'Le restaurant est bon, mais n'y restez pas.'

We smiled, shrugged, said au revoir, and drove around the streets of Lyon before finding a little cafe on the outskirts, and after coffee, rolls, and jam, our optimism returned. We

CHAPTER 13

passed lovely stretches of hills and countryside on our way to Languedoc-Roussillon. After checking in at our pension in Uzès, we wandered around the market town in the warm evening, looking at the shops and stopped for a drink in the central square shaded by plane trees. Some artists had set up their easels to paint the arches bordering the square, and we wandered over to look, standing a little way back so as not to appear intrusive.

'Do you mind if we have a look?' I asked.

'You're welcome,' said Bea, one of the artists, who was English.

'Do you sell any?' asked Jim.

'Yes, we do, often to local people. Would you like to see some we have for sale?'

We arranged to visit Bea and her friend Eunice at their house near the square, so after a shower and treating our bites with ointment bought from a chemist shop in Lyon, we got ready to visit the two artists and enjoy the warm evening. We walked along the narrow, cobbled streets to where Bea and Eunice lived, in a stone house with shutters, theirs painted a dark blue, matching Jim's shirt. They welcomed us into a large, airy room with a tiled floor, the walls covered with paintings, and through an arch, we could see their studio. Bea offered us kir cassis and a selection of olives, vol au vents, and little truffle canapés.

'I think we've both fallen in love with France,' said Jim.

'This is a lovely part of the country, and we wouldn't live anywhere else,' said Eunice, with intense brown eyes.

'Come and see if you fancy anything to buy,' said Bea, her short fair hair touching her glasses, making Jim wonder how she could see to paint.

Bea's medium was watercolour, while Eunice was mainly a portrait painter in oils. Jim chose one of Bea's, a watercolour of light and shadows from trees around a courtyard, the house in the background, its shutters half closed in the evening light. I thought of Mum's clever use of colour and how her artwork was as good as the two artists we met in France.

'This is wonderful and will remind me of our trip to France,' said Jim.

I stayed quiet and hid my tears.

CHAPTER 14

Every morning, as I lay in bed, Bea's painting of the lavender fields in France reminded me of Jim. He had stood behind me as I was daydreaming from the window in Uzes and rested his hands on my shoulders.

'I have something for you,' he said, and I took the watercolour painting wrapped in brown paper. It was beautiful, the lavender colour vibrant but blending perfectly with distant houses and hills of France. I wondered how he'd bought it without me knowing, but maybe it was when I rested one afternoon. He said he was going out for a short while and then sneaked it back when I was sleepy from the wine at lunch: a delicious serving of salade nicoise, followed by a plate of local cheeses and French bread. I love French food, tastier than ours and am inspired to base all my cooking on their cuisine.

I carefully removed the roll of film from the camera, took it to be processed and couldn't wait to relive our French experience. The first slide I picked was one of me leaning over the rail on the ferry, and I popped it into the little viewer and held it to the light, my grumpy expression thinking about Jim's departure. There were several of him looking out to sea and one or two of the shoreline as we sailed out of the port. The slides of our picnic en route to Lyon were hilarious.

SHE TAKES HER CHANCES

We'd spent time driving around trying to find a shop to buy food, and when Jim veered off the main autoroute, we came across a little village with a small supermarket and bought bread, camembert, a bunch of grapes, bottles of red wine and mineral water, paper plates and a knife. It was a case of 'let's go on a bit further until we find a better spot', but we plumped for a grassy patch under a clump of trees. We had nothing to sit on, but the ground was dry, and I found a sheet of paper in my suitcase to serve as a tablecloth. There were several slides of me eating and Jim drinking from the wine bottle, and one of him bending over the map to find the best way back to the main road. We tried to set the camera to take both of us together, but we weren't quick enough, and it turned out blurry. There were a few of Bea and Eunice and their artwork and one of Jim and Eunice standing together, Eunice looking sideways at Jim. I don't remember taking it, so perhaps Bea picked up the camera and snapped them. Eunice appeared to fancy Jim as she flirted with him, but I didn't mind, as we'd probably never see them again. Jim took two of me, starkers, with my bug bites. I looked forward to when Jim was on leave, and he would see the slides if I could borrow a projector. Whenever I saw the airmail letter sitting on the mat in the hall, I felt excited, especially his first letter from Muscat.

Muscat
October 1967

My darling Julia

I was disappointed not to have seen you the weekend before I left. I woke that morning with a

CHAPTER 14

sore throat and shivers, but ignoring the symptoms, I packed a bag ready to make the trip to your village near Salisbury. Fifteen miles outside Lincoln, my car broke down on an empty road. The engine stopped, although there was plenty of fuel, and however hard I tried to get it to start, the engine was dead. I searched for a telephone box to call the RAC and saw one by a group of shops. I pulled open the heavy door, the musty smell hitting me full on, and saw a note stuck over the coin slot that said, "OUT OF ORDER". Walking back towards the car, I saw a woman bending over a flower bed in her front garden and stopped to ask if I could use her phone. She understood when I told her the distance I had to travel and showed me where to make the call. I dialled the RAC, and after a wait, the mechanic arrived and checked the engine, but he couldn't fix it and towed me to the nearest garage. He offered to give me a lift back to the Officers' Mess, and I spent the next three days in bed, taking aspirin and not much food, feeling rotten. I was so sorry, my dearest, I didn't make it.

I have left Bahrain, an island radiating heat surrounded by a deep blue sea in contrast to the white buildings. I have been kitted out with shorts, a shirt and desert boots to suit the environment and advised by the outfitter to always check the inside of the boots in case of a lurking scorpion. I was incarcerated in a building for two days, sitting exams for my promotion, but I am now relieved to be in Muscat at last.

SHE TAKES HER CHANCES

My living quarters are air-conditioned, with an ample-sized room, an en suite shower, and enough space for my books, records and personal effects. The painting I bought in France hangs opposite my bed, reminiscent of our time there, my dearest. I have met the rest of the squadron, who are all great chaps, and the army people whom I'll be in contact with. I have already been on one mission to drop supplies, starting at six in the morning and finishing at midday, when the cockpit is stifling. We also fly at night, but there are no brightly lit runways, only light from gooseneck flares or headlights from a stationary Land Rover. The abundance of exotic fruits is unbelievable: papaya, grapes, tangerines, guava, dates and figs are all grown successfully because of the ancient irrigation system or falaj, where water is sourced from underground wells or wadis and distributed through channels down the hillside to farms, gardens and areas that need water.

Much of Oman is a wild, uninhabited, rocky country, hot and dusty. I've seen goats, camels, oryx, ibex and the gracious gazelle wandering free, as well as marine life, including stingrays, leaping from the water alongside whales and dolphins. I love the country but miss you terribly and reminisce about our times together before dropping off to sleep.

All my love
Jim

CHAPTER 14

Holland Park,
November

Darling Jim

I can feel the atmosphere from your descriptions and long to be there with you. There were no emotional farewells, only the memory of France, elusive like a Monet painting, the last time we were together. Like you, I have your picture in my room at the flat, a part of you close by, to be admired and loved.

I am sitting in bed after seeing a film with Babs and her boyfriend at a film club they belong to. A strange, rather cold film called The Pumpkin Eater with Peter Finch and Anne Bancroft. I hope I'll never feel as disorientated as the woman played by Anne Bancroft when she fell in the department store.

I'll tell you about my jazz dance class. I bought a leotard, black tights and dance shoes and went to the class with Maggie who lives in Shepherd's Bush. The class was in a municipal building near her flat, and it was like entering a ballet school with one wall of the room covered by mirrors and another, a practice bar, where they flexed in preparation. The class was for beginners and mixed ability, but when I mentioned my disquiet to Maggie, she said not to worry as most of them were beginners. Terry, the class teacher, sashayed in, greeted us with, 'Good Evening, Ladies,' and directed us to the bar for warm-up exercises before taking our places to learn the dance steps. He was a good teacher and used to be a classical ballet dancer with a company in the North but left due to a back injury. I concentrated on the steps, left leg behind the right one, right one in front of the left, arms synchronised with leg movements, a turn one way, then the other, the music provided by a pianist on the piano similar to the one I play at the club. The hour went by too fast, the class finished, and Terry said, 'See you all next week.' Maggie said she and another girl had a drink afterwards, so I tagged along to a coffee bar where the three of us gossiped about the class. We were working towards a series of dance routines for a concert at a church hall, and I practised the dance steps every evening, hoping Terry would choose me for the performance. Another friend of Maggie's wanted to join the class, and as there was a space, she came too, but I was so embarrassed for her. I introduced her to Terry, and she attempted to follow the steps but found it difficult and had to stop to watch the rest of us. The confident ones in the front row preened and turned in front of the mirror, while those further back were the followers. A week later, we had to demonstrate a leap, followed by a turn, across the room in front of the class. I waited nervously, and when Maggie, before me, finished in record time, her legs flying, I gave her a little clap. But when it was her friend's turn, she fell awkwardly, her legs splayed out, and I hoped she hadn't broken any bones or sprained any ligaments. I rushed over to see if she was alright, but she nodded and slowly got up, looked upset and hobbled away to sit down. She had a few bruises but no breaks and never went back.

CHAPTER 14

We had the date for our jazz dance show at the church hall and worked hard to perfect the routine. The dances were either in rows or small groups, and on the stage, Maggie was at the front while I was further back. The programme was varied with poetry readings, piano, clarinet and violin solos, two short comedy sketches, a longer, more serious one, and our dance performance, the last item on the programme. Terry gave us last-minute advice, and we waited poised behind the curtain for the music to start, and we were away. Any doubts I had about forgetting the steps disappeared, and when we'd finished, the audience cheered and shouted encore, and we obliged them by dancing the final routine again.

I hope you weren't bored reading that long account, my dashing pilot. I wish you were here to listen to my anecdotes, and I look forward to more fascinating tales from your elusive place.

All my love
Julia

Muscat
Darling Julia

Unfortunately, I got sunstroke and spent a day in bed with a temperature. They called the doctor, but his diagnosis was to rest and drink plenty of water. I felt nauseous and quite unwell but have recovered now.

SHE TAKES HER CHANCES

I was fascinated by your jazz dance experience and would love to have been there, in the audience, watching the movement of your lithe body. I would have stood up, cheered and joined the others shouting 'encore'. Instead, I was on a rescue flight to an overturned, crashed lorry carrying a group of army personnel, but before we landed, a runway had to be made, marked out by stones found lying around so the aircraft landed safely. We use aircraft for ambulances, and on this occasion, we transported a few passengers to the hospital at the base, a 45-minute ride. The other incident involved my forgetfulness (I was thinking about you, my darling). I failed to check my fuel tanks and had to crash land on the stony ground without the luxury of a makeshift runway. Fortunately, others saw the accident and towed me back to base, and I put it up my sleeve for a dinner party story.

Knowing how much you like coffee, I must tell you about a coffee ritual among the native dwellers here. When entertained, you sit in a circle on the floor, checking you don't point the soles of your shoes at the host, as it's bad manners. Bowls of figs and peaches are on offer but only eaten with the right hand, leaving the left hand free to do other things. Coffee is ground and brewed, emitting a wonderful aroma, and served in small cups the size of an egg cup, thick, black and unsweetened. The guest drinks three lots of coffee, but on the fourth offering, he shakes the

CHAPTER 14

cup to say no more, but it is refilled and passed to the next person. Shall we hold an Arabian coffee party and follow the strict customs of the Omani people?

All my love
Jim

Holland Park

My darling Jim

I am so sorry to hear you've been ill and wish I'd been there to wipe your brow and give you sips of water. Thank God you have recovered.
    I love your stories. Please don't stop telling me as much as you can. It sounds like a fascinating place, although I am sure flying is difficult and hazardous. When I saw another airmail letter on the mat, I was surprised you'd written again so soon, but it was for my flatmate, Babs.
    Now I think only of you.

All my love
Julia.

SHE TAKES HER CHANCES

Muscat

My beautiful Julia

I wish you had been here last weekend when a group of us took a 15-mile trip up the coast in an Arabian dhow. We set off at 4 a.m., and as we sailed into the sunrise, we saw hundreds of fish leaping out of the water, a school of dolphins swimming under the bows, jumping up in front of the boat, and the beautiful manta rays somersaulting in front of us. It was dusk when we beached the dhow, and we made up our beds on the beach while the cook and bearers prepared a delicious curry. We retired to bed under a sky studded with stars and a new moon, and I imagined you close beside me and made a wish! We filled our next day with sailing, water skiing, fishing and swimming but stayed away from the poisonous sea snakes. In between, we had tasty meals and plenty of beer, which I kept in the water. At lunch on the second day, we saw an old turtle with seaweed and barnacles growing on his shell, so thick he couldn't dive, and we left him to die.

All my love
Jim

CHAPTER 14

Holland Park
6th January

Dearest Jim

What a wonderfully exotic scene you paint, sleeping under the stars and seeing so much wildlife! In contrast, I am working under the London grey skies and thinking of you in the Omani heat, flying dangerously in a stifling cockpit. I look forward to more fascinating descriptions.
    Please write soon.

All my love
Julia

Holland Park
13th January

Dearest Jim

I am getting very worried. I haven't heard from you for over two weeks, which is unusual as you write at least every week and sometimes more frequently. I hope all is well.
    Please write, my darling Jim.

All my love, as always
Julia.

CHAPTER 15

When I hadn't heard from Jim for a while, it was like déjà vu after Russell had disappeared. Is it something about me that triggers men to cease communication? I knew something wasn't right. I thought he may have met someone else, but the likelihood of single women lurking in the dunes was remote. I was tempted to ring Rich but didn't want to appear too desperate. After I'd come in from the copywriting course feeling whacked, the phone rang, and it was Rich.

'Julia, I'm sorry, but I've some bad news about Jim. He's had a serious flying accident and is in a hospital in Bahrain, in the burn's unit.'

'Oh, my God, Rich. How bad is he?'

'He's alive, but the burns are serious, although with the right care, he'll survive.'

I was so shocked I could hardly speak, and when Babs saw me, she looked concerned.

'Julia, is everything alright? You look very pale,' she said, as I'd slumped on a chair by the phone, head in my hands. She poured the dregs of a bottle of brandy into a glass and handed it to me.

'Drink this. You've had a shock,' Babs said and handed me the glass of brandy. I sipped it slowly, feeling the

CHAPTER 15

warmth flow like liquid velvet. Rich said I could write to him at the Bahrain hospital, and that evening, I wrote and posted a letter.

Holland Park

Dearest

Oh, Jim, I can hardly express my shock and sadness when I heard from Rich about your accident. You must have been in such pain physically and mentally, and my heart breaks for you. I am thinking of you in the hospital, trying to imagine what it is like, and hope the wards are air-conditioned and not stifling. Our life path can change without warning, and we have the dilemma of what to do next. I wonder if you will fly again with your injuries as you have told me how strict they are. I hope so, as I know how much you enjoy it.

I would love to hear from you, but I expect it's difficult for you to write with your poor burnt hands. Perhaps a nurse could write it down for you if it isn't too personal! A short note to reassure me you are recovering, albeit slowly. Always in my thoughts, dear Jim.

Love and kisses,
Julia.

As I knew very few details of Jim's terrible accident, I was surprised and pleased to receive his account from a

SHE TAKES HER CHANCES

Dictaphone tape typed by one of the nurses. She had typed a short note from him as a prologue.

Dearest Julia

Here is my description of the crash for you to read.

Muscat 1968

The evening before my fateful day, I received a concerning letter from Dad about Mum's health. I loved hearing news from home, but the news in the letter was worrying. Mum had stopped eating, had no energy and wouldn't leave her bed. Her hands constantly shook, and whenever Dad wanted to speak to her, she turned away and refused to respond. The doctor had examined her thoroughly, but there was no diagnosis for her condition. He suggested she may be overtired and was heading for a breakdown. She was always busy with the house, seeing her friends at the gardening club, helping at the Church, or meeting for coffee or lunch. I mention the letter because the distraction of Mum's health could have contributed to my accident. I stored it in my desk drawer and prepared for a day's flying.

My first briefing was to fly four passengers in a Beaver, one of my favourite aircraft, a robust one designed for short take-off and landing. Not only does the aircraft take a maximum of nine passengers, but it was also used for freight, such as

CHAPTER 15

food and medical supplies and the all-important mail. I touched down on the short airstrip, left the aircraft and walked across the airfield to meet a brigadier, taller than me, with a booming voice and a stocky colonel. Mrs Brigadier was nearly as tall as her husband, and Mrs Colonel was small and round. After introducing themselves, they settled down, with Mrs Brigadier by a window and Mrs Colonel beside her husband. I checked the controls and took off to the East over flat desert terrain for two hours until we reached the Gulf of Oman. My passengers left the aircraft while I climbed back into the cockpit and continued to the base, but when I arrived, the air conditioning generator had broken down. My room was like an oven, so the only option was to sleep outside. I dragged out the camp bed, stored in my room, set it up under the stars, and covered myself with a heavy blanket to soak up the early morning dew. I awoke with a headache, but after two painkillers I kept by my bedside, I threw off the cover, inhaled the cool morning air, and made my way to the crew room, where the squadron finalised their trips for the day.

'Morning, Jim. Want a coffee?' one of the pilots called to me.

'He hasn't time for that,' said another, coming through the door.

'Just seen a group of illegal immigrants 40 miles down the coast that need surveillance.'

'I'm on my way,' I replied.

SHE TAKES HER CHANCES

'Don't forget your gloves,' they called after me., but I was halfway through drinking a litre of water and intent on donning my flying suit and helmet.

I walked out to the two-seater, single-engine piston provost on the tarmac and climbed into the cockpit. I fixed my mask and was thankful there was enough room for me and a large area at the back for the fuel tank. I checked the controls and radio, adjusted my mask and helmet, and took off towards the rising sun. The light shone on the dark mountain crags around Muscat, silhouetted against the morning sky, and once again, I knew how much I loved this empty, wild country.

Beside the wadi, the line of immigrants moved slowly, weighed down by backpacks or bags full of their belongings, while some of them carried young children on their shoulders or in their arms. A few had dragged their feet and were separated from the rest, while others had climbed higher up and stood in an untidy group looking around. A band of conmen had coerced them to catch a boat from Pakistan to get to Mecca, but they had ended up miles away in the neighbouring mountains. I put the aircraft into a climb but grazed spiky plants and grasses growing among the jagged rocks on the harsh mountain slopes. But when I ran out of airspeed, I had a sense of dread, warning me that disaster was imminent.

I desperately tried to control the aircraft but collided with the mountainside and felt the full impact against my chest. I had to get out fast to

CHAPTER 15

escape the flames and was furious I hadn't brought my flying gloves. I pushed my weight against the canopy, scrambled out and stumbled away from the burning wreckage, my hands on fire, looking for a rock so I could drag off my helmet. It was suffocating me. When I found a large, pointed one, I struggled and pulled, but it was impossible, and I watched the helmet roll down the slope out of reach. I heard an aircraft buzzing overhead and tried to extract the heliograph from my pocket to signal, but my hands were so painful I couldn't dislodge it and gave up.

The hostile expanse stared back at me, the pain spreading to my legs as I tripped and floundered over the loose boulders on my way down to the coastal plains. My inner voice repeated the mantra that I must get to the sea and salt water to cool my burns, but the relentless midday heat danced a slow tango with me. A cloud enveloped me as I fell onto the stony ground, and through the mist, I saw a coffin and a country church and heard music bathed in green light and knew I was hallucinating. A young goatherd whispered close to my face, 'Do you want dates and milk?' No milk, I said, so he pushed a handful of dates into my mouth, one or two falling on the ground. The glint of the sea, like a mirage, encouraged me to continue in the emptiness, and as I put one foot in front of the other, I had the sensation of walking through quicksand, with a pain so severe I was numb and couldn't feel the pain at all. The mantra to get to the sea continued, and when, at last, I reached the water's edge, I passed out into the shallow sea, and darkness swallowed me whole.

A concerned Squadron Leader paced the crew room floor, muttering to himself. He had received my earlier messages about the immigrants but needed an update.

'I can't contact Jim. His radio's dead, and he's been gone for several hours, and we've heard nothing,' he said to the anxious men, waiting to hear news of me.

'We'll send out a surveillance aircraft. It could be a 'worst-case scenario'.

One of the pilots, John Chesham, was chosen to search for the wreckage.

He prepared himself for the worst with a sinking feeling he couldn't shake off. Flying over the mountain ranges, he saw a blackened mess and a scattering of aircraft parts over the dried-up slopes and radioed back to base.

'I've found the wreckage, and no one could survive that. I suggest the Navy assist and sail along the coast to look for a body.'

The captain of the naval dhow summoned two of his crew, and with their eyes trained on the beach, they sailed along the coast looking for anything resembling a casualty until the eagle-eyed captain saw my human shape kneeling in the water. He pointed and shouted, 'Boys, over there. I think it's him.'

They sailed towards me, unconscious in the water, and tried to be gentle as they pulled me

CHAPTER 15

out, but when they carried me into the dhow, I screamed so loud they must have heard me in the mountains. At the harbour, they moved me into the waiting ambulance and transported me to the base hospital, bumping over uneven ground, where I received emergency treatment for the burns on my hands, back, arms and legs. I had sedation before the two-hour flight to Bahrain, but I had no recollection or memory of that crucial time.

The large white hospital building, with its arched entrances, was my refuge for healing during the critical weeks after the accident. My wounds were dressed and redressed by the caring nursing staff, but the first days were touch-and-go as I went in and out of consciousness. Sometimes, I heard low voices at my bedside and had flashes of the buffeting, flailing aircraft and the desperation to prevent the crash. I had a vision of Julia trying to call me on an out-of-order phone with no dial tone or my parents anxiously staring down at me from a great height. I got to know the senior nurse in charge of my treatment and the doctor, who visited me daily to check my progress. Two nurses treated the burns on my back, but when they turned me, I moaned in pain, although they always apologised and said how sorry they were. My room was on the ground floor with a window overlooking a small courtyard with one red flower poking out of a plot of dusty greenery.

During the third week, when I was improving, John Chesham, the surveillance pilot on detachment *in Bahrain, came into the hospital to see me. I was strong enough to handle a visitor and was happy to see someone from my life in Oman. He hesitated at the entrance to the ward, looking around for my bed and beamed when he saw me sitting up.*

'Good to see you alive, old chap! When I saw the wreckage, I feared the worst. Black bits everywhere,' he said, sitting beside my bed.

'I still have nightmares, but the burns are healing. I could kick myself that I forgot my gloves.'

'We shouted at you when you walked out, but you didn't respond.'

I remembered Dad's letter and hoped Mum had recovered, but I imagined they were worried about me and my accident.

'You'll be in the air again once you have healed,' John said.

'It'll take a while, but I'll be flying again one day.'

John brought a bag of books for me to read, but I wasn't sure I was up to that. He put the bag in my locker and asked if there was anything else he could bring the next time he visited.

'Fresh fruit would be very welcome, although I'm not allowed any booze. I could do with a beer, though. I'm parched.'

John gave me a sip of water through a straw and said a beer was something to look forward to. It was good of him to come and visit me, and I looked forward to his next visit.

'I'll see you again, Jim, old fellow, before I leave Bahrain,' were his parting words.

CHAPTER 15

Jim's first-hand account of his accident brought the traumatic experience alive and I could almost feel I was there. I could understand and sympathise with the trauma he went through, and knew he was strong, resilient and dedicated to his flying career, which would stand him in good stead for his recovery.

CHAPTER 16

I had a surprise phone call from Ian at work. He had an appointment in London and wanted to see me during my lunch break. He suggested we meet at twelve-thirty outside my office. I froze from head to foot. What did he want? I was suspicious but had to see my stepfather, or I would never hear the end of it. I couldn't concentrate the whole morning and longed for the day to finish. He was waiting outside five minutes early, wearing a well-cut suit, his hair still dark without noticeable grey strands. We caught a taxi to his Club and sat in a hushed salon with sofas that sunk beneath our weight and he ordered coffee and biscuits. I looked at him, waiting for him to speak.

'Now, Julia, how is the job progressing?'

'Very well, thank you, and no problems. The company wants me to enrol in a copywriting course.'

'If you had an English degree from Oxford or Cambridge, you'd be able to get a much better job.'

I didn't reply as I was sick of his mantra and wondered what else he had to say. He dropped three lumps of sugar into his coffee and slowly stirred.

'I don't want your mother making trips to London. If you want to see her, come home if that's not too much trouble.'

CHAPTER 16

We hadn't arranged anything definite for Mum's visit to London, but she must have mentioned it to Ian. Don't worry, Ian, I said to myself. We'll find an opportunity. I looked around at the other occupants, who looked like business executives, talking in low tones interspersed with throaty laughter suggesting dirty jokes.

'And where does she do her painting? She can't magically produce them out of nowhere.'

'I don't know. Maybe Mum paints in the Village Hall. What does it matter? She produces some excellent artwork.'

'It does matter. Mother's place is at home, not wielding a paintbrush somewhere else. She can give it a rest for a while.'

I was agitated and had to leave the stifling room and return to work. Mum can't possibly give up her art and will have to continue doing it secretly.

'Have you met any men since you've been in London?' he said, looking up from his cup of coffee.

'I'm friends with an air force pilot, and we've been to a rugby match.'

I didn't think Ian was interested in rugby, but I hoped it would keep him from asking more questions. But there was no such luck.

'Where is he stationed?'

When I told him, he asked if I'd been to see him, and I mentioned the summer ball.

'Are we going to meet him? You could invite him to Thornfield.'

'I could, yes, if we find a free weekend.'

I tried to imagine Ian talking to Jim. He would admire his discipline and be in awe of his flying career but might be jealous of Jim's flying expertise, though that was only conjecture.

'Please extend an invitation from us, and let us know,' Ian said, putting another sugar lump into his coffee. He finished the last drop, and I hoped he had no more questions as I had to return to work. Fortunately, he had another appointment, so hailed a cab outside the Club, and I was never so pleased as to see my desk!

Babs had been on a week's holiday in Boston visiting friends, and I was excited to meet her at the Tube stop on Saturday. The flat was lonely without her and quiet, with no one to discuss Jim's accident and give me support. I wished Mum and Helen lived nearby so I could pop in and talk to them about it, as phone calls are not the best way to communicate. I called them and spoke to Ian, who was unfriendly and passed the phone to Mum. She was very concerned and sympathetic about Jim and was glad that Babs was only away for a week.

I couldn't mistake her unruly head of burnt umber curls, coming up the escalator at the Tube station, holding a brightly patterned overnight bag. She had a clumsiness, as though she was lopsided, but her smile lit up her face, and her wave was larger than life. She talked about her escapades, her words tumbling out, until I told her to slow down. I asked if she'd managed to find Russell's address when she was there.

'It was a dead end. The taxi driver stopped in a rundown area of Boston with dilapidated buildings, areas of wasteland and no residential properties to speak of. He asked me to check the address as he said it was unlikely to be on that street, but he'd wait while I went again. I walked

CHAPTER 16

down the deserted street, carefully looking at each shack, and eventually came to a small gas station. A man in a vest with tattoos on his arm stood by the petrol pumps and asked me if I was lost, but when I told him the address, he said it didn't exist. I couldn't get back to the taxi fast enough. Fear gripped me, sending shivers down my spine.'

'Thanks, Babs, for doing that. It was brave of you. What is Boston like apart from rundown scary parts?'

She described it as a lovely city surrounded by water, which added an extra dimension to its charm. There was a large market called Faneuil Hall, and another one called Quincy Market, where visitors could purchase various foods and products. Additionally, several popular fish restaurants by the harbour created a lively atmosphere.

'Are you still keen on Russell?' Babs suddenly asked.

Not particularly, because I've met Jim, but I think of him mainly because he's a mystery.'

'I think you still fancy him!' said Babs.

Either Russell gave Sylvia the wrong address, or she gave me the wrong one on purpose. It could be either, but maybe Sylvia fancied Russell and didn't want us to have any more contact with each other.

I had cooked spaghetti Bolognese, an ample meal for Babs and me before we went out for a drink. Although she had just landed in the country, Babs was running on adrenaline and was keen to go to a pub. We left the dirty dishes in the kitchen, dressed in light summer clothes and caught the Tube to the Denmark Pub on Old Brompton Road, an old haunt of ours.

The evening was warm, and Babs said it was good to be in London again. As we made our way to the pub, she commented how different London was from Boston with its hotchpotch of roads, unlike the American grid system. When we arrived, people were stood outside to avoid the crowd, although inside, Babs had to fight her way to the bar to order two shandies. Luckily, I saw a group of people leaving a table, quickly grabbed it, and asked a woman to clear the empty glasses and clean the cigarette ash and spilt beer from the table. I looked around to see if I recognised anyone, but it was a mass of heaving bodies and above the hubbub, Babs told me about a man she'd met in Boston whom she fancied, but knowing Babs, it would be a flash in the pan, and she'd get bored.

We saw Maggie in the pub with her Welsh rugby-playing boyfriend, who stopped briefly to talk to us. But the noise level was so high it was difficult to hear anyone. She called out, 'See you at the dance class', and went to join her Welshman at the bar.

'How was the show?' shouted Babs.

'It went off brilliantly, and everyone called for an encore. Maggie is a brilliant dancer, but I am just average,' but when I looked across the room, my heart stopped. It looked like Ian standing near the door talking to a group of men. I had my contact lenses in, and they'd blurred a little, but it looked very much like him. What's he doing in a London pub on a Saturday? I grabbed Babs's arm, spilling her drink.

'I think my stepfather is over there by the door.'

I wasn't sure it was him, but I shivered in the warm pub. It looked like Ian, and when he half-turned his head, I thought it was.

'Do you think he's seen you?' said Babs.

CHAPTER 16

'There's such a crowd in here, possibly not, although we've seen him.'

They were finishing their pints of beer and putting the empty glasses on a table.

'Looks like they're leaving,' I said, as the three men made a beeline for the door.

'What does he look like?'

'Medium height, neatly dressed.'

'Let's follow them,' Babs said excitedly.

'Follow? You must be joking! How, in a taxi? Perhaps they're on foot. We'll be lucky to hail an empty cab.'

We pushed through the crowd onto the street and saw them crossing the road and getting into a car. We had to move quickly to hail a cab, but fortunately, the car didn't move off, and they were talking inside. A taxi with its light on passed us, but the one behind it was free. We ran across the road, and Babs put her head through the driver's window.

'Can you follow that car over there,' Babs said, breathless.

'Whatever you want, Miss,' he replied.

We opened the heavy door and flopped down onto the seat. The other car moved off, and we followed it through one street, then up another, round corners, with crowds getting in the way as they crossed the roads. At one point, I thought we had lost them at the traffic lights.

'Sorry, ladies. It was red, but I've got them in my sights,' the taxi driver reassured us.

We caught up with them and arrived in a rundown part of London. I peered through the window to work out where we were and realised it was Kentish Town. The car stopped outside a small, terraced house on a narrow street, and we asked the taxi driver not to park too close. If it was Ian, what was he doing in this part of London? Perhaps he led a double life, and Mummy was involved with someone shady. Heavens above, I hoped not.

'I'll make a note of the address,' I said. I fished a piece of paper from my bag, found a pencil and wrote it down: 11 Cathcart Street. When the three men had disappeared into the house, we asked the cab driver to take us back to Holland Park. We thanked him, and Babs gave him a good tip.

'Good night, ladies,' he called out.

'He did well with that ride,' said Babs.

'I'm going to ring Mum and see if Ian's home.'

'What, now? Will she be up?' Babs said.

'They have an extension in the bedroom.'

The phone rang twice before Mum picked it up, sounding tentative.

'Mum, it's Julia. Just ringing to see how you are.'

'It's late, Julia, and I'm just about to get into bed. Is everything all right?'

I had to ask about Ian before she finished the call. She said he was at a conference in London and would be back on Sunday. So, it could have been him in the pub.

'We'll come back tomorrow,' I said in the spirit of the moment, but in the cold light of day, I had lost the enthusiasm to return to the address where we thought Ian (if it was him) had gone.

Babs was keen to go and said she'd pay for the taxi ride again, as she had lots of spare cash. But we caught the Tube and walked there, as the weather was still warm and made

CHAPTER 16

a day of it. We settled in a cafe over coffee and a sandwich and studied the A-to-Z book to find the street.

It was hot walking. People had opened their doors to let in the cool breeze and were sitting on their doorsteps chewing the fat or daydreaming on their own. We trudged along dreary roads with hardly any greenery, grey and shabby, although the sun was shining, and had to stop to look at the map to sort out the jumble of streets. Babs said Boston's roads weren't always on the grid system, and some were more like London streets. We eventually arrived at the house, although it looked deserted, and we wondered if anyone was in. Young children were playing at the end of the street, skipping or throwing a ball, and their voices in the hot sun created a dream-like quality.

'Shall we knock and find out, or leave it?' I suggested.

'I'll be the spokesperson. We've come this far,' said Babs.

Since there was no knocker, we knocked on the door and heard a voice shouting inside. It took a while for a woman holding a baby to open the door. In the hall was a clutter of shoes and toys, with a bicycle leaning against the wall.

'Can I help?' she said, balancing it on her hip.

'Sorry to trouble you,' said Babs, 'but we're looking for a friend, Ian McClain, and wonder if you know him?'

'Who? Never 'eard of 'im,' she said with a cockney twang.

'Would your husband know him? He's an old friend of ours,' I said.

'Reg,' she shouted, 'two girls asking about an Ian someone.'

Reg appeared in his vest, dripping with sweat, and shook his head. 'Don't know anyone of that name. Try next door.' He slammed the door shut, and a crack in the door widened.

We knocked several times until we heard a chain rattle, and a woman in bedroom slippers and hair curlers peered out through a crack in the door.

'Yeah?' she said, wheezing with a phlegmy cough.

When we asked the same question, she looked confused but opened the door wider and invited us to come in. We entered the dark hall that smelled of damp, mould, and fried food.

'I'm deaf. You'll have to shout,' but when we repeated the question, the woman knew nothing about Ian McClain.

It all looked suspect, and if the man was Ian, it added another concern about him to my list, and the most serious one.

'Shall we try the house on the other side before we go?' I suggested.

Their door was open, and three boys were playing outside.

'Do you live here? Is your Mum in?' we asked the oldest looking one.

'Robbie, go and get Mum,' he said to another boy who ran inside and returned with a young woman in shorts and a ponytail. Babs asked the same question to the woman, who looked more friendly and approachable.

'What's he look like?' she asked.

'Dark-haired with a bent nose,' I said.

'I think there were men there last night, but I don't know their names. The people next door aren't very friendly,' she added.

'Do groups of men visit them?' I asked.

CHAPTER 16

'Yeah, they come and go, but that's all I know. Are you from around here?'

'No, the other side of London,' I said.

'Thought so,' the girl replied.

At least we have an address if it was him, so not all in vain,' I said when we were out of earshot. We dragged ourselves back to the Tube station and were relieved to be home. At least we had our small, shaded garden to relax in.

I was very concerned if it was Ian we followed, although Babs couldn't confirm my suspicion as she had never met him. What was he doing in Kentish Town with two shabbily dressed men on a Saturday night? Perhaps I was mistaken, and it wasn't him at all, but as he was out when I rang, it was more likely to be him. I hoped I was wrong, but my eyes weren't too bad, and I was sure it was him. I made a mental note to tell Helen to see what she thought, although not being there, she probably would have leaned towards caution.

CHAPTER 17

I woke on Saturday morning to a ping-ping sound at the back of the house, the rain coming down in sheets, dripping through a hole in the guttering onto a metal box. I couldn't think where I was and lay there trying to work it out. Once I was properly awake, I wandered into the kitchen to see Ian sitting at the table with a boiled egg and Mummy sorting out the toast.

'Are you ready to go, Mum?' I asked.

Jim had left the Bahrain hospital and was now in a military hospital 50 miles away. Ian had offered to take me in his new car, a Jaguar, to show off and suggested Mummy came too. The weather was abysmal, and on the way, the wipers could hardly sweep away the water fast enough, and when we eventually found a flower shop, we bought blue irises and some grapes from the greengrocer. The hospital looked grey and more like a prison when we swept around the drive to the entrance, past an island of grass with flowerbeds in the middle.

I pushed open the main door and asked the way to Jim's ward, trying to memorise the instructions from the receptionist. I passed store cupboards, patients on trolleys, busy wards, nurses hurrying past, and finally had to ask a porter to direct me. I was nervous and imagined a patient

CHAPTER 17

swathed in bandages, unable to move or speak, but when I arrived at the ward, a nurse showed me an annexe where he lay pale but relaxed, considering what he'd been through. The nurse took the flowers, found a space among the others on the shelf and spoke quietly to Jim. He looked surprised to see me, and when the nurse helped him to sit up, he was careful not to move his bandaged hands. The ward was hot, and when I removed my coat, the nurse spoke to two more visitors. I recognised his mother, who had lost weight, and his father, who carried a large bouquet of pink and white roses for Jim.

'Ah, the girlfriend,' said Hilary when she saw me. Her hands shook quite noticeably, but she must have improved.

'It's Julia, Mum,' said Jim.

'Hello, Julia. Very nice to see you again,' said his father, Francis.

'Aren't we all going to be too much for Jim,' Hilary stuttered, looking concerned.

'We could go and find a doctor to chat to and give Julia some more time,' said Francis.

'See you in a little while, darling,' Hilary said.

Judging by the number of flowers by Jim's bed, there must have been an influx of visitors.

The squadron pilots had been and tired him out, Rich and Poppy had visited another time and so had his younger brother. I was going to ask Jim about flying again after the accident, but his parents returned with the nurse before I had a chance, and as he was only allowed two visitors at one time, I arranged to visit him the next day in the afternoon. We sped home in the Jaguar with Ian puffed up and proud, and I assumed the company was doing well for him to afford such a smart car.

The following day, Mum dug out the L plates and bravely let me sit in the driver's seat of her Hillman Minx, and I drove the last few yards to the hospital entrance. Before I visited Jim, Mum suggested I practised parking, and the three-point turn in a quiet street nearby, and she would show me the note she found under the bed. We drove up and down a few streets and found a cul-de-sac where I parked at the end. She handed me the note that read: *"Meet me at the gallery at six pm. F."*

'That could mean anything, Mum,' I said trying to reassure her.

'But who is F, and why are they meeting?'

'It's probably to do with a business meeting and the gallery is a landmark.'

'I'm not convinced,' she said.

'I'll do the three-point turn and we'll go to the hospital,' I said, putting the key in the ignition.

I managed the turn without touching the kerb and when I finally took the driving test, I passed the first time and, excited beyond belief, I planned to save up and buy a car.

When I arrived at the ward, Jim was out of bed and sitting in a chair, ready to greet me. He'd eaten half the grapes I'd brought the day before and said he could only force the hospital food into his mouth.

'Will you be able to fly again when the burns have healed?' I asked, hoping his reply would be positive.

'There will have to be a full investigation of the crash, which could take a long time, but if there are no complications, the answer is "yes".'

'Will you go back to Oman? You've only been there four months.'

CHAPTER 17

'No, I doubt that very much, but the Royal Air Force and flying are my career, so I shall do everything to continue.'

As the afternoon progressed, his eyes started to close and at times he dozed on and off.

'I have nightmares about the crash and different emotions of frustration, anger, depression and then fatigue. Seeing you helps me, Julia.'

I held his hand gently to be sure I didn't press too hard on the burns.

'And what about you? How is the piano job?'

'I gave in my notice.'

'Any particular reason?'

I thought someone who went to the club was stalking me, but I wasn't sure, and Jim would think I was neurotic. I had seen him on my train a few times, but there may have been a valid explanation.

'I wanted a change,' I said, the only answer I could think of. 'How is your mother, Jim?'

'She has improved, as you probably saw when she visited me yesterday, but she hasn't recovered completely and has days in bed, not eating or speaking. She isn't asleep but is motionless in bed, apart from her shaking hands.'

The nurse arranged the pillows and made him comfortable while I went to find Mum waiting outside the hospital.

What a difference a week made. On my next visit, Jim had more colour and walked about the ward, stopping to talk to the other patients he'd befriended, particularly one pilot who had ejected from his aircraft too near the ground and broken most of the bones in his body. He lay strung up to pulleys, tearful, waiting for his wife to visit, but when I left, he was chatting to a young woman who was probably her. I knew this visit would be my last, and walking to the exit, I felt more hopeful about Jim's condition. Mum thought I looked more relaxed this time and was pleased there was an improvement. When his doctor agreed to discharge him, his parents came to take him home to recuperate before he returned to work. His recovery on the surface was excellent, but the trauma may have affected him in more hidden ways.

Before Jim visited me in the flat, I cleaned it thoroughly, especially the bathroom and kitchen, until it was spotless. Babs was away with the man she'd met in Boston, who had come here to see her, so I had the flat to myself. When I saw Jim outside with a bunch of red roses and a bottle of champagne, I could hardly believe it was the same person. He'd found a parking space and walked, without limping, to the front door and said he'd go to the shops after lunch to buy ingredients for the surprise dishes he would cook. I saw the scars on his hands and arms, but his mobility had improved, and his face was unmarked. He looked well, happy and rested.

While Jim prepared dinner, I had a long soak in the bath with calming salts and shut myself in the bedroom to get ready. I could smell delicious cooking aromas wafting from the kitchen, making my mouth water. But despite my relaxing bath, I felt apprehensive and thought about the disastrous dinner I had had with Russell before he stormed out. I know my cooking might have been partly to blame, but that was certainly not the whole picture.

I found two glasses at the back of a cupboard, and Jim pulled the cork, poured the fizz and said, 'To us, Julia,' crinkling his eyes in the muted light. Our candlelit dinner started with borscht soup followed by boeuf bourguignon,

CHAPTER 17

bubbling in the pot. We smiled and raised our glasses, and I congratulated him on his culinary skills.

There was a brief silence before he said: 'We should get married, and then we can do this every evening.'

'One day,' I said, enveloped by a rush of panic.

'I'm serious. I mean soon. I am asking you to marry me.'

I looked down at my plate and wondered if I'd heard correctly. I wasn't expecting a marriage proposal, as settling down wasn't on the agenda.

'Jim, I'm not ready yet. I need to progress more at work and study for a degree.'

'Marriage wouldn't stop your study. I would be there to support you.'

'And for me to support you. I'd need to devote time to air force life, entertaining, attending functions, and that sort of thing. There would be no time for study, and where would I go? The RAF station would be nowhere near a university or place of learning.'

'Have you thought how difficult it would be working and studying at the same time?' Jim continued.

'You're already set on your career path.'

'If you truly loved me, you wouldn't hesitate.'

'I do love you, Jim. I missed you so much and was devastated when I heard about the crash.'

I took a few mouthfuls of the boeuf cooling on my plate and a good swig of wine.

'Please think about it, Julia. You're the one I want to be with.'

To lighten the mood, I played a Dave Brubeck jazz record to accompany the cheese and fruit with a glass of port. We danced to the Beatles and Beach Boys before sharing a nostalgic hour, looking at the slides of France in the viewer and holding them up to the light. But the gloom never lifted as I slept in my single bed, and he had the put-you-up on the floor.

The next day, I woke with a headache, took two aspirin, and made a pot of coffee while Jim slept until the smell of breakfast woke him up. The day was a mixture of clouds and blue skies, and with a car at our disposal, we decided to visit Hampton Court Palace and drove into Surrey to the house steeped in the brutal history of Henry VIII's reign. The ghosts of Jane Seymour and Catherine Howard are said to haunt the Palace, but we didn't see them. We wandered through the gardens, bypassed the maze, and found a shady spot to eat a picnic I'd prepared with leftovers from yesterday.

Jim was anxious to return to the station, so he packed his overnight bag, kissed me goodbye, and as I watched him drive away, I wondered what our future would bring. I knew I'd made the right decision, but the depression hung over me for a long time. How ironic to receive a letter a few days after our difficult conversation, so different from the letters he wrote from Muscat.

Wednesday

Dearest Julia

I know from our conversation at the weekend that if you are not ready for marriage, I can't force you. It would be better if we didn't see each other and, as I write, I know separation is the only way. I hope you find fulfilment in whatever path you take.

Love Jim

CHAPTER 17

When Babs saw me in floods of tears, the dropped letter on the floor, she waited for me to explain. I picked up the letter and gave it to her to read.

'I'm so sorry, Julia, it's ended like this,' Babs said.

Getting ready for work on Monday was a struggle. I was so distracted I put on a navy-blue shirt and grabbed a brown skirt out of the wardrobe, and in the office cloakroom mirror, I saw my mistake. Part of the hem hung down, but when I searched through my desk drawer and found a safety pin to pin it up, it didn't look right, and I wanted to go home and change.

'You look down, Julia. Is everything alright?' Annie said when she saw me.

'Jim and I have split up.'

'Oh no! I'm sorry. You seemed so solid. What happened?'

'He wanted to get married, and I'm not ready yet.'

'I'd marry Paul like a shot if he asked me,' she replied.

A few weeks later, I bought The Times from the news vendor outside the Tube station to check the Situations Vacant column, and quite by chance, turned to engagements and weddings. When I saw the notice, I couldn't take it in.

Mr and Mrs H Moreno of Buenos Aires, Argentina, announce the engagement and forthcoming marriage of their daughter, Marta, to Flight Lieutenant Jim Maddox, the older son of Mr and Mrs F Maddox of Wye, Kent.

I read it three times to make sure it wasn't my imagination. Maybe it wasn't him, although he'd mentioned an ex-girlfriend from Argentina. I rang Poppy to see if she knew anything about it.

'Rich told me yesterday. I was going to call you, but knowing how upset you'd be, I chickened out. I could come down this weekend.'

'Yes, come and stay. Is Marta back here? It's happened so quickly.'

'I'll tell you what I know when I see you.'

It was even more hurtful that Poppy and Rich knew about the engagement, and I had to read about it in the paper. Babs joined us for lunch, and the conversation turned to Jim.

'I hope our chat at the summer ball didn't influence your decision,' Poppy said, who had arrived that morning.

'No. I'm just not ready for marriage, and it's happened so fast with the ex-girlfriend,' I said.

'I think he'd contacted her from Muscat, according to Rich. His parents liked her, especially his mother. They may've had some influence,' said Poppy.

'I'm so stunned I can hardly think. Jim can't have deep feelings for me and suddenly marry somebody else. And all those letters he wrote; perhaps mine were duplicates of the ones sent to her.'

'Men are different. What about the saying: "How happy I could be with either, were t'other dear charmer away," Poppy quoted, although she couldn't remember where it came from.

I showed them the engagement notice, and Poppy's analysis that he wanted the warmth of a home and a loving wife instead of the impersonal Officer's Mess made sense.

'Maybe he was never sure of you, Julia, and sensed you were not ready for marriage, hence the renewed contact with the ex-girlfriend,' Babs suggested.

'It's just as well I didn't agree to marry him then.'

CHAPTER 17

Poppy stirred her coffee and put the spoon gently in the saucer and looked at me.

'How do six months or a year in Australia appeal? Dad and Aunt Dora have suggested I go out there with a friend to live and work for a few months. There are plenty of temp jobs going in Sydney, apparently.'

'That sounds exciting, Jules, and you can tell me if the water does run anticlockwise down the plughole,' Babs said, laughing.

'I'll let you know,' I said, my mind racing.

I thought about the possibilities of the plan and could see it working. I got on well with Poppy, and we would be good travelling companions. But the upheaval would be enormous, and there was a lot to think about.

'I'll leave it with you, Julia, but the offer is on the table,' said Poppy.

That night, I took a pad of paper to write to Jim, but the blank page stared back at me. I knew my decision was right, but I hated to think of him with someone else. I tortured myself with thoughts of the wedding plans, a picture postcard bride, bridesmaids, page boys, a packed church, resounding music and the honeymoon. They would set up home together, albeit a married quarter, and sleep in the same bed. Our relationship had ended so abruptly, and it seemed only yesterday I had visited him in the hospital, worried how I would find him and praying his burns would heal without complications. I was devastated.

CHAPTER 18

After Jim's devastating blow, I went home for the weekend to think about Poppy's offer to go to Australia. I pondered the pros and cons. It was an attractive invitation, but I wouldn't know anyone except Poppy, who had her family for support. On the other hand, I might always regret not taking up the offer and miss out on an exciting adventure. I was nervous telling Mummy but chose a time when we were together by the fire.

'I've got some sad news, Mum,' I said.

I told her about my split with Jim and his engagement to an ex-girlfriend. She was very sympathetic and supportive and understood why I was upset. We talked at length about how I felt but telling her about Australia was challenging.

'You've got your job and nice flat, Julia. You'll get over Jim in time.'

'Yes, I know, Mum, but Poppy has asked me if I'd go with her to Sydney, Australia, for a few months to live and work.'

Mummy was quiet and looked pensive and I thought she was going to be emotional and beg me to stay. I was surprised by her reaction.

'I'll be sad if you go, but it's your decision. It would be a new experience for you, so I'll understand if you accept.'

CHAPTER 18

What a wonderful, philosophical mother. Ian didn't appreciate how lucky he was.

There was some good news. After Helen and Steve's unhappy break up, when Helen had a hair-brained idea to work in a children's hospital in Edinburgh, in the middle of their wedding preparations, she changed her mind and knew she had made the wrong one. The matron where Helen worked had found an opening in a more local children's hospital, and Helen took up the offer. The wedding plans were re-ignited, but when Helen told Ian, in the kindest way possible, that she wanted Grandpa to give her away, he was not pleased and scaled down his financial contribution to the wedding. There were no bridesmaids, traditional bridal wear or a long guest list. The ceremony, in the village church, was beautiful and simple, followed by a reception at Thornfield, arranged by Mrs Tidey, as she had done for Mummy and Ian. Twenty guests joined the couple in the celebration, and they left for their honeymoon in Andalucia, floating on clouds of joy. I was delighted for my sister and relieved. Helen and Steve should be together; a separation would have been skewed and wrong, and living within easy distance from Mum and Ian, was ideal.

I had to make up my mind about Australia by Christmas. We planned to travel in January to enjoy the Australian summer, and as an early Christmas present, my wonderful grandpa generously offered to pay my fare. I began to be excited and tried to ignore my nagging guilt of leaving Helen with the situation at home, despite her ability to deal with difficulties with tact and maturity. Ian liked Helen, and later, Helen told me he had helped her financially when she was training. I felt guilty about leaving Mummy, but it didn't mean I would spend the rest of my life there.

'Helen and Steve are living close now, Mum. That's a vast improvement to living in Scotland.'

'Thank God for that,' she said.

They had rented a house, about a 15-minute car journey from Thornfield. It was convenient for Helen to travel to the hospital and for Steve to get to work. They had settled into a routine, and although Helen's hours were erratic, Steve understood and fitted in accordingly.

Back in London at work, I had to hand in my notice. On Monday morning, I knocked on Susan's door. She was concentrating on editing a piece and looked distracted. Had I chosen a bad time?

'Yes, Julia, is this important?'

'Sorry to disturb you, Susan. I can come back later.'

'No, you're here now.'

I suddenly felt tearful and hesitated, finding the words difficult to express.

'A friend has invited me to travel with her to Australia for a few months, so sadly, I must hand in my notice.'

'That sounds like an exciting adventure, Julia, but we'll be sorry to lose you. You have been an asset to the Company, and I can give you a good reference for the future. Your leaving date will be a month from today.'

When I told Annie, she started crying, which made me well up, and we arranged a lunch date before I left. My five years at Pericles Publishing had been varied, to say the least, with memories of Russell and all our ups and downs. When the staff learnt of my departure, they all wished me luck and said they were sorry to see me go.

CHAPTER 18

I was also sad, but the memory of working there would fade as time went on.

Babs had pre-empted my decision to accept the offer and had put out feelers to find my replacement. She was sure I would decide to go, especially after the trauma of Jim's engagement. Babs had asked around, and a young woman at the theatre had agreed to share the flat with her. I thought she'd find someone without too much trouble, as it was a comfortable flat, in a nice area. I'd miss Babs a lot as we'd had some fun together, but I wouldn't be surprised if I saw her in Sydney.

I think Clare was jealous. 'Why do you want to go so far away? Supposing you hate it there and don't have the fare to come home? You won't know anyone apart from Poppy, and she's got her family,' Clare said, shifting in her seat with the cat on her lap.

She was echoing my negative thoughts, but I ignored them. She could have been pleased for me and more positive, but her attitude made me more determined to go than ever.

'If I don't like it, Clare, I can come home. It will be an adventure to visit another country, albeit far away.' I paused, but there was no response.

'When I have somewhere to live in Sydney, perhaps you'll come and visit me?' I said provocatively.

'It sounds like you'll be there for a long time,' she said, taking me seriously.

I may be if I am successful in studying for a degree. Perhaps this is fate, and Poppy's offer was pre-destined.

'Somebody from work told me about a university in Sydney that takes mature students.'

'That's what I mean, Julia. If you study for a degree, it will be at least three years.'

'Nothing has been decided, Clare. The unknown awaits me,' I said, trying to lighten things up.

When Ian found out, he said how foolish I was not to accept Jim's proposal and waste my life going to some God-forsaken place on the other side of the planet. I told Ian about the university in Sydney that accepted mature students, but that invited even more criticism.

'I can't think a university in Australia is a patch on the ones here. You'll end up with a fake degree.'

'That's rubbish, Ian. The University of Sydney was founded in 1850. I realise that's more recent than Oxford or Cambridge, but it doesn't mean the degrees are worthless.'

Before I left, Mummy and I visited Helen and Steve in their rented house on the outskirts of the village. It had three bedrooms, enough space for visitors or if a little person came along. Helen asked me how many people I had told about my trip. I said quite a few, but some people only mentioned the downsides of my decision, which was not very encouraging. She said they were probably jealous and wished opportunities like that had come their way. She advised me to accept the offer with pleasure and not to worry about leaving Mother's domestic life behind.

'Steve and I live close to Thornfield and are there to help. You go and enjoy your trip and the new experience and have confidence that we'll be able to rectify any problems Mum might have.'

The day of departure was raw and getting dark when Ian drove us to Heathrow Airport. Mummy decided to come, although initially, she said it would be too upsetting.

CHAPTER 18

We walked into the concourse looking around for Poppy and spotted her standing with her mother and stepfather, looking around for us.

'Ah, here we are,' Ian said, anxious to get going. 'We'll be off and leave you to it. Have a safe journey, Julia, and let us know when you arrive.'

We watched them walk to the exit and disappear to pick up the car. Poppy's mother and stepfather hugged her closely, shook my hand and left the building. Airside, we wandered through the shops to buy a book to read on the flight. Poppy's was The Franchise Affair by Josephine Tey, while I chose The Edible Woman by Margaret Atwood, her first novel, before we boarded the Boeing 707 aircraft. Having never flown before, I looked up at the vast aircraft, and felt my nerves gripping me, making me want to run back into the airport building and home.

We had booked non-smoking seats, and I chose the window seat, but when we were airborne, cigarette smoke wafted down to our area, making a non-smoking choice laughable. As soon as we heard the roar of the engines and felt the gathering speed on the runway to lift off, we knew there was no going back. I watched the London lights recede as we flew over our capital city and into the darkness to the other side of the world. We slept on and off until Poppy nudged me and said we had to get out.

'Where are we? Sydney already?'

'No, Bombay, and we have already stopped at Cairo while you were asleep,' Poppy said knowingly.

We left our belongings and followed the other passengers to the exit, down the rickety steps, and out into the hot, humid air, a sort I'd never experienced and caught a bus to the airport building, teeming with passengers from all corners of the earth, and it was hotter there than outside. We sat together, groggy and half-asleep, until we boarded the aircraft again and took off for Singapore. But when the plane started to jump about, the captain announced we had to fasten our seatbelts because of turbulence, and I hung on to my armrest for dear life, but it didn't settle my nerves until it was smooth again. After that, I could hear the rhythmic thrum of the engines around me, each mechanical whir igniting a flicker of anxiety. I couldn't stop worrying that one of them might go haywire and explode at any moment. I held my breath, hoping against hope for a smooth journey ahead.

Fortunately, we were both awake when we approached Kingsford Smith Airport, Sydney, and took in the deep blue water of Botany Bay, our noses pressed to the windowpane. I was very excited. The runway looked too small to take our large aircraft, but we slowly descended to prepare for landing and as we bumped down onto the tarmac, brakes full on, Poppy and I held hands, united in our adventure. I wondered why we had to remain in our seats when a man in uniform walked up and down the aisle, spraying a substance and making us cough and sneeze.

'Why are they spreading that stuff everywhere?' I asked.

'They always spray the aircraft cabin as a safeguard against infectious diseases,' said the woman beside me, who needed a wash.

'It smells disgusting,' I said.

At the immigration desk, we had to wait behind a yellow line before being called, and when it was my turn, the officer stared at me and then stamped my passport.

CHAPTER 18

Poppy was the first to see her luggage on the carousel and grabbed it while I missed mine and watched it disappear, waiting for it to come around again. Poppy found a trolley, and we walked out to a crowd waiting in the arrivals area.

'There's Dad,' she shouted, pointing to a sea of faces.

I followed her to a tall man wearing light-coloured trousers, although several men wore shorts. He formally shook my hand and said, 'Welcome, Julia, to sunny Sydney, and please call me Martin. I hope you had a good flight. Sasha is at home with the kids.'

It was hot walking to the car, the bright light making my eyes water, so I was pleased I'd brought my sunglasses. The harbour bridge loomed huge and metallic, busy with cars, buses and trains on tracks parallel to the road, and on the water, a large container ship sailed under the harbour bridge, joined by different kinds of ships and boats, big and small. We passed Fort Denison, a sandstone turret on a small island in the harbour that, in the past, was a place of punishment for convicts, and in the distance, a liner with migrants on board had docked, and the passengers were slowly leaving the ship faced with their first sight of Sydney, like us.

CHAPTER 19

Once off the Sydney Harbour Bridge, we drove north through residential roads lined with widely spaced bungalows, surrounded by the native bushland, and through the bush, we glimpsed the harbour in blue patches. Martin stopped the car outside a single-storey house with a verandah in the front where you could sit in the shade away from the heat. A stone path, flanked by dense bushes, led to the house and up a few steps to the front door where Aunt Dora, Martin's sister, stood in the doorway, straight-backed and dark-haired, to invite us into the cool of her house. Dora led us along a central passage into a sunroom at the back, with a door into the garden. We crossed an area of grass to a small building, or granny flat, comprising a bedroom and an open-plan living room with a kitchen and bathroom. Martin put our luggage in the bedroom, with two single beds and enough space in a wardrobe for our clothes. We sat on the beds, exhausted, staring at our suitcases, and had no energy to unpack them until the morning. Martin said his goodbyes and left us to settle in.

We yearned to wash away the dirt from travel and have a good night's sleep. There was only a shower in the bathroom, but we had to get used to the knack of getting

CHAPTER 19

the water to the right temperature by twisting the dial to the exact position. If not, the water was either piping hot or freezing cold, but when I finally got it right, what joy standing under the warmth, washing away the grime, turning one way, then the other, to cover the whole of me. I didn't know anyone in England who had a separate shower, only one over a bath. We couldn't wait to get into a proper bed, find our night clothes in our cases, lie under the clean sheet and rest our heads on the soft pillow. But as I lay there, I could still hear the drumming of the engines and felt the motion of the aircraft, and thought I was still on board the plane instead of hoping to fall asleep. Poppy had curled up like a dormouse, her back to me, and I was sure she was in the land of dreams. I couldn't believe I was on the other side of the world, in the Southern Hemisphere and had escaped the English winter for their hot summer. I was thankful that I had such a lovely travelling companion and wondered how long we'd be sharing Dora's flat.

I remembered nothing after thinking about Poppy until I awoke to a scratching noise above as though it was coming through the roof. I looked across at Poppy, but she was faintly snoring, so I grabbed the bedside clock and saw 0530 illuminated. But what was the loud scratching in the roof space? I thought it might be a large bird, but it sounded more like a squirrel. The noise was so loud I wanted to wake Poppy, but instead, I quietly opened the door to the garden and sat outside in the soft air, although it was still dark. There was no sound, and I breathed in the cool of the early morning before the heat hit the city and enjoyed the gradual symphony of birdsong until its coda, the kookaburras' laughter, broke the peace.

I was ravenous, as we hadn't eaten for hours and were too tired the night before to have anything, although Dora had offered us a meal. She had put a few breakfast items in our little kitchen, but I preferred to wait for Poppy. I went back to bed and lay under a sheet until Poppy shook me, asking my preference for breakfast.

'Did you hear a scratching in the roof?' I asked her.

'No, I was dead to the world. It was probably a possum, and they can cause a lot of damage with their sharp claws, but they are protected, so we must leave them alone,' she said, yawning.

I wondered what a possum looked like and if I would see it when it emerged from its home.

The day was going to be hot, so Dora suggested doing our shopping early to escape the midday heat. I had only brought a few summer clothes, and none were suitable for the temperature in Sydney. Poppy was more prepared, but she also needed to do some shopping. Dora took us to a large department store, much like one of ours, and we came out with two sleeveless summer dresses, T-shirts, bikinis, sandals and flip-flops – or thongs, as the Australians call them. In the cosmetics section, we bought skin cream for sun protection, foundation, lipstick and eyeshadow. Later on, I noticed children and adults with peeling backs from sunburn, and it was evident they hadn't used protection against the sun.

On our return, we stopped at a supermarket and purchased meats, salad produce, fruit, vegetables and Australian wine. Food was cheaper and more plentiful, with an irresistible variety of fruits and vegetables. Potatoes, parsnips, and artichokes were often twice the size of our

CHAPTER 19

British ones, making it hard to find tasty small carrots, potatoes, or tomatoes, and making it impossible to buy berries like raspberries. Dora tossed the salads in a lovely oil and lemon dressing, much nicer than the sort of dressing they had back home. It was the Mediterranean touch that mainly Greek immigrants had brought with them.

We had an invitation to a barbecue on Sunday at Martin and Sasha's house, and I was interested to meet Sasha and see where they lived. I wanted to return to the department store to buy a snazzy outfit for the party, but Dora said there was a little boutique within walking distance, and she drew a rough map showing us the route. We passed more bungalows, a few with rose beds and watered lawns, others that were deserted with brown, patchy grass, and the blinds pulled down on the front windows.

We had to cross the main road to get to the shops, and in the small parade, there was a milk bar selling different flavoured milkshakes, a delicatessen displaying meats and cheeses run by a Greek couple, a chemist, and a 'bottle' shop selling alcohol. On the corner stood a butcher's shop, the plastic strips for the door hanging limp in the heat. At the other end of the row of shops was the boutique.

'Are you Dora's niece?' said a husky smoker's voice belonging to a thin, lined woman wearing well-tailored grey trousers and a sleeveless silk blouse.

'Yes, and this is Julia, my travelling companion.'

'Welcome to Australia. How long are you staying?'

'It's flexible, but at least six months,' said Poppy.

I wondered how long I would be in Australia and whether I'd travel back with Poppy. I was facing an unknown future, which was rather exciting.

SHE TAKES HER CHANCES

I had chosen a floaty dress in a swirly turquoise pattern, while Poppy's choice was a plain orange skirt and matching top, and I was pleased we had found something suitable.

'Are these for a welcome party?' said the husky-voiced shop manager.

'Yes, a barbecue at my stepmother and Dad's house.'

'Your purchases are perfect,' she said.

When we'd left the shop and stood outside, Poppy said, 'You'll have to get used to direct questions. They like to file you away if you know what I mean.'

I knew what she meant and had come across it a few times. I wished we'd driven, as the walk back to Dora's was a slog through the deserted streets. The evening was warm, and she'd set up a little table and chairs outside for us to rest and enjoy the shade, the chorus of cicadas drowning our conversation.

'There are two poisonous spiders to be wary of,' Dora said suddenly. 'One is called the redback spider and can be seen in suburban gardens. It has a small red dot on its back and a deadly bite.'

'Is there an antidote for it?' I asked, looking nervously at a nearby shrub. I didn't want to get bitten and end up in a hospital.

'Yes, there is an antivenom, fortunately. The other dangerous one is the Funnel Web spider, which is large and hairy but usually hidden under rocks, and you very rarely see them, which is fortunate as there is no antidote. There are other scary-looking spiders, but they are harmless.'

I didn't fancy seeing either of these spiders, but if I had to choose, I would prefer to see the possum.

'What about poisonous snakes, Dora?' I asked, wanting to get the dangerous bits over with.

CHAPTER 19

'Yes, Julia, there are some highly venomous ones. The Death Adder is deadly and tends to disappear into piles of leaves, so you could easily tread on it. The Eastern Brown Snake is also venomous and aggressive and frequents urban areas, with its bullet-shaped head, but you rarely see that either. The Red-Bellied Black Snake is not so deadly or aggressive, but it would be best to avoid its bite.'

I didn't know which was worse, snakes or spiders, but we should be aware of them. We were quiet after Dora's spider and snake lesson, and I wondered if we'd ever see them, but she said, in all her time in Australia, she'd never seen a snake and only once saw a red-backed spider. The evening was still warm, and our bedroom was stifling, but we had to turn off the fans as they were too noisy and disturbed our sleep. We couldn't open the windows because of the flies and the room was hot, but despite the discomfort we fell asleep. Luckily, the weather forecast was for a 'cool change' or the Southerly buster, opposite to our warm wind from the south.

Residents would go outside and stretch out their arms to feel the first caress of cool air, and then it would roar through, flattening the heat, pushing it northwards until it disappeared, leaving the cooler temperatures for a few days until they rose again. I thought about the scratching possum and how hot he must feel in the roof space, but when I saw a gap under the roof tiles, I guessed I'd found his exit, and he was roaming around somewhere.

I wanted to tell Mummy we'd arrived safely but was too embarrassed to ask Dora if I could use her phone to call them. It would be expensive, and I had to choose a convenient time.

Instead, I wrote a letter.

SHE TAKES HER CHANCES

Sydney
4th January 1969

Dearest Mummy

After a long and tiring flight, with several stops, when we had to go through the palaver of landing and taking off again, Poppy and I are settling in at Dora's granny flat. It is scorching, and with the bright light from the cloudless sky, I wear sunglasses most of the time to help with the glare. We have already been shopping to buy summer clothes. There is more choice of fruit and vegetables than at home, but some clothes are old-fashioned in the large department stores.

Dora seems a lovely lady, quiet and serious but very hospitable. Her flat is small, but there is enough space for both of us. It is separate from her house at the far end of the garden, mainly grass with brightly coloured shrubs and flowers. The bird sounds are extraordinary and so different from our tweeting dawn chorus, particularly the kookaburra with its loud cackle. Martin and Sasha have invited us to a barbecue on Sunday and I will meet Poppy's two little half-sisters. Martin met us at the airport and seemed pleasant and welcoming.

I miss you a lot, Mummy, and was sad seeing you leave the airport building when we went through to departures. I hope the weather isn't too cold and there is no snow. It's all so new and different here, and I feel like a stranger, although

CHAPTER 19

Poppy, Martin and Dora are English and have lived here for some time. However, everyone is friendly and helpful, which makes things easier. I hope you are doing lots of painting while I am away. Please write as soon as you can, and lots of love to Helen and Steve, and regards to Ian.

Much love

Julia

It would be hypocritical of me to send love to Ian as he was so scathing about my trip. I won't miss him at all, but worry about the situation at home.

CHAPTER 20

Martin and Sasha's house was in a cul-de-sac, brick and painted white, with a small front garden and no fence to separate it from the road. The house next door was a wooden bungalow with a verandah, while tall gum trees and large shrubs hid the house opposite.

Sasha stood at the door, taller than Poppy and me, her mid-brown hair shoulder-length, pushed back from her face with a large clip. She led us through airy rooms, the walls adorned with a stunning collection of original paintings. There were indoor plants in large pots scattered throughout the space, adding a touch of natural beauty to the already impressive atmosphere. We left our bags and wraps in the cloakroom downstairs, and from a balcony upstairs, you could see a fenced-in swimming pool, pristine and empty, waiting to be enjoyed by agile swimmers. The barbecue was set up on the terrace, through the open French windows, ready to be fired up and tended by the men.

'Come down when you're ready. I must entertain,' Sasha said, watching us with long, narrow eyes.

We freshened up, and I took my handbag in case I needed my sunglasses, which I wore pretty well all the time, even when it was cloudy.

CHAPTER 20

'Hello, darling,' Martin said to Poppy, 'and hello to my dear sister, Dora. Julia, it's good to see you looking so pretty and refreshed. How about a daiquiri?'

I'd never had one before, but I was always willing to try a new cocktail.

The mixture of rum, lime juice and sugar were moreish and tempted me to have a second one.

'Hello Poppy, welcome, and this is your friend, Julia?' said a tall, good-looking man, who was an old family friend of Martin's.

Martin and Sasha's two small girls, Briony and Molly, ran around a grassy part of the garden, throwing a ball and jumping into a paddling pool. They were blonde, bleached by the sun, but Briony's hair colour had a red tinge. She was eight, two years older than Molly, although Molly was the bossy one. A few couples were stood drinking cocktails, catching up on the local gossip, and calling out to the girls to see who dropped the ball first.

Poppy introduced me to neighbours and friends of Martin and Sasha, and we followed them to the barbecue, attracted by the charred, earthy smell of the steak and sausages. The men stood above the smoking food, turning it as if they had hunted and caught the animals, with the women tucked away in the dessert department. I took a plate from the pile and helped myself to a piece of steak, eggplant, sweetcorn and a helping of dressed green salad, and sat with Poppy and Dora on garden chairs, balancing the plates on our laps. I met Dresden, a man in his 50s, broad-shouldered with thick, light brown hair, and he fetched a glass of red wine for me and white for Poppy and Dora. Dora didn't eat meat and had a piece of barbecued

John Dory fish instead, and while we were chatting, there were shouts from the guests leaping into the water and the little girls' over-excited voices, saying they didn't want to go to bed and running into the pool hut, to hide.

'Did you bring your swimming togs?' Dresden said.

'No, I didn't think of it. Did you?'

'No, I prefer to stay dry,' he said with a slight shiver.

Dresden took my glass and went for a refill. When he returned, we somehow got on to the subject of higher education, and he mentioned Kingsford University taking mature students. Our conversation encouraged me to apply to start the next term, the beginning of their academic year, but we were interrupted by the next-door couple, who had changed into bright yellow swimming gear, the woman in a bikini and her partner in swimming trunks. They had dived into the deep end and raced each other the length of the pool.

'Anybody coming in?' she called.

'We're having a dessert instead,' said Poppy.

The dining room table was heaving with loganberry and pear flans, cheesecake, chocolate torte, a bowl of tropical fruit salad and jugs of cream. I chose a slice of flan, and Poppy opted for the chocolate torte.

'You can use towels in the pool hut if you decide to go in,' Sasha said when she swept past us to collect her two girls for their meal and bed.

I made my way to the dining room to get a second helping of flan, but when I looked into the room, two of the guests drew apart as if they were in an embrace, and I wondered if it was "that sort of party". The woman wore a low-cut, black and silver dress, and the man was well-built

CHAPTER 20

and tanned. I was not sure they saw me, and I retreated and made for the pool area to watch a couple throwing a ball to each other and a girl floating on a Lilo.

As I stood there, two other guests raced each other, their legs and arms churning up the water.

'Not tempted to go in, Julia?' a voice said beside me.

Martin's friend Austin exuded an earthy aroma that drew me to him but made me uneasy.

'No, not this time. I prefer the sea.'

'So do I,' he replied.

I was interested in his response as most people liked swimming pools and at once felt a connection. When I was a young teenager, Clare and I had gone to an indoor swimming pool, and a boy pushed my head under the water and kept it there. I choked and struggled, but when I came to the surface, I couldn't see the boy anywhere. I asked Clare if she knew who he was, but she didn't know his name, and ever since, I have hated indoor swimming pools. I didn't tell Austin that story, and he wandered away to chat with Martin, who was pouring more drinks for his guests who were still there. Most of them had left, and Sasha came over to join us as the girls were already in bed.

'At last, I can relax,' she said. 'I hope you've all had enough to eat and drink.'

'It was delicious,' everyone said.

We sat with the last remaining guests, some making the odd, fatuous comment or contributing to the perfunctory chat to extend the evening into the early hours. Dresden had already left, but he had suggested that Poppy and I would like to catch a ferry to a fish restaurant on the beach and have lunch, and we both accepted the invitation. Dora said she didn't want a late night, and as it was midnight, we collected our bags and wraps, thanked Martin and Sasha, and made our way to the car. You could still hear the calls of two people in the pool, mixed with the sound of a distant owl.

Before I went to sleep, I thought about the enjoyable day and how friendly everyone was. Although Australia had a parochial and small-town feel, the mixture of warmth and water created a kind of glamour fuelled by the abundance of good food and wine.

Poppy was making me jumpy. She was very excited because Rich was coming to see her on Sunday, and he was to join Poppy, me and Dresden on our trip to the fish restaurant near the beach. Poppy and I wore a bikini under our dresses in case we wanted a swim, and we packed towels and beach shoes in our canvas bags bought from a shop near one of the harbour beaches. When a tall, tanned man crossed the garden with Dora to where we were sitting, I recognised Rich. He said Hi to me and stopped in front of Poppy, and they gazed at each other, lost for words. I went inside and left them but later joined their chatter at the garden table as if they'd never been apart. When Dresden arrived, we collected our belongings and went to his car, Rich in the front seat to stretch his legs and Poppy and me in the back. Poppy looked flushed and leant towards Rich, her hand on his shoulder, directing the conversation towards him, while I felt uneasy wondering how much of our talk at lunch would involve news of Jim.

'We'll catch a ferry from Circular Quay to Watson's Bay,' Dresden said, 'and then you can see the city from the water.'

It was all so exciting, riding a wave of excitement in a kaleidoscope of colour and pattern, but once again, I was on edge about hearing news of Jim.

CHAPTER 20

The terminal was busy with people running to catch the ferry and others making their way to the exit. We stood on the pier and waited for the yellow and green hulk to dock and let off the passengers so we could find seats on the deck. It was a relief to feel the breeze from the water on another hot day, the patches of white foam reflecting the blue and green, and as the harbour bridge receded, we passed properties built near sandy bays with the bush as a backdrop. Sailing craft surrounded us on our journey, from small yachts crewed by one or two people to larger boats, the sails flapping in the sea breeze until we reached the tiny landing stage of the stop before ours. The ferry slid to the edge, and two workers threw the gangway down for departing passengers to cross before we cruised to our destination. Dresden led the way to the fish restaurant, a few yards from where we landed and a stone's throw from the beach.

We grabbed an empty table at the front.

'Well, what is everyone having?' Dresden said.

'Lobster for me,' said Rich.

'I'll join Rich and have lobster,' said Dresden.

Poppy and I studied the menu together, me dithering and Poppy knowing her choice.

'Barramundi,' said Poppy.

'Snapper for me,' I said, not knowing what it would taste like.

Restaurants allowed you to bring the wine of your choice, and after the waiter had uncorked ours and filled our glasses, we raised them and wished each other good cheer.

'The fish you girls have chosen are local to us, as plaice and cod are for you,' said Dresden.

'Where do you work, Dresden?' Rich asked.

'I'm a graphic designer in the marketing department of a company based in the suburbs. I understand you're an air force pilot, Rich,' Dresden continued.

'Correct. I am now at a station in New South Wales, which is a change from Lincolnshire. I miss my old mate, Jim, but he's doing well after his bad accident.'

I nearly choked on my fish and swallowed a mouthful of wine. Rich suddenly stopped and looked at me.

'Where was the accident?' Dresden continued, unaware of the tension that was building.

No one spoke, and I wondered if Dresden noticed anything different. Poppy glanced at me and sipped her wine but didn't comment. I felt sick.

'In Oman where he was stationed. He was badly burnt but has recovered well,' Rich said abruptly.

'It must have been a traumatic experience. Was Jim a good pilot?' Dresden went on.

'Excellent pilot,' Rich said.

The waiter brought the dessert menu, and Dresden suggested pavlova, New Zealand's national dish, but according to him, Australia thought it was theirs. The pavlova oozed fruit, meringue and cream, a rich swirl of colour, and as we felt in a celebratory mood, we ordered coffee and liqueurs. We had a few bites of our dessert, and you could hear the clink of spoons as we scooped up the mixture.

'He must have found Oman fascinating and a huge contrast to Lincolnshire,' Dresden continued.

'They are certainly different. The county is mainly flat and ideal for flying,' Rich replied.

CHAPTER 20

'Lots of sky,' I added, intent on moving away from the subject. I couldn't stand hearing Jim's name mentioned any more than it had been.

'I have cousins in Scotland, and I must visit them one day,' Dresden said.

I relaxed a little as we moved away from the heat of Oman.

'Wonderful scenery, with mountains, hills and lochs, although there are also RAF stations up there,' Rich explained.

We settled the bill, and I was relieved to take off our shoes and walk along the beach, the sand caressing our toes. Dresden asked me if there was a problem with the pilot who crashed his plane, as we had looked awkward when he asked about him. I didn't elaborate but said he was a friend, and we'd separated under difficult circumstances.

'Perhaps I shouldn't have mentioned him,' Dresden said.

'Don't worry, Dresden. It's no big deal,' I said, trying to lighten the day. 'How about we go for a quick swim, Poppy?'

We whipped off our dresses, ran into the warm water, and swam out, lay on our backs to float with only a ripple to keep us buoyant, hoping there were no poisonous jellyfish underneath or basking sharks, gnashing their teeth.

The men had walked to the far end of the beach, and when we'd had enough, we came out and lay on our towels. I asked Poppy to rub sun lotion on my back, and when she'd finished, I did hers. The wine had made us sleepy, and the distant calls of swimmers, the gentle surge of the waves and the whisper of the silver gull merged into my dream of walking through a forest of blackened tree stumps after a bushfire and remarking on the bright green shoots appearing out of the destruction. I saw a house burnt down to blackened dust and wondered what had happened to its owners.

'You've been asleep, Jules. We need to find the men,' Poppy said, pushing my shoulder and gathering her belongings. My arm felt numb from lying on it, and my shoulder had turned a deep crimson from the sun, but during the night, I had a touch of sunstroke and woke feeling sick with a splitting headache. I took two painkillers, but they didn't work, and I was sick anyway. My arm and shoulder felt raw and painful when I dressed or moved my arm, and although I dowsed them in vinegar, it didn't help, so for the next few days, I wore long sleeves to protect myself from the sun.

We walked along the beach to some rocks at the other end but couldn't see the men. The hot glare blurred the distant figures, and we thought they might have caught the ferry without us. Only the seagulls replied when we called their names, so we decided to return to the restaurant as a starting point and back there, we sat in the shade to wait. Dresden had the ferry tickets, so as a precaution, Poppy and I pooled our money to ensure we had enough for the fare if they had gone ahead.

'They're over there,' said Poppy, standing up and pointing to the far end of the beach. The two men walked towards us as we trudged over the sand, and when they approached, Dresden was laughing at Rich, telling him something.

'Where have you been, girls?' they said in unison.

'Looking for you,' I replied.

'Hurry, or we'll miss the next ferry,' Dresden said.

CHAPTER 21

When Dora saw my sunburn, she let out a long breath. 'That looks sore, Julia. I'll give you some lotion to soothe and heal the burn. With your type of skin, you'll need to be careful.'

I knew that but couldn't help falling asleep on the beach. The lotion was cooling, and for a while, it helped. We had a late breakfast before another hot day as the "cool change" hadn't arrived.

'How does working in a bookshop appeal before you start Kingsford University?' Dora advised.

My application to read Psychology and French had been accepted by the university, much to my relief. Fortunately, I had packed my A-Level certificates to send with the form.

'I'm all ears,' I said.

'A friend, Pam, is looking for someone to help while her assistant is recovering from surgery. Would you be interested?'

I thought it would be an appropriate environment for me before university and a little source of income. There were no student fees, only an amount to subsidise the Student Union. I wanted it to work out as the extra money would be helpful, although I was very grateful to Grandpa, who had offered to support me while I studied, and he'd already paid my fare to Sydney. Ian had no intention of being my benefactor, and no surprise there!

Dora took me to meet Pam at her bookshop on Saturday afternoon. It was next to a Methodist Church on a quiet road and comprised two main rooms, the front stocked with new books, while the back room had shelves of second-hand and antiquarian books.

Pam was waiting for us in the shop, a round-faced lady with grey hair and glasses.

'I will show you the different sections,' she said, and I followed her around the shop as she pointed them out. Fiction was at the front, followed by cookery books, travel, history, sport, education and other non-fiction categories.

The two windows that faced the road provided the light, but as there was no natural light at the back, ceiling lights and lamps were on. Pam opened the shop at nine in the morning and closed at five in the afternoon and she usually got in between eight and eight-thirty in time to prepare before opening.

I studied the different shelves and titles and hoped I would remember them. Pam showed me a kitchenette with a small stove, worktop and fridge next to a cloakroom, both rooms on the other side of a door behind the cash desk. Along a passage was a storage room.

'How do you feel, Julia, about working here? Or do you want to go away and think about it? You can start on Monday. My assistant will be away for at least six weeks recovering from abdominal surgery,' Pam said, taking her glasses off.

I said I was happy to accept the job, and the evening before I started, I prepared a packed lunch of a ham and

CHAPTER 21

tomato sandwich, a peach and nectarine, a bottle of lemon cordial, and a piece of fruitcake Dora had made. Martin kindly gave me their VW Beetle car as it remained in their garage, untouched. He and Sasha had their vehicles, and Martin said it was better driven than gathering dust. On my first morning, I travelled with the rush hour traffic, cars coming from all directions, blowing their horns and shouting obscenities.

When I arrived at the shop, there was no parking outside, and the first space I found was at the end of the road behind an old van. Pam was going through the accounts when I got in.

'You look flustered,' she said. 'Sit down for a while. We don't open for another fifteen minutes, and I'm pleased to say business is healthy.'

'Parking was difficult, but I found somewhere in the end,' I said.

At first, there were no customers, but when Pam went shopping, a young mother came in, pushing a small boy in a stroller or pushchair, as we'd say.

A little girl of about four years old was hanging on to the handle.

'Good morning. Do you want to browse or need any help?' I asked.

Her eyes looked tired and her hair fell lank to her shoulders.

'I'm looking for a thriller by Len Deighton, something File? It's for my husband's birthday.'

I looked along the row of his books and took out *The Ipcress File*. I hoped it was the one she was looking for.

'Is this the one?'

'Yes, and one by Patricia Highsmith, *Strangers on a Train.*'

Authors with names beginning with "H" were in the next section, and we had a copy in stock.

The little boy started whining for ice cream, and the small girl said he had to wait.

'Just shush, Bobby, stop whining, or you won't get anything.'

The little girl pushed his shoulder, and he started screaming.

'Leave him alone, Carrie, or you won't have any ice cream either.'

They were both shouting, and I couldn't wait for them to leave the shop.

'I'll have both books. Sorry about the kids. They're probably tired and hungry.'

We moved over to the desk, and she paid the correct amount in cash. Books were more expensive in Australia compared to home.

She smiled. 'Thanks. At least I have something for my husband.'

'Enjoy his birthday,' I said as she left the shop with her two quarrelling kids.

I felt exhausted, and it wasn't even ten in the morning, but when Pam returned, I made us a coffee. Our next customers were a couple looking for a book on Fiji as they had booked a holiday there and were interested in its history. We had one book in stock, but they decided to leave it and said they'd try the large bookshop in the centre of Sydney. They bought another book about Papua New Guinea, as they knew someone who travelled there

CHAPTER 21

on business. When it was time to close, I returned the books to the shelves while Pam dealt with the till and cash.

'We did reasonably well today. How did you get on, Julia?'

'I enjoyed it once I started, but dealing with people is tiring.'

Pam said she was thinking of setting up an area for serving coffee, but that would be even more stressful.

The day I was late for work at the bookshop, there was a car accident when two cars collided, not giving way to each other at the junction. One of the cars looked a write-off, its bonnet squashed flat, and the other vehicle was on its side. Two ambulances were there, blue lights flashing, the paramedics loading the casualties into the back. Although several cars had stopped before me, I could see where the accident had happened and why it had caused a long tail-back. We had to wait for the ambulances to move and for the police to do their work.

When I arrived, Pam was deep in conversation with Sasha, but they both looked up when they saw me and Sasha's comment, 'Better late than never, Julia,' didn't start the day well.

'Don't worry, Julia, traffic accidents happen almost daily, especially in rush hour, so go and make yourself a drink and relax for a while.'

Pam was helping Sasha find a book for her Book Club meeting the following week. They chose The Stepford Wives by Ida Levin, but ironically, Sasha was the last person I could see as a "Stepford Wife". Perhaps that's why she chose it.

I went into the kitchen, poured myself a cup from the coffee pot, picked a biscuit from the tin and sat on the only seat there, waiting for Sasha to leave. Pam advised me to ignore Sasha and her cryptic comments, but according to Pam, I unnerved her, which puzzled me, as I didn't think I was intimidating, but how we appear to others is different from how we see ourselves. After Pam had gone to the bank with the shop's takings, I had a surprise customer. A tall, straight-backed man came in, and although I recognised him, I had to think where we'd met. He knew my name, and when he said he was Austin, I remembered him at Martin and Sasha's party and our brief exchange by the swimming pool. He was looking for 17th-century French poetry books that wouldn't be easy to find.

'I know Pam has antiquarian books in stock,' I said. 'But I'm not sure we have what you're looking for. They would be in the back room.'

He followed me in, and we stood together looking along the shelves but only found ones published in the 19th and early 20th centuries and nothing on French poetry.

'Never mind, I can look elsewhere,' he said.

We went to the front of the shop and saw a woman concentrating on a book about cake-making. Austin hovered and suggested we go to Lucia's wine bar near the shop when I was free. I had often wondered what Lucia's was like and hoped the opportunity would materialise.

'I'll be in touch, Julia,' he said, and as I watched him leave, I wanted to see more of him.

I asked the woman at the front of the shop if she needed assistance, but she said she'd take the book and hoped it would give her some baking tips, as she was the cake-maker for Church social events.

CHAPTER 21

I wondered how many more customers we'd get that day, but what a shock I got later in the afternoon.

My next customer was a tall, thin woman wearing large round sunglasses. She requested two books on art theft, The Baron and the Missing Old Masters by John Creasy, and Clutch of Constables by Ngaio Marsh, but they were out of stock.

'We can order them for you,' I said.

'Oh, don't bother. I can try somewhere else as I need the books in a hurry,' the woman said, marching out of the shop and slamming the door. She nearly knocked Poppy and Dora over when they came in after having lunch at Lucia's Wine Bar. Wine bars were popping up like mushrooms in Sydney and a trendy alternative to the typical Australian pubs frequented by men. Some were small and intimate, but Lucia's was large and often crowded, being a popular place for lunch. Poppy had the afternoon off for working overtime one evening and had tickets for a Magritte exhibition at the Art Gallery of NSW. They were valid for any day, and as the shop closed at five, she knew I'd be free.

'The exhibition sounds interesting, Poppy. I'd love to go,' I said, looking at Pam to see if she still needed me in the shop.

'Go and enjoy yourselves. It's about time I shut up shop,' Pam said, flapping her arms like a bird.

'I've got an appointment with a customer about a stained-glass window and must hurry, or I'll be late,' Dora said, opening the shop door.

We climbed the steps to the art gallery, passing the neo-classical frontage and through the galleries of permanent exhibits to the Magritte exhibition in a spacious room to view the artworks. We bought a programme and stood in front of the first painting called *Golconda, a Whimsical Landscape,* the canvas filled with different-sized bowler-hatted men floating past terraced houses to the sky.

'What is your analysis of this one, Julia?' Poppy asked, covering her mouth with her fingers.

'Humanity, living in cities, with no individuality, following each other like sheep, but are fooled, thinking it's heaven because of the blue sky.'

The next painting was a mermaid with a woman's legs washed up on the shore.

'This is a strange one. Sinister. Debunking the romantic idea of a mermaid, perhaps?' I said, not sure what it meant.

'I think it's depressing,' Poppy said.

'The artist is a cynic.'

'I suppose *Ceci n'est pas une pipe* is saying art is an interpretation and not reality, and I suppose it is,' Poppy said.

We stared at The Therapist. Did the therapist feel imprisoned rather than the patient?

But one of the birds outside the cage probably represented freedom. We agreed that Magritte often depicted people as faceless to accentuate the message behind the painting.

Although the exhibition wouldn't appeal to everyone, the gallery had filled up. We started discussing "The Lovers", a claustrophobic picture of a man and woman kissing, covered in white sheets.

'He doesn't have much hope for humanity,' I said, but when I looked around, I did a double-take to check I hadn't seen a ghost. A man and a woman were chatting at the far

CHAPTER 21

end of the gallery, and the man looked like Ian, but I had to be careful because I didn't want to get into the habit of thinking I saw people I knew, and it wasn't them. But when the Ian lookalike glanced in our direction, I was certain it was him. I felt sick and faint and wanted to run away.

'You wouldn't believe it, Poppy, but my stepfather is on the other side of the gallery talking to a woman.'

'Are you sure, Julia? What on earth would he be doing in Sydney?'

'I've no idea, but he is coming over to speak to us.'

He mumbled 'Hello' and introduced himself to Poppy. I was speechless and waited for him to explain what he was doing there.

'Did you receive Mother's letter about my visit to Australia?' he said in an unfriendly tone.

'I haven't received any letter, Ian, and I presume Mother knows you're here.'

'Of course she does. As I said, she wrote to you over a week ago to say I was coming.'

I wondered if he was telling the truth although the mail in Australia can be pretty hopeless.

'When did you arrive? Are you on business in Sydney?' I asked, hoping he wouldn't snap at me.

'I've been here almost a week, and I leave tomorrow. I thought you might have called my hotel, but I can see now why you didn't.'

I could only sigh with relief that I hadn't received the letter, but why didn't he call Dora's number? Mum has it in her address book – but perhaps she hides it away somewhere. I wanted to ask him what his business was in Australia, but he had something else to say.

'I have one of Mum's paintings to give you and I'll leave it at the hotel reception, and you can pick it up tomorrow. My flight leaves early in the morning.'

I was thankful he was going the next day and I wouldn't have to see him again in Sydney. Before he left us, he said, 'Have you enrolled in that second-rate university yet?'

I was so insulted I didn't feel like answering the question. Poppy had moved to look at some more paintings, and I couldn't wait for him to leave. The woman he was talking to was still in the same position at the far end of the gallery, and without saying any more, Ian went over to join her.

'I can't get over him being here and in the same gallery we're in. I need a drink after that,' I said.

'I'll buy you one, Julia, and we can do a postmortem on your tense meeting,' she said, raising her eyebrows.

I needed a whole bottle and couldn't get my head around Ian being in Sydney. I wondered if Mum knew about his trip to Australia or whether that was a lie. I could ring Mum to find out, if Dora wouldn't mind my using the phone and I'd offer to pay for the call. Over a glass of wine, we discussed Ian being in Sydney and I gave him the benefit of the doubt that he was there on legitimate business.

'He's an architect, so I suppose the company could be expanding geographically,' I said.

'He looked mean and tight-lipped,' was Poppy's opinion of him. I nodded in agreement but had the nagging thought that he was doing something underhand.

CHAPTER 22

After my shock at the Gallery, Dora suggested we have a picnic in the Blue Mountains, about an hour's drive west of Sydney. Martin and Sasha had asked Dora to have their girls for the day while they visited friends, so it was a day out for all of us. We drove through vast stretches of gum trees, their tall, thin trunks and messy branches, a grey-green uniformity stretching either side of the road. There were hundreds of different gum trees, but they all looked the same to me. True to their name, the mountains looked blue, hazy and mysterious and when we arrived in the nearest town, deserted except for a few pedestrians wandering in and out of shops, the misty blue was still there. Dusty paths and rocky steps took us to a place suitable for our picnic and near a lookout over the vast area. In the distance were the Three Sisters, an unusual rock formation, sharp and craggy, representing three aboriginal women who married three forbidden brothers from a neighbouring tribe. The colours changed depending on the season and time of day, and for us, they glowed with patches of pink and orange, the reflection of the light and sun. We sat on rugs to take in the view while the girls marked out squares for hopscotch in a patch without grass and found stones to play the game. When it was time to eat, Dora reached for the picnic basket, opened the creaky lid and unpacked rolls, cheese, ham, cucumber, tomatoes and fruit. She laid them out and opened the cool box for water and wine.

'Can we have ice cream before the other boring food?' asked Molly.

'No, rolls come first; there are ham and cheese with either tomato or cucumber. Ice cream is last,' Dora said.

'Daddy lets us.'

'No, he doesn't,' Briony retorted.

They had hard-boiled eggs and asked Dora to unpick the shell, who did it with her deft fingers, keeping the egg whole. Rich poured the wine into cups we'd brought and split open a packet of crisps. The air was pleasant, cooler than when we started our climb, and the smell of eucalyptus was as intoxicating as the wine.

Rich looked at me and I knew he wanted to say something controversial.

'That must have been a surprise to see your stepfather in Sydney, Julia,' Rich said, looking intrigued.

'To say the least, I had no idea he was coming.'

'Odd you didn't receive any warning by letter or phone.'

'Mum said she had written to me but I'm not sure who had Dora's telephone number. Ian said he'd lost it, but Mum said it was in her address book.'

I thought maybe Ian had posted the letter later than he said, and when he was in Sydney, he purposely didn't call. I'm convinced seeing him in the art gallery was a coincidence, so he wasn't expecting to see me.

'Poppy said he's an architect,' Rich said, 'so perhaps he was looking at buildings in Sydney. Long way to come, though.'

CHAPTER 22

'He never tells Mum anything about his work, and she doesn't ask.'

'What did you think when you first met him?'

'I never took to him, Rich. He was pernickety from the start.'

'What about Helen?'

'She was more accepting of him. Helen's more laid back than I am.'

As we'd finished the picnic, Poppy and Rich wanted to check in at the hotel, and Dora said we should pack up and walk back to the car. Briony and Molly asked to finish their game, and Dora gave them a few more minutes. Rich and Poppy went on ahead while Dora and I leant over the railing and took in the expanse of tree tops and steep rock faces and the different sounds of native birds. The loud cheep of the noisy miner, the galah with its pink chest and the haunting tune of the bellbird. The sounds filled the air, and it was a wrench to leave and wend our way back to Sydney. We packed away the picnic and, on our return, remarked on the lizards darting between the stones, and we caught the rare sight of two tiny rock wallabies jumping about and disappearing into the undergrowth. The girls ran ahead, up and down steps cut into the sandstone.

'Stay with us,' called Dora.

Briony ran back, but Molly continued, so I went after her to make sure she didn't fall, but sadly, she did, and tumbled down the steps to a lower level.

'My leg's bleeding. It's agony and I want Mummy!' Molly screamed.

Dora and I rushed down, her screams echoing around the rocks. Dora grabbed a tea towel she'd packed with the food and wrapped it around the gash, but the blood quickly seeped through the towel and soaked Molly's dress. Dora picked her up, and we ran over bumpy, stony ground to where we had parked the car. She found a T-shirt in the car boot and bound the wound tightly, gradually stopping the flow of blood, and I helped by pressing on it while Molly lay on the back seat, her head on my lap. When Dora drove into the town, we looked for someone to direct us to a hospital.

'Excuse me, but is there a hospital near here?' Dora called out to a man in shorts.

'Down this road, second turning on the right, Benton Street, and the hospital is at the end. There'll be a sign.'

After following his instructions, we reached a low building with several extensions. Dora carried Molly through the main entrance and spoke to a nurse who took them to a consulting room to see a doctor.

'Will Molly be alright? I'm scared,' Briony whimpered.

'Don't worry, Briony. We'll wait here. I'm sure Molly and Aunt Dora won't be away long. Once the doctor has treated the wound, Molly will feel a lot more comfortable.'

Briony was restless, so I found a book for her to read about a tractor on a farm and descriptions of different farm animals. After an hour, Dora and Molly, with her leg bandaged, came into the waiting room with a doctor.

'No breaks, but the wound was deep, so she had six stitches,' the doctor said.

Dora asked to use the hospital phone to call Martin and let them know.

'They didn't sound too happy about it,' Dora said, looking concerned.

CHAPTER 22

'Once they see Molly's leg isn't broken, and it's not as bad as it might have been, they won't be so frantic,' I said hoping to appease Dora.

Molly fell asleep on the journey home, but Briony said she felt car-sick, so we had to stop for her to get out. Although she looked pale, she didn't vomit, and after drinking some water from the cool box, she recovered, joined her sister and fell asleep. Martin and Sasha were waiting for us outside the house, and carried Molly inside, where she sat with her leg on a footstool enjoying the attention.

'You must keep your eye on Molly. She's accident-prone,' Sasha told us firmly.

'It was excruciating, Daddy. Can I have a treat?'

'We'll see, young lady.'

They made an appointment with the doctor the following week, and the prognosis was good. Molly was the most popular girl in the class, with a bandaged leg to show off to her friends, but when it healed and the bandage came off, everything went back to normal.

Poppy and Rich returned the following day, all smiles and sparkly eyes, and Poppy displayed a diamond ring on an elegant finger that caught the light in a rainbow of colours. They had got engaged in the Blue Mountains, sitting on a rock and watching a waterfall cascade down the steep escarpment, after a long walk along rocky paths. I was delighted for them and not in the least surprised, and I looked forward to a beautiful wedding, except for the possibility of seeing Jim again, as Rich's best man. I thought Jim would be the likely choice if he was free to travel, but it would also mean meeting Marta, the woman who had taken my place.

We celebrated the engagement in a renovated Victorian house converted into a restaurant, the original features of architraves, ceiling roses and fireplaces still intact. We met in the small bar on the ground floor for pre-dinner drinks. Black and white photos of Hollywood stars from the early 1900s, some of whom I recognised, like Vivien Leigh, Ingrid Bergman, and Humphrey Bogart, adorned the walls, and added to the ambience of the house.

Poppy looked radiant in a low-cut dress, her blonde hair brushing her shoulders. After champagne and cocktails to toast the couple, we climbed the stairs, passing other tables in nooks and crannies, to the balcony room at the top of the house that had a view over the tops of buildings, the Sydney lights shining like a mass of pinpricks.

We sat at a long table with Poppy and Rich at either end. Sasha had done the table plan, and I found my place card next to Dresden, and opposite Austin. I would have preferred to be next to Austin, so we could have a conversation, but sitting opposite him was better than nothing. I sat with my back to the balcony and enjoyed the soft breeze and the distant sounds of the city. Vases of red roses and blue delphiniums added life and colour to the room, and small dishes of crudites, to be dipped into a mayonnaise sauce, were already on the table, before the main meal. We had made our choice from the menu a few days before to make it easier for the catering staff, and I'd chosen a chicken casserole with a salad, while others had chosen a lamb casserole or a vegetarian dish. Rich held the floor and talked about their forthcoming wedding in a church in the city, and the reception at a club he belonged to.

CHAPTER 22

'Several air force friends will form a guard of honour, and Briony and Molly will be Poppy's bridesmaids,' Rich continued.

'Will your family be able to come?' Dora asked.

'I hope so. My parents have moved to a retirement complex in Phoenix, Arizona, and enjoy the warmer weather, although it can get very hot.'

'My wife and I went there on holiday and were fascinated with the tiny flowers that sprouted at the top of the cactus,' Austin said.

Austin's remark made me sit up. Had his wife died, or was she alive, living somewhere else? His mention of a wife changed my mood and made me wary.

'The flowers open at night and only last for a day, but there are several blooms during the season,' Rich explained.

'You'd have to be quick to see them,' someone piped up at the other end of the table.

'Who's going to be the best man?' Sasha asked.

'Jim, who has accepted the invitation,' Rich replied, not looking at me.

A cold shiver travelled down my spine, but I wasn't going to ask if his wife would accompany him. I toyed with the idea of making an excuse not go to the wedding, but they'd all be suspicious, unless I was seriously ill.

'Is his wife coming too?' Sasha asked with a slight furrow on her brow.

'Yes. They have both accepted the invitation,' Rich said quietly.

Poppy said her mother and stepfather would make the journey. Although I'd only met them briefly when I went to the RAF ball, I liked them and looked forward to seeing them again. But I was right, Rich had already asked Jim to be his best man, and he had accepted, and would travel to Australia with Marta. Rich knew I'd be nervous seeing Jim again, but that didn't stop him. I didn't think anyone else at the gathering knew my history with Jim, except Rich and Poppy, and I didn't imagine they had told anyone. Dresden knew there was a connection from our conversation at the fish restaurant, but he didn't know the details.

Austin looked at me across the table, and I knew we were attracted to each other, although he was listening intently to Poppy talking about her family. The dynamics around a table of people were always complex. Still, on this occasion, we were well-balanced, with no one dominating the conversation and everyone involved in their immediate group.

'Will it be a traditional wedding, Rich?' Dora asked, suddenly.

'Yes, probably in an old church in the city with a guard of honour consisting of guys from the squadron and Poppy's father.' Jim's name was mentioned again and when I heard his name, I put my fork back on the plate and gulped my wine. The chatter around the table was happy and animated, while I felt isolated and abandoned, only thinking of Jim.

I grabbed an opportunity to ask Poppy about his wedding. She was standing in the hall waiting to leave.

'Before you go, Poppy, did you attend Jim's wedding?'

She smiled at me as much as to say; I was wondering when you would ask.

'Yes, Rich was the best man, unsurprisingly, but there was friction between the parents.'

'Tell me more,' I said, feeling secretly pleased.

CHAPTER 22

'Marta's parents wanted a Catholic wedding, but Jim didn't want to convert to the faith, which he had to do.'

'Did they marry in a church?' I asked.

'Yes, the village church near Jim's parents. Marta looked lovely, I have to admit, but you could feel the tension. Her parents were cold but polite and hardly spoke to Francis and Hilary despite the language barrier. They looked displeased and left the reception early.'

Well, at least it wasn't all plain-sailing and hunky-dory, which was only a slight relief.

'Where was it held?' I continued.

'In the garden at Jim's parents'. The weather was gorgeous, hot, and it was well-organised.'

'Were there many guests?' I asked, vowing it would be my last question.

'About fifty.'

I didn't want to hear much more about the wedding as it made me sad. Jim and I were suited to each other in so many ways, and I hoped I hadn't made a terrible mistake and will never meet anyone else as compatible.

CHAPTER 23

Poppy spent the week before the wedding at Martin and Sasha's to finalise arrangements and be close to her two half-sisters, Briony and Molly, who were the bridesmaids. On Poppy and Rich's wedding day, I could hardly concentrate on getting ready, thinking of seeing Jim and wondering how we'd react. Fortunately, I was alone in the flat and could get dressed without sharing the bathroom or bedroom. I stood for ages under the shower, playing out different scenarios in my head, from a dramatic altercation with Jim, who declared his undying love for me in the church, to no recognition of me at all.

After my lengthy shower, I put on my dressing gown and lay on the bed to cool off and hoped I hadn't made a mistake turning down Jim's proposal. Of course, it was too late to worry about it, and I should be thankful I was doing what I had planned. Half of me wanted to back out of the wedding altogether, but I would never forgive myself if I missed their wedding. I felt nauseous but probably hungry as I hadn't eaten breakfast. I popped a slice of bread in the toaster, made a drink and sat at the kitchen table, idly spreading the toast with butter and marmalade, and taking small sips of coffee from a large mug. I was in the middle of a memory of Jim and me in France, inspecting our bed

CHAPTER 23

bug bites, when Dora called from the garden asking if I was nearly ready. She wanted to get there early to sit near the front, so I finished the coffee and sat in front of a mirror to do my make-up. Although it would be a challenge, I had to look as stunning as possible. However, when I had finished the transformation, with eyeshadow and mascara applied, I crossed the garden to the house and called out for Dora. She came out looking very smart, and we both congratulated ourselves on how lovely we looked.

When we arrived, there were plenty of empty seats, and we sat behind Poppy's immediate family, her mother and stepfather, who'd come from England, with her sister and husband. I looked across at Rich's side of the church and caught a glimpse of whom I thought was Marta, Jim's wife, tall and elegant with a hat not dissimilar to mine. I fiddled with the Order of Service, distractedly reading it from cover to cover, until Rich and Jim walked down the aisle, handsome in their uniform, and stood by the altar rail.

The organ played soft background music, accompanied by low chatter, as the congregation waited for Poppy and Martin to come and join the bridegroom. When the music suddenly burst into a triumphant sound, all heads turned to Poppy, who looked out of this world in a slim-fitting, beautifully cut silk dress, the train held by her two little bridesmaids in pink, looking intent, walking with straight backs, and Martin, her father, beside her.

Towards the end, a group disappeared to the vestry to sign the marriage register. I looked over at Marta, who was talking to one of the officers, although he was doing most of the talking, and all I saw of her was a bobbing black hat. When they reappeared from the vestry, the organ music reverberated around the church, and I couldn't stop thinking of my time with Jim, not regretfully, but with nostalgia, and wondered if he was thinking the same thing. But when the air force chaps walked out of the church at the end of the service to form the guard of honour, Jim looked straight ahead with no acknowledgement I was there at all. Outside the church, a crowd of onlookers gathered to watch the officers with their swords raised, to make a canopy for Rich and Poppy when they walked out into the sunshine. The group of spectators stood still, pointing and talking in low voices, marvelling at a spectacle they probably had never seen.

Afterwards, Dora and I sat on a seat and watched the performance of the wedding photographs. It took ages, with the photographer arranging different groups, changing their position, making them look at the camera and smile, with him standing nearer or further away to take the shots. The main players were Rich, Poppy, the bridesmaids, the best man and the parents, but in some photos, the photographer included Marta, and she shyly faced the camera in her large hat. The same group of spectators were still there, enjoying Act II.

We assembled in a private room at the RAC Club, filled with flowers and a table adorned with a vast spread for the wedding breakfast, congratulated the beaming couple, toasted their happiness and wished them a long life together. Jim never once looked in my direction but was in a group from his old squadron and their wives or girlfriends. I peered across the room to catch a glimpse of Marta, who seemed to smile a lot and occasionally contributed to the conversation. She glanced to where I was standing, and I wondered how much Jim had told her, but when I was

CHAPTER 23

chatting with a couple I had met at Martin and Sasha's, Dora introduced us. I thought she looked pregnant and was taller than I expected, with large brown eyes and a strong accent when she spoke. She was enjoying their visit and looked forward to going to Melbourne after the wedding to stay with a relative of Jim's, and I felt a pang of jealousy that they would do so many things together as a couple. That day, Austin was my saviour. We sat together on a small couch with a drink and a plate of canapés, and he told me about his wife, who had died from a head injury after a car accident. She was driving, and the doctor said she could have had a brain haemorrhage, causing her to swerve and crash into a brick wall, the only small blessing, as no one else was involved.

In retrospect, that was an intimate, sad event to tell me at such an occasion, but after all the champagne on offer, you'd tell anyone anything. In return, I informed him that Jim was an ex-boyfriend but omitted the marriage proposal and the details. But I wished I hadn't said anything, as he immediately asked me a loaded question.

'Is it difficult for you to see him married to another woman?' he said boldly.

I bit my tongue and decided not to say anything more about him.

'I have hardly seen him today and have only briefly met his wife. I'm more interested in talking to you, Austin,' I replied.

I felt satisfied I had put Jim to rest as far as Austin was concerned, so I asked him where he lived in Sydney. I didn't know the area, but he suggested he'd take me there and show me his house.

'Will you stay in Dora's flat now that Poppy is married?' Austin asked.

'I'm not sure. An old school friend plans to come to Sydney to live, and I suggested she share accommodation with me. Dora's flat is small for two people, and I may look for somewhere else.'

Austin was about to say something when Jim's father, Francis, came and asked how I was and congratulated me on my university acceptance. I wasn't sure how he knew, but obviously, someone had told him.

'Where did you live before Sydney?' Austin asked, handing me a seafood canapé.

'London. I shared a flat with another girl.'

'How old were you when you went to London?'

'Nineteen, after I'd done A-Levels.'

His interrogation felt like an interview, but I didn't intend to answer every question he asked if I didn't feel like it.

'That's young to leave home and live independently in a big city.'

'It wasn't unusual. Lots of girls went to London to live and work.'

'What was home life like, Julia?'

I didn't feel in the mood to answer a personal question and explain the situation at home.

'Not perfect, but I miss my mother and sister.'

Afterwards, I felt as though my path had taken me to a black hole, and to forget, I thought about Austin. I found him attractive and interesting but had a vague notion that I was walking on a precipice, although I ignored the feeling and didn't listen to my inner voice.

CHAPTER 23

Austin and I had to pause our chat to hear the speeches. Everyone shuffled to get comfortable, and Martin stood to start the proceedings. He looked very dashing in his wedding suit, welcomed everyone present and thanked the organisers of the glorious event. Martin lauded Rich and said he was delighted to have him as a son-in-law, married to his beautiful daughter, Poppy. He loved his friendly, open nature and his wicked sense of humour. Everyone grabbed their champagne glasses and raised them for the toasts. He read out a pile of telegrams from people who couldn't attend, mainly because of the distance, and all the while, Sasha gazed lovingly at her husband, and I knew she adored him.

Rich also thanked everyone who had come to celebrate the happiest day of his life. When he was given the posting to flat, boring Lincolnshire, he was disappointed and depressed, but when he met Poppy, Lincolnshire changed into paradise, and he thanked the Royal Air Force for his good fortune.

Then it was Jim's turn, as the best man, to speak. My heart fluttered uncontrollably and missed a beat when he stood in his uniform. He said Rich was a loyal friend and an excellent pilot, and he was delighted Rich had joined the squadron. He had introduced him to cricket, but Rich couldn't warm to the red ball and had more success with rugby. Rich loved the oval ball and played the game when the opportunity arose. Finally, Rich and Poppy were the perfect couple, and he wished them a long and happy life. I wondered what Rich had said about Jim and Marta when he was Jim's Best Man, but it was probably better that I didn't know, although one day, I might take the plunge and ask Poppy.

After the speeches, the waiter brought a traditional wedding cake with a little bride and groom sitting on the top in the icing. Poppy deftly cut the cake, and everyone cheered and toasted again. A waiter whisked it away and cut it up into neat squares, and we all had a piece of the dark, fruity cake and another swig of champagne.

Towards the end of the reception, it looked as though I wouldn't have any contact with Jim, but I was wrong. I saw him when he came out of the Men's when I went to the Ladies', and my heart missed a beat.

'Julia,' he called.

I began to walk on but turned round and saw Jim looking at me.

'I hope you're happy in Australia and enjoying university,' he said, with an expression I couldn't read.

I didn't know what to say, as anything would have sounded forced and false.

'I am, Jim. And how is married life?'

'Great, and I'm flying again.'

'Good. You gave a good speech today.'

He paused and said, 'Thanks, Julia. It's good to see you. Take care of yourself, and all the best.'

It was the strangest conversation I had ever experienced with someone I was once close to, and then, so far apart.

I returned to the cloakroom and cried buckets, ruining my make-up.

My hands shook when I opened my powder compact to repair the damage. I waited a while before going back to join the crowd, but everyone was oblivious to me when I entered the room, except Austin.

CHAPTER 23

'There you are, Julia. You suddenly disappeared!' Austin said, offering me a glass of wine.

'Just went to freshen up. Rich and Poppy will be leaving soon for Fiji,' I said.

When the party finished, we all went our separate ways. Dora and I found each other and left the building. I didn't see Jim and Marta leave, which was a blessing, although I didn't exactly look out for them!

'You seemed to be getting on with Austin like a house on fire!' Dora said, giving me a cheeky grin. But then her expression changed.

'Just be careful, Julia,' she said, slowing down her words.

I chose to ignore her, the worldly woman I was.

CHAPTER 24

An unopened airmail letter from Helen lay on the table by the front door. I had been distracted by Jim's presence at the wedding and hadn't got round to opening it. During the night after the wedding, I suddenly awoke thinking about him standing beside his wife, touching her arm and talking to her in low tones. It was hard to digest, and only the thought of Austin made it a little easier. To stop thinking about Jim, I slit open Helen's letter with a knife from the kitchen, and her first sentence helped lift my spirits with surprise and joy.

Dearest Julia

Our main news is that we're expecting a baby in December, and you'll be an aunty. I was sick at first, but now I've settled into feeling well and hungry, and my little bump is growing. I am still working at the hospital and will do so, as long as I can, before the birth. We are delighted, and Mum is very excited and getting used to the idea of being a granny.

Apart from that, she is well, although apparently, a heavy easel fell on her at Dot's, giving

CHAPTER 24

her a bruised face, but fortunately the bruises are fading, and we can hardly see them now.

Ian is working all the hours God sends and has bought a new Jaguar in exchange for the other one, although Mum still has her Hillman Minx. Ian remembered Clare when she called in and was interested in her degree from Southampton University and her job. It was lovely to see her again, and it was thoughtful of her to visit. She told us about her plans to visit Sydney, and I hope it all works out for her. You must be looking forward to Clare coming now that Poppy is married and has left Sydney.

Steve is doing well in the company, and they promoted him to a more senior position. We are buying the house we rent as the owners want to sell. So, our lives are changing. And how are you, dear sister? I hope the course isn't too demanding and your brain is well in gear! I also hope you enjoyed the wedding and weren't upset seeing Jim again. We all miss you and think of you in that sunny country.

Much love, Helen

I had a nagging thought about Mum's bruised face and hoped it was just the easel and not something to do with Ian, although it wouldn't surprise me. He could be horrible to Mummy and nasty to me. I had to accept that the falling easel caused the bruises, not something more sinister. But what was Ian doing in a Sydney art gallery thousands of miles the other side of the world when Poppy and I went to the Magritte exhibition? It was a long way to come to look at architecture, but I gave him the benefit of the doubt that he was on legitimate business. I was sure it wasn't to see me unless he was checking up, but I wondered what would have happened if I had received the letter about his visit. I wouldn't have contacted him, but he may have wanted to meet me.

On Sunday after the wedding, I missed Poppy and thought of her and Rich married and enjoying a far-flung Pacific Island. I missed the sound of her sleeping in the other bed, her untidy pile of underwear and the gap in the wardrobe where her clothes had been. She had taken away a photo of Rich, making the bedside table look abandoned. One thing, there was room in the bathroom for my toiletries, but the little flat looked empty. I wandered into the living room and found it too tidy, the cushions put at odd angles and the bare counter staring back at me, with Poppy's ceramic coffee set of cups, saucers, jug and sugar bowl missing, leaving me to drink my coffee from a chipped mug. Now that Poppy had left, I had to find alternative accommodation so Clare could have her room, as the set-up at Dora's wasn't ideal. For a short while, it had worked with Poppy and me sharing a room, but Clare needed her own space and not a "sleepover" arrangement.

I didn't get dressed until lunchtime, spending time reading one of my textbooks on narcissism. I wandered outside and looked at the house, wondering if Dora was in. I wanted to tell her Helen's news, but I didn't have to wait long as she came over to the flat and suggested we take a picnic lunch to a nearby park by the harbour. The day was fine and warm for late April, the Australian autumn, and

CHAPTER 24

after she packed some lunch, we took the ten-minute walk along the path to Berry Island and spread ourselves on the grass by the water.

'As Poppy is now married, what are your thoughts about staying in my flat?' Dora asked after we'd taken a few bites of a sandwich.

'I was thinking about it earlier, Dora. Now that Clare has planned to come here to live and work, I should move to a larger property with two bedrooms. Would this leave you in the lurch with no tenants?' I asked, concerned.

I was glad she had broached the topic as it was uppermost in my mind.

'That's understandable, and don't worry about my being without tenants. Sasha knows of two second-year students looking for accommodation, and they may be a possibility.'

I had always thought that Sasha would be the type to come up with a solution, as she was good at networking and in with the latest news.

'There is a property in this area available to rent,' Dora continued. 'It's a Victorian, end-of-terrace house with two bedrooms and has been renovated. It's not far from here, and we could go and look at the outside and see what you think.'

I liked the description and hoped it had a lacework balcony and exposed sand stock brick.

Before seeing the house, Dora asked me if I had settled into Sydney life and how I was finding it.

'My adventurous side thinks it's all new and exciting. The course is going well, and I've met a few older students, making me feel less of an alien.'

When Dora asked me if I felt homesick, I told her about Helen's pregnancy, and news like that made me wish for home.

'So, to answer your question, Dora, I suppose I'm in two minds, but I wouldn't want to go back home permanently just yet, and anyway, I have to finish my degree course first.'

'Tell me about your sister, Julia.'

'She's two years older than me and a trained nurse.'

'When did she decide on a nursing career?'

'She has always wanted to be a nurse. She used to play doctors and nurses when we were kids, and I was always the sick patient.'

'Same with me,' Dora said, smiling.

What a long way Helen had come, from cancelling the wedding to getting married and being a mother. Chloe, Steve's sister, and I were never bridesmaids, and I wondered whether I would ever be one, or more importantly, a bride.

When I told Dora I was to be an aunty she was delighted for me. I was excited about Helen's prospective motherhood and my "auntyhood". I imagined taking my nephew for walks with the dog, the pantomime at Christmas, or special treats to eat at his favourite cafe, or taking my niece to the ballet, shopping for girlie things, or the pantomime. My thoughts of home helped to obliterate any misgivings about Jim, and I wished I was there to hug them all, bar Ian. I felt sad that I wouldn't be nearby for the birth or possibly babysitting, but being in Australia was my decision, so you can't have the best of both worlds. Helen would be an excellent mother, sympathetic but firm as well. It had made me question motherhood, but I wasn't ready, although I'd hoped, one day, motherhood would come my way.

CHAPTER 24

I was intrigued about how Dora had come to live in Sydney and was surprised by her reply. She paused for a long time, and I began to wish I hadn't asked her. After a broken engagement, Dora had decided to follow her brother, Martin, and live in Sydney. I waited to hear if she would elaborate on the engagement, and when she looked at me, I realised she wanted to continue.

'He was an orthopaedic surgeon at the hospital in London where I worked as a theatre nurse. We became very close and decided to get married. But before we had arranged a definite date for the wedding, he accepted a job in America and broke off the engagement.'

'That must have been heart-breaking, Dora, and a terrible shock for you.'

'It was. I had a nervous breakdown, was unwell for a year or more, and had to give up work. The hospital gave me sick leave, but it took a long time to recover, although I managed to return to nursing at a different hospital.'

I felt for her, making me feel guilty for not accepting Jim's proposal and possibly causing him heartache. But I never really knew how Jim felt after I said I wasn't ready for marriage. His brief letter and subsequent engagement to Marta told me nothing about his true feelings.

After our rather sad conversation, the day turned cloudy, making the usually blue water look grey. We gathered up our things and walked the short distance to the house that Dora had mentioned.

The house was on a tree-lined street at the end of a row of three similar houses with balconies at the front. We stood outside, and I hoped the people living there weren't in, as it would have looked suspicious with two people staring at the outside of your house. The frontage was small but tastefully renovated, painted white, covering the brick on the outside walls. There was a door to the balcony above and a Victorian-style window below, with the front door in natural wood, instead of an ugly screen door on so many properties. A colourful shrub was growing in the small front area, which set it off nicely.

'It looks lovely, Dora, from the outside, so I look forward to seeing the inside.'

'Inside is just as nice. I know the people who own it, and I helped them with colour schemes. Does Clare have a travel date?' Dora asked.

I didn't think Clare had got that far, as she had to give in her notice at the shipping company where she worked and the flat where she lived.

'No, she hasn't yet. I imagine it would be another six weeks before she is ready to travel.'

'You're welcome to stay at the flat until you have some firm dates.'

'Thank you, but what about Sasha and the students?'

'Don't worry about them,' Dora said. 'They will have to wait until it's vacant.'

I suddenly thought about Dresden and realised I hadn't seen him for a while.

'By the way, have you seen Dresden, Dora?' I asked.

'He's met someone.'

'Really? Who is she?'

'He, as in a relationship.'

I had wondered about Dresden in that respect, but then I'd dismissed it.

'Have you met him?'

CHAPTER 24

'No, but he's a nurse at a large teaching hospital and ideal to help Dresden with his diabetes.'

I was glad Dora told me, as it made his aloofness easier to understand and stopped me from saying the wrong thing.

I was set on the house we'd seen and hoped Dora would soon arrange for me to see the inside. When we arrived back at Dora's, she called the owners, and they arranged for me to visit the following afternoon after lectures. It was as delightful inside as outside, with a large living area leading into a breakfast room, kitchen and sunroom at the back, which I thought would be a good space when I was a counsellor. I had found an evening course and when completed, I could combine counselling with a degree in psychology.

Upstairs were two reasonably sized bedrooms, with a very small one at the back that could easily be a study. There was a bathroom upstairs, which was a bonus, as many houses like that had bathrooms on the ground floor. The courtyard at the back had flowerbeds and a lemon tree, and I liked the idea of picking lemons in the garden. The present tenants had arranged to move out in about six weeks, so a moving date was feasible, and Dora said the owners were happy for us to be tenants. My next job was to contact Clare to see how her plans were shaping up.

Dora had prepared a rich vegetable soup with home-baked bread, suitable for a cool Australian evening, and we settled down to enjoy the supper. She had turned on her electric fires, warming the house and making it cosy. Having arrived in Sydney in the summer, I was spoilt, but Dora said that the winters in Sydney never dropped much below fifteen degrees, unlike Melbourne winters, which could be much colder.

That evening, when I returned to the little flat, I felt the emptiness, and when I opened the bedroom door, I missed Poppy terribly. I was probably tired and needed some sleep, especially after a heavy day with back-to-back lectures and in-depth tutorials. Zoe and I had arranged to meet for lunch the next day, which was something to look forward to, and I hoped that Austin would ring me in the week.

CHAPTER 25

It was warm the Saturday Austin and I went to the beach, but being autumn, the summer heat had quietened down. He drove north up the coast to a sandy beach where he had booked lunch at a restaurant overlooking the golden stretch. We ordered seafood with a crisp, chilled wine, and Austin poured me a glass and wished me luck with my studies. He wore an open-necked shirt, and a silver coin caught the light.

'What is the medallion you're wearing, Austin?'

He fiddled with it, turning it round in his long fingers, looking down to see its face.

'It's a Maria Theresa dollar and still currency in parts of Africa and the Middle East.'

He took it off and passed it to me. I traced the raised outline of the woman on the coin, Maria Theresa of Austria, who ruled Austria, Hungary and Bohemia in the 18th Century, the only woman to reign in the Habsburg Empire. The coins are minted with the same date of 1780,' he explained.

When Austin said that he and Madeleine had found it in a market in Rabat when they travelled around Morocco, I felt a pang of jealousy. I imagined them walking together in the crowded casbah, looking at the well-stocked stalls spilling out jewellery, ornaments, textiles, and pottery surrounded by the clamour of the tradespeople pressurising you to buy their wares. It was a rich and crowded scene full of different aromas. They were being jostled by the crowd, wanting to buy a souvenir or in the market for the experience.

'When is your friend arriving?' he suddenly asked.

I told him she hadn't fixed a date, as she had a few things to sort out.

'I have a small, empty house that needs renovating before it's habitable. Perhaps you'd be interested in renting it when the work is complete.'

'Thanks for the offer, Austin, but I have already agreed to rent a house near Dora.'

'Well, if that doesn't work out, the offer is there.'

'Why is the house empty?' I asked, curious.

'My wife was a sculptress and used it as her studio, but after she died, I lost interest in doing it up.'

I didn't want to live somewhere that had belonged to his wife, who had died in such dreadful circumstances.

'Why not do it up anyway and rent it out?' I suggested.

'You've inspired me, Julia. Perhaps I'll put the wheels in motion.'

From the restaurant window, I saw tiny figures lying on the sand or paddling at the water's edge and one or two heads bobbing far out to sea. I wondered if the sea was cold to swim in, but as I hadn't brought my costume, it didn't matter. After lunch, we made our way onto the beach, and Austin fetched two folding chairs from the car, and we sat like film directors until I slid onto the sand and lay there, enjoying the sun on my face. I drifted into a half-sleep about

CHAPTER 25

Austin in the market with me, his arm around my shoulder, buying me a Moroccan necklace.

'Would you like to come and see where I live?' he suggested, the first time he'd invited me to his house.

I came down to earth, gathered my belongings while he folded the chairs, and walked to the car. We left the beach, drove to a suburb near the harbour, and stopped outside a sandstone house with a verandah at the front, single-storey with shutters, the rooms light and furnished with comfortable sofas and cushions, soft-coloured rugs and wall pictures, painted by Madeleine. On the sideboard, I saw a photo of a pale-faced woman smiling at the camera, and Austin said it was during one of her happier phases. We sat inside as the air had cooled, and he suggested a drink. I chose Campari and soda, and he had a whisky, and to accompany the drinks, he brought bowls of olives and savoury crackers from the kitchen. I sat next to him on the sofa and kicked off my shoes. He looked at me intently, pulled me towards him, and we kissed until I heard the telephone ringing in the hallway. We didn't stop, but it went on ringing until Austin went to answer it. He chatted for ages so, feeling restless, I found my shoes and wandered into a garden of neat flowerbeds and a recently cut lawn. A group of gum trees stood at the other end, their untidy branches hanging over an ornamental pond with two fish swimming slowly among the fronds. I was mesmerised watching the fish and jumped when Austin put his arm on my shoulder.

'Come back inside, it's chilly out here.'

'What are the fish called?'

'The two you see are Koi.'

'The colours are vibrant. Are the fish difficult to look after?' I asked.

'They are more difficult than some pond fish. You must watch them and give them the right food.'

Austin took my hand, his fingers curled around mine and led me back inside the house. We sat together and leaned against the rounded cushions.

'I hope you don't think I'm too old for you, Julia.'

'It's not the age, but the person,' I said, making him smile.

'I don't feel an age gap, and you have a maturity beyond your years.'

I was interested he said that because sometimes, I thought I was young for my age, compared to Helen.

'My father dying when we were young made us grow up quicker,' I suggested.

'It must've been hard for your mother.'

'Mum started working when we were teenagers, which was a big surprise. She always seemed vulnerable and adrift.'

I remembered how astonished Helen and I were when Mum announced she was looking for a job. I didn't think she would get it off the ground, but when she'd announced a company had offered her a job as a secretary, I was amazed.

'She must have an inner strength,' he said.

Although she was vulnerable, she could be stoic, although deeply sensitive.

'And then marrying the boss was difficult to take. Ian and I clashed from the word 'go', and moving to a different house was also an upheaval,' I said

'Was it in the same neighbourhood?'

'No, more in the country and much bigger than our little cottage.'

CHAPTER 25

'How did you clash?' he asked.

'He liked to have control and for us to toe the line, especially his wife and stepdaughters. I had my ideas, and he didn't like that.'

We discussed our parents, although the memory of my father was hazy. He listened with interest about Mother's marriage, Ian's control over her, and how she dealt with it by escaping into her art. His father was distant and strict, and his mother, unfulfilled. She'd won a scholarship to the London School of Music, but her father forbade her to go, as he didn't want her living in London.

'What a waste, but at least women have more freedom now to follow their path.'

'Are you close to your mother?' he asked, neatly taking out an olive stone.

'Mum was closer to Helen when we were young, but we have a connection now, and I know she misses me. She's a brilliant artist, despite Ian trying to thwart her.'

'How does she manage to do her art?'

'She paints in a friend's studio or down in our cellar.'

That made Austin laugh, and he made jokes about bacchanalian orgies with Ian's wine collection.

He kissed me again, and I felt as if I might be in his house forever, and I panicked. I wanted to leave, but instead, I accepted another drink. He got up, went over to the sideboard and poured a generous Campari and a drink for him. He brought the glasses to the sofa and handed me my drink, and I marvelled at its rich, red colour. We settled down again, but when he put his hand on my back, I thought he was about to unzip my dress and I shifted away from him. I started to feel dizzy and wondered if I could walk to the car. When we kissed again, I had the sensation of drowning and would never reach the surface, but suddenly, his tabby cat rushed into the room and jumped onto the sofa, breaking the spell. He was a big cat with a round face, and Austin picked him up, took him to the kitchen and shut the door.

'I have to go,' I said, tentatively.

'Stay a bit longer, Julia. I love your company.'

I had to be resolute, or he would have persuaded me to stay the night. He tried to lead me back to the sofa, but I told a lie and said I had to leave as I'd forgotten my keys and didn't want to disturb Dora when it was late. He sighed and looked annoyed, having to drive to Dora's instead of seducing and taking me to his bed. I refused to feel guilty, but in a way, it was a shame to leave his warm, comfortable house for my sad little flat, and under different circumstances, I could have stayed in his guest room. I presumed he had one.

'Are you ready to leave now, Julia, so you're not too late for Dora?'

'Where is the bathroom before I go?' I asked, knowing this would make him even more annoyed. But I was dying to go with all that liquid.

He pointed to a door along the passageway, and when I opened it, I smelt a strong aroma, probably of an aftershave. There was a separate shower and bath with a collection of soaps and shower gels to choose from and several towels on a rail. I noticed he had more than one toothbrush in a jar and several tubes of toothpaste. After I'd emptied my bladder, I opened the bathroom cabinet above the basin, where he kept a supply of pills and other medication. I saw

CHAPTER 25

several different types of painkillers, but there were bottles of pills I didn't recognise, and I made a mental note to look them up. I was being very naughty, snooping around his bathroom, but I also noticed a bottle of perfume that could only belong to a woman unless he was a cross-dresser. A life drawing in charcoal of a nude woman with large breasts and a cloth hiding her pubic area hung above the bath in a frame of dark wood, and it gave an extra dimension to the bathroom.

'Are you alright, Julia,' he called and knocked on the door.

'Sorry, for being so long. I was admiring the life drawing you have in there.'

'One of my wife's creations, although she mainly did sculptures.'

'Do you have any sculptures in the house?'

'Yes, and there are one or two in the garden, but I thought you were in a hurry, Julia.'

I followed him out to the car and waited for him to start the engine, but although he turned the ignition key several times, the engine was dead.

'Oh bugger,' he muttered, 'the car has been playing up lately, and now it won't start.'

I knew I was fated to stay there and hoped I was right about a guest room.

'I'll show you your room, Julia. The bed is ready to sleep in.'

When we went back inside, I called Dora, who took a while to answer.

'Are you alright, Julia?'

I told her Austin's car wouldn't start and she said, 'See you tomorrow, Julia, and take care,' as if she'd been asleep.

Austin showed me the room, gave me a towel and said with a smirk that I already knew the vicinity of the bathroom. I still felt dizzy, forgot to remove my makeup, drank a glass of water and firmly shut the door, wondering where his bedroom was. I slipped between the cold, ironed sheets and adjusted the pillow, all the while the room spinning each time I turned my head.

I awoke in the guest bed, hungover, with a headache, and wanted to get back to the flat as soon as possible to shower and go to bed to get a good sleep. I got dressed, and in the mirror, I had smudged my mascara onto my cheek, my face powder was blotchy, and my hair was a tousled mess. I ran a comb through the thatch and wondered how I would get home. I opened the bedroom door and stood in the passage, wondering if he was still asleep, but when I smelt coffee, I walked to the kitchen, and he was preparing breakfast with his back to me.

'Julia, good morning to you,' he said, turning round. 'I see that you're up and dressed. How does a cup of coffee and toast appeal?'

'Thanks, Austin, but I must go home now as I didn't sleep well. Is there any transport close by I could use?'

'I'll call a taxi for you.'

I sat in the hall on a chair with a tall back, feeling cold and tired and couldn't wait for the taxi to arrive. When it stopped outside, he said: 'Sweet dreams, Julia. I'll call you.'

After thirty minutes, I was back at the flat, showered, in bed and asleep.

CHAPTER 26

During the week, I received a letter from Clare with her arrival details at the end of June. Fortunately, I was moving to the house at the weekend, so I'd be prepared by the time she arrived. I said goodbye to Dora's little flat, which was a helpful start to my Sydney life, and although I treasured good memories of sharing with Poppy, I was pleased she was happy and married to Rich. Martin said he'd hire a truck for the furniture he had promised me, as I didn't have enough to warrant a removal company, and the house was part-furnished, anyway.

The morning after the move, I awoke confused. The bed was facing the wrong way, and the window was on the opposite wall. I heard a screeching outside, drew the curtains to the balcony and saw two currawongs having an altercation. They looked like our magpies but were a different species and eventually flew into the neighbouring trees to continue their argument. The balcony overlooked the empty street except for a black cat sitting on the wall opposite. I went downstairs into the kitchen and put the kettle on before opening the ugly screen door to the courtyard, but it was starting to rain, and large, grey clouds rolled past, bringing dampness into the house. I closed the door to keep in the heat from the stove, turned on the electric fires in the sitting room and prepared breakfast. The phone rang, and it was Dora checking the move had gone smoothly.

'What's it like waking up in a house with a balcony?' she said with a chuckle.

'I was disorientated when I awoke to noisy birds and almost fell down the stairs thinking I was back in the flat.

Dora laughed and said she missed me in the flat, and her house and garden felt deserted.

'When do the students move in?'

'Next weekend, all being well.'

When Dora had interviewed the students, they were quiet and respectful, and she hoped that was an accurate impression.

I concentrated on preparations for Clare's arrival and ensured there were hangers in the wardrobe and new bed linen and blankets for her bed. I'd bought a tall freestanding mirror, so I didn't have to struggle to hang it on the wall and Mum had given me three of her unframed landscape paintings. I took them to be framed by a friend of Dora's and chose one of them for Clare's room, a landscape of purples and reds with a white frame. I hung the other two in the sitting area and an arty print of London Bridge by the dining room table. Clare's room overlooked a path at the side of the house with a gate leading into the courtyard.

I hoped it would all work out for us, but I've known Clare since schooldays, and we've always got on well together. The time whizzed by before her arrival, and I packed in lots of reading. Zoe was intrigued by the house and said she had a set of dinner plates and bowls she didn't want and hoped they would come in handy. I suggested she visit the

CHAPTER 26

house after our Wednesday tutorial, and yes, the dinner set would be handy as I didn't have much crockery, only what the owners had left in the cupboards.

'I love the house, Julia, and the balcony sets it off beautifully,' Zoe said.

I unlocked the front door, hoping I'd left it tidy, and Zoe followed me in and remarked how wonderful it was to have a fireplace and thought Mother's paintings fitted in perfectly. We went to the kitchen, and she remarked on the little breakfast alcove and how it added character. I unlocked the door to the courtyard, and Zoe raved about the lemon tree, so I gave her a few lemons to take home. She wanted to see upstairs and thought the bedrooms were larger than she'd imagined.

'You must come round for dinner one evening and meet the family. Ours is a typical Australian bungalow style, although there are many Victorian-style terraces like this in Sydney.

I checked a map for directions to the airport and hoped I wouldn't get lost on the way. The journey was roughly 45 minutes, and her flight arrival time was early evening. Austin had offered to take me to the airport, but I preferred to go alone, as I hadn't seen Clare for two years, and she'd feel more comfortable with only me. The evening she landed was clear and sunny, a typical late winter's day in Sydney if she was awake to appreciate it.

It didn't take me long to pick out Clare from the crowd, pushing her trolley, tired and baggy-eyed from jetlag, looking everywhere but at me, jumping and waving to attract her attention. It was like old times to see her, and once we'd squashed her luggage into the car boot, she relaxed. She commented on how long and tiring the flight was and mentioned the awful spray they used before you were allowed to leave the aircraft. It reminded me of our journey and how it had taken a week to have a proper night's sleep. When we arrived at the house, we both hauled her luggage up the stairs as she'd packed most of her worldly goods. I showed her the bathroom and my room and then left her to unpack and settle in, but I knew everything would be put away neatly and in order, unlike me, whose drawers were a jumble. When she appeared downstairs in a long, thick cardigan, her arms folded, as if she was in the frozen North, I asked if she felt cold.

'Yes. We've had lovely hot weather at home, and it's the contrast.'

'The houses here are not well insulated because the winter is short and mild compared to ours. I'll light the fire, and you can sit near it. Are you hungry?'

'No, we had a tasteless meal on the plane, and now all I want is sleep.'

I ran her a hot bath, poured in bubbles, gave her towels and left the shepherd's pie I'd made for the following night. At least she'd brought a warm dressing gown and a hot water bottle to keep her cosy. I got myself a snack and started a psychology assignment to be completed in a week, while Clare went to bed.

On Monday morning, I left Clare to acclimatise herself while I was at lectures most of the day. She was still asleep, so I left a note explaining where everything was and a spare door key if she decided to go out. When I arrived home, a large display of pink and orange flowers stood in a vase on the mantelpiece. She'd bought a cake from the bakery,

CHAPTER 26

made a pot of tea, and put it on a little coffee table I had found in a local second-hand shop. She looked rested but wore the thick cardigan, switched on the electric fires, and lit the fire in the grate.

'I hope you weren't cold in the night, Clare?'

'No, warm as toast. I enjoyed the raucous bird song when I awoke. It's very different from our little twittering birds.'

'What a lovely welcome, Clare!' I said, pointing to the flowers and cake. 'Perfect after a day of brain work.'

'I also bought a paper, although it took the shopkeeper a few minutes to understand when I asked for The Sydney Morning Herald,' she said, shaking her head.

'Sometimes they pretend they don't understand an English accent. Yours will dilute in time.'

I couldn't imagine Clare with an Australian accent, but who knows? I didn't think Dora had one, but I detected one in Martin, but then he had an Australian wife to influence him.

'I hope I don't end up sounding Australian. You don't, although I've detected a slight twang.'

'I think it's using different terminology rather than the accent. I've noticed that with Dora.'

'Tomorrow I'd like to go to employment agencies. I found a few in the paper.'

'I'll drop you in the city when I go in tomorrow. You could catch a bus back, or we'll arrange to meet.'

However, Clare's experience at the employment agencies was unsatisfactory as there seemed to be nothing in finance at an executive level. I suggested she should "temp" as a secretary/typist to get her foot in the door of a company. She signed up with an agency to find a temporary job as a stopgap before looking for permanent work. After taking her details, she was sent to a construction company to temp as the secretary to the Finance Director. Her typing wasn't brilliant, but she got by being quick and intelligent, and she was offered the job for six weeks before the permanent secretary started.

'How was work today?' I asked her one evening when she came in after me.

'Tedious, and I hate the American spelling.'

'Isn't it an American company? I don't use the American spelling when I do assignments.'

She didn't sound very happy, and when I asked what the boss was like she said he was dull and fussy, and the rest of the staff asked too many questions.

One afternoon, when I came in from lectures, Clare was still out. She'd had a day off from work, and I assumed she was shopping, but when it got to six in the evening, I began to worry and wondered why she was late. I'd prepared a vegetable casserole of carrots, celery, parsnips, sweet potato, onion, and a selection of beans and put the dish in a low oven. It was getting dark, and the shops would have closed.

I went to the front of the house and looked up and down the road to see if she was coming, but there was no sign of her, although my looking wouldn't have made any difference. I was getting very concerned and didn't know what to do. I set a deadline of seven-thirty and if Clare hadn't come in by then, I'd have to think seriously of contacting hospitals or the police. She had only been in the country for a week, and anything could have happened, but I was sure if Clare needed help, she would

CHAPTER 26

have called me, and I could have picked her up. If she was lost, she could always ask for directions. I called Dora, who said she would drive over if Clare hadn't come in by the deadline, and we'd discuss what to do. I started feeling sick with worry as the evening darkness fell and imagined her injured somewhere or kidnapped by a dubious gang. I turned on the television to see if there were any local accidents or catastrophes, but the news was mainly international. I was on the verge of calling Dora again when I heard the key in the front door, and Clare, looking dishevelled, walked in. She was breathless and sat down before either of us said anything.

'I was so worried, Clare. Why are you so late?'

'Long story,' she said when she got her breath.

She had checked her bag at the bus stop and had found her purse was missing, but when she returned to the shop to see if she'd left it there, the shop was closed.

'Julia, I had no money for public transport, so I had to walk back, but as it was getting dark, I got lost and had to ask the way several times. People were very helpful, but I kept ending up in dark streets with no idea where I was.'

'How horrible for you.'

'I'll return to the shop tomorrow to see if anyone has handed it into Lost Property.'

'Let's have supper and a glass of wine to relax.'

We sat at the dining room table near the open fire, enjoying the vegetable stew and the warmth of Australian red wine.

'Have you heard from Colin in New York?' I asked, remembering he was living there.

'My brother is having a ball, as far as I can see.'

'What about Alex?'

'He loves it there too. My parents aren't happy with the two of us out of the country.'

'At least Helen is near home, and Mum, almost a granny, is happy,' I said, thinking of them all.

'Helen said Ian chatted to you about your job when you visited them.'

'Yes, I was surprised he even remembered who I was. He was friendly, but his voice had a different tone when he spoke to your mother.'

I thought, what a bastard! He could appear so pleasant and friendly, and people had no idea how nasty he could be, especially to Mum. He had a split personality, and his nastiness to me was very upsetting. And what was he doing in the art gallery? That was very odd and a coincidence I saw him at all, not having received Mum's letter. Was he really on business or up to something else?

The next day, Clare returned to the shop, but they hadn't found her purse, so she assumed someone had stolen it from her bag when it was open or took it when she put it on the counter. Clare didn't waste any time opening a bank account, and being paid every week made her feel more secure. At breakfast one morning, she put down her cup of coffee, looking worried.

'Julia, I'm not sure about living in Sydney. The job is boring, and I feel I don't fit in.'

'Give it more time, Clare. I felt like that at first. It's very different from home, and you won't have that temporary job forever.'

'I'll give it until Christmas,' she said, but she looked doubtful, and I desperately hoped she would stay.

CHAPTER 26

After a few weeks, Clare and I settled into a routine, and either I gave her a lift in the morning to work, or she caught the bus. One morning, her boss called her into his office and offered her a more senior position with a higher salary. She terminated her employment with the Agency, started her new job with the company, and looked happier than I had seen since she arrived. She also started going out with someone from the company. His name was Kevin, but everyone called him Kes, and I couldn't wait to meet him.

CHAPTER 27

On Saturday, Austin suggested we spend an afternoon on his yacht and sail around the harbour. I jumped at the invitation. I'd never been sailing before, but I was always ready for a new experience, although I felt nervous and hoped I could help with the ropes without doing anything stupid. I showered and changed, used an exotic-smelling soap, a good deodorant and my favourite perfume. Since living in Sydney, I'd bought several bikinis, and that day, I wore a green pair under a sundress and put a pair of knickers in my bag. I wore sneakers for climbing on and off the boat and navigating around the deck. The temperature was perfect, not too hot, but beautifully warm, with a slight breeze and a few clouds to break up the endless blue sky.

When I arrived at Austin's he came out rattling his car keys, and we drove to the marina where he'd moored his yacht. We walked to the bobbing boats and stopped at a 35ft yacht, painted white, with "Madeleine" in blue on the hull. It didn't take too much brain power to guess she was christened after his wife. I thought again of the tragic way in which she'd died, so going on the boat had a poignancy that was hard to shake off.

I stepped onto the salt-blanched deck, and he handed me a life jacket to wear all the time on the boat. He gave me

CHAPTER 27

a conducted tour and showed me where the toilet was, the galley, a tiny kitchenette, and a table where you could sit and eat. I noticed a burn mark on the table and wondered if he smoked. I'd never seen any evidence of it, so maybe it was from a friend. Austin had to prepare the boat for sailing before we left the marina. He explained to me, in simple terms, what he had to do, and I watched him open the hatch and take out the headsail and position it at the front of the mast, before it was unfurled when we sailed. He said we'd use the outboard motor to move away from the marina, into the harbour. He asked me to take the tiller, while he continued to prepare the boat. I was honoured he'd asked me to do that, and when he'd untied us from the marina, I felt I could do anything, as we zoomed away from the resting boats.

Austin checked the wind, and as we sailed, I felt a camaraderie with the flotilla of boats, big and small, as we sailed towards the harbour bridge and the half-completed opera house with its concrete blocks and unfinished "sails". It was an extraordinary building but would look a lot better when the construction was complete. There was just the right amount of wind for sailing, and I felt on top of the world as we skimmed over the water, passing other boats on the way. Austin was a good sailor, and I wondered if he'd been in the Navy.

'Are you relaxed about jumping off the boat when we reach the sheltered cove? 'He said.

'I'll give it a go. I have my bikini on, so I'll be ready.'

'Good, because we'll be cruising to the sheltered beach shortly.'

Once more, I took in the whole vista of the foreshore and the amazing harbour that stretched as far as the eye could see. The harbour was popular at the weekend, and he recognised a few owners of their boats and called out, waving at them.

'Mind the boom, Julia, and duck your head, or you'll get a thump,' he said before he turned the boat. We sailed towards a quiet cove and dropped the anchor, and out of the wind, the air was calm and all was quiet. Austin said he'd go first, which meant I would be left alone on the boat.

'Will I be safe on my own?' I asked with a tremor.

'You'll be quite safe, and I won't be in the water for long.'

He entered the cabin and changed into swimming trunks, exposing his tanned, well-toned body and legs. As I watched him jump off and swim away from the boat, his arms and legs moving confidently, into the distance, I thought about the men I'd been out with. I was younger when I knew Russell. He was charming, but full of secrets and I often wondered what had happened to him and whether I'd ever find out. Jim was different, more open and direct, but when I had moments of regret about him, I recalled his lack of persistence and the smooth transition to marrying Marta, diluting my regret. Did he want me, or simply a wife?

It was hard to describe my relationship with Austin. I found him interesting and sexy, but because he was thirty or more years older than me, I was in awe of the age difference as well as his charm. I pictured Ian with the three men and was sure he'd be intimidated by Austin, but doubted they would ever meet. He would have liked Jim but not Russell, although Mother would have liked both. It was a pity Jim's car had broken down and he never got to Thornfield, but did it matter?

CHAPTER 27

I was relieved when Austin reappeared and climbed back onto the deck, dripping wet, his dark hair flattened, making his brown eyes look more prominent.

'Now it's your turn, sexy,' he said.

I slipped off my dress, and he handed me the life jacket to wear again to make me feel more secure. I went to the jumping-off point, looked at the deep blue-green water, and hesitated, wondering if I had the courage, but I couldn't get that far and not jump in. I tried to forget the time I was held under the water at the swimming pool when I was a teenager.

I took a deep breath and jumped. At first, it was cold, but as I swam away from the boat, the water warmed up and caressed my arms and legs, and it felt like heaven, quiet and soothing. I wondered what lay underneath me in the water, and hoped the sharks weren't basking, waiting to bite off my toes. It was the first time I'd jumped off a boat to swim, and it was probably bravado, not wanting to appear cowardly in front of Austin. I was tempted to swim to the little beach, but it was a fair distance, and I might not have reached it.

I turned and swam back towards the boat and climbed the small ladder up to the deck. Austin took my hand, hauled me onto the rocking "Madeleine", wrapped a towel around me, and kissed my cheek and the back of my neck. We sat together on the gently rocking boat before he went to the cabin to get two glasses of champagne.

'You're a good swimmer, Julia. Madeleine didn't like deep water and would never have jumped off the boat.'

'I was more nervous than I looked,' I said, feeling sleepy.

I drank the bubbles, feeling them flow through my veins, and entered another level as if I had been swept along on an invisible wave to unknown territory.

'There's a Greek restaurant near the marina. Are you hungry?' he said, bringing me down to earth.

I was ravenous and tipsy from the champagne.

'Julia, you have wonderfully expressive eyes,' he said, looking at me with half-closed eyelids.

'I normally wear contact lenses but have taken them out to swim.'

'I wouldn't have noticed,' he replied, giving me the hooded look.

We sailed back to the marina, and despite feeling sleepy from the wine, I had to help with the ropes, although I was confused about what to do. I was sorry to leave the water and our sailing trip, but I hoped he would invite me again to join him on his yacht.

The restaurant was buzzing and full of Greeks when we entered, but we found a quiet table at the back. We ordered moussaka and a bottle of Retsina, and I tried to soak up the alcohol by lustily eating the Greek dish. It was comfort food with a delicious topping, and I thought, again, how more adventurous the cuisine was here than back home.

'Did Madeleine often come with you on the yacht, Austin?'

'Yes, she loved sailing but wasn't a good swimmer.'

'Did she smoke?' I asked, thinking of the burn on the table.

'Why do you ask?' he replied, looking puzzled.

'Oh, I just wondered.'

'Yes, she did, and too much. Her fingers were pale brown where she'd held too many cigarettes. I did as well, but I gave it up a few years ago. People were odd if they didn't smoke.'

CHAPTER 27

I remembered the first and last time I tried a cigarette and hated it.

'What about you, Julia?' he said, reading my mind.

'No, I've never smoked. I only tried it once.'

A boy offered me one at a party, and not wanting to appear strange, I took it, breathed in, and nearly choked to death.

When we arrived at his house, the cat was waiting on the doorstep and darted in for his food when Austin opened the front door.

'I'll have to feed him, or he'll be a nuisance,' he said, going to the kitchen and getting a tin of cat food. I followed and watched him open the tin with the tin opener, his nimble fingers putting the contents onto the cat's plate. As I watched the cat eating, Austin came up behind me, slid off my dress and led me to the bedroom. As he lowered me onto the bed, I was malleable and unresisting, with this practised and smooth lover, his long fingers in the right places. I fell into a hazy sleep, feeling the boat's rocking motion, and slept for about two hours.

When I awoke, I had a terrible thirst and longed for a glass of water. I looked at Austin's sleeping back, trembling from his loud snores, slipped out of bed, put on knickers and my bikini top, and crept to the kitchen. All the worktops were empty and clear unlike mine that displayed jars of rice and pasta, packets of cereal and miscellaneous kitchen items. I looked in several cupboards for a glass, but when I found the right one, a glass fell out and smashed onto the tiles, scattering pieces everywhere, and I hoped I hadn't woken him. Without wearing shoes, I had to be careful not to cut my feet and try to avoid the broken pieces, large and small, while I looked for a broom to sweep them into a pile. I opened a broom cupboard, but in doing so, I cut my foot, and the blood oozed onto the floor making red streaks on the tiles. It revived a memory of when Mum did the same thing before Ian came to lunch for the first time, to meet us. Was this a bad omen? I must not be superstitious, but sometimes you can't help it when you're unsure of the future. I tore off a piece of paper towel, wet it, cleaned the bleeding cut, pressed it hard and hoped it would stop. I swept up the broken bits, big and small, found a dustpan and brush, and poured the bits into the rubbish bin under the sink. I found another glass, filled it with tap water, and drank all of it.

The telephone in the hall started to ring, but it wasn't my business to answer it, and I thought he would hear it and get up. But he went on sleeping, and the phone eventually stopped.

I looked at my watch and suddenly remembered Clare and I had arranged to see a film that evening. By then, it was too late, but she'd be wondering where on earth I was. I dialled our number, but it was engaged. I kept trying, but there was always the engaged signal, so I assumed she was having a long chinwag with Kes. After I'd put down the receiver for the fourth time, Austin appeared in his dressing gown, yawning.

'What are you doing, Julia? Are you trying to call someone?'

'Yes, Clare, at home. We'd arranged to go out this evening.'

'Forget that and come back to bed,' he said, taking my hand.

CHAPTER 27

I had to get dressed and go home as soon as possible, or Clare would be frantic. I hoped he wouldn't be too persuasive, and I'd weaken.

'I need another glass of water,' I said. 'The wine and Greek food has made me thirsty.'

He led me into the bedroom again and sat me on the bed while he went to the kitchen to get my water. I hoped there weren't any stray pieces of glass on the floor that I'd missed, as I wasn't sure whether to tell him about the broken glass. While he was gone, I found the rest of my clothes and bag, went to the bathroom and locked the door. I filled the basin with warm water and washed, using my hands as best I could, and came out dressed and ready to leave.

'I wondered where you were, Julia. Here's the glass of water and what was the broom doing out of the cupboard?'

'I'm sorry, but one of your glasses fell out, and broke.'

'Never mind. I hope you didn't cut yourself.'

'I cut my foot, but it's stopped bleeding. Thank you, Austin, for taking me on your boat. I really enjoyed it.'

'Would you like to borrow a book on sailing?'

'Yes, and I could learn more about it,' I said.

He went to his study and returned with "A Beginner's Guide to Sailing" and handed it to me.

'Hopefully, next time, I'll know what to do.'

He didn't reply, and after he'd kissed me, hoping I'd weaken again, I drove home as fast as I could, but when I arrived, Clare was standing on the doorstep, frowning with fury.

'Where have you been, Julia? You could've called me!' she said, snarling.

'I did, Clare, several times, but the phone was engaged. Who were you talking to?'

'I didn't use the phone,' she snapped.

I investigated and found it had moved off its cradle, which accounted for the engaged signal. Clare stood in front of me.

'The place was a mess when I came in. I've tidied the kitchen and some of the sitting room, but what about all your study papers and university stuff scattered everywhere? I didn't know what to do with them,' she said.

'Leave it all. I'll sort it,' I said, wondering why Clare was so irritable.

I didn't think it was too bad. A pile of books was on the floor by a chair, my notes folder was on the coffee table, and another file was on the kitchen table, but all the papers were intact. I took all my notes to the bedroom, ran a bath and wallowed in warm, soapy water, thinking of Austin's kiss and how sexy he was.

CHAPTER 28

I had missed a period but wasn't too concerned as I was never regular. Once, I forgot to take two contraceptive pills when I was involved in a long assignment, and it messed up my cycle. Every day, I checked if I had a period, but nothing appeared. My breasts started to feel different, sort of lumpy and slightly enlarged and all the time, I felt distracted, not being able to concentrate with the nagging feeling I was pregnant. But as the time passed, no period appeared, and I began to be frantic with worry.

A wave of nausea came over me during a lecture, and I had to rush out, excusing myself along the row. On my way to the toilets, I was nearly sick in the corridor but reached the toilet bowl in time to "chunder", as the Australians say, but because I kept feeling queasy, I put my head in the sand, convinced I had a tummy upset. There were no lectures that afternoon, so I went straight home to bed, and when Clare came in, she said she'd go to the shops and get something to eat. I managed a light meal, but the following morning, I was sick again. Clare joked about my being pregnant, and I had a horrible feeling she was right. I was ill several times over the following weeks, although I managed to attend lectures and tutorials.

I thought of the yacht trip and how intoxicated I was with the drinks, the sun, and the thrill of the adventure. When the nausea started, I was almost sure I was pregnant but the only way to find out was to make a doctor's appointment. A few months previously, I had joined a GP surgery in the area, so I called and made an appointment to see the doctor. So that he wouldn't suspect, I wore a silver band embedded with a small green peridot stone on my wedding finger. Mum had given it to me when she was going through a birthstone phase, and according to her it was Leo's gemstone. I felt anxious and annoyed with myself for being careless, although it didn't mean I wanted to be childless in the future. I dressed in a demure skirt and blouse and waited for the doctor to call me into the surgery. He addressed me as Mrs Langley and took a urine sample, but I had to wait two weeks for the result, and it was the longest two weeks I had ever experienced.

Every morning, I could feel a change in my breasts, and not long after, I began to feel different everywhere. When I returned for my second appointment, the doctor said the test was positive, but when he told me, I wasn't surprised.

'Is this your first baby, Mrs Langley? You have exciting news to tell your husband this evening,' he said.

He looked at me quizzically when I didn't respond.

'I'll refer you to Mr Samuel Saunders, a gynaecologist, and you'll have the baby in the hospital where he practises.'

I could barely concentrate on my work, thinking about being pregnant. By my calculation, I would be due in December, at the start of the long summer holiday, with the opportunity to bond with the child. I thought carefully about the practical issues and whether there was room in

CHAPTER 28

the house for a baby. The small bedroom would take a cot and a small wardrobe, and we had outside space for a pram. However, I was under no illusion that studying and caring for a baby as a single mother would be easy. Clare said she would help, but I couldn't expect her to disrupt her routine with feeding, changing and general infant care. She could take it for a walk in the pram and help like that, but it was my responsibility.

But where did Austin feature in all this? My main task was to tell him, but I had no idea how he would react. If, for example, he suggested marriage, would I accept? The answer was yes, for the sake of the child. We were compatible, and I found him attractive, but were those ingredients enough to marry someone?

I made an appointment to see the specialist for a consultation. His rooms were in a suburb north of where we lived, and my appointment was for an afternoon when I was free. The building was on a main road, and when I entered the foyer, I took the lift to the third floor and walked along the corridor, looking at each door for his name. I found his brass plate, gently knocked and waited. When no one came I knocked again until his secretary, a woman in her 40s, opened the door.

'I am sorry, Mrs Langley, but Mr Saunders is running late, but he shouldn't be long.'

I sat in the reception area and looked around at the other patients. There was a woman about my age, who looked as if she'd give birth in the waiting room, and another older woman with, I presume, her husband. I picked up a leaflet from the table about family planning and different types of contraception. It mentioned the coil, which sounded like mediaeval torture, and according to Zoe, it was. She said it was very uncomfortable, kept slipping out and gave her an infection, and finally, she had abandoned it and gone on the pill. I hadn't told her about my pregnancy and missed the opportunity when she asked if I'd recovered from my sickness.

After I'd read about every form of contraception under the sun, Mr Saunders called me into his room. I decided to be honest with him as he came across as a sensitive, caring man, so when he called me Mrs Langley, I corrected him and said, 'It's Miss.'

'Ah, I see. I presume you know who the father is.'

'Yes, but I haven't told him yet, although I intend to soon.'

'Is he married?'

'He is a widower. His wife died in a bad car accident.'

'Has he talked about marriage to you, Miss Langley?'

In retrospect, he talked a lot about Madeleine, his dead wife, and was probably deeply affected by her death and was still in love with her.

'Would you consider adoption?' Mr Saunders said suddenly.

I was shocked and insulted that I would even consider handing my baby over for adoption.

'No, I want to keep it.'

'Are you able to support it?'

I didn't know whether he thought I had no money, or his questions were linked to adoption.

I wished I hadn't been so honest and worn the Peridot ring.

'I'm sure the father would support the baby financially, even if he didn't want to marry me,' I said, raising my voice.

CHAPTER 28

'Think about adoption. A stable, married couple, who can't have children, would give it a good upbringing and a loving home.'

Did he think I wouldn't give it a loving home, be a bad example, and not fit to bring up a child?

'I know I will always want to keep it,' I said firmly.

'I'll examine you now, Miss Langley.'

I lay on the bed, and he pressed around my abdomen and said all was progressing well.

'I'll see you in a month. Make an appointment with my secretary and take care.'

I took the lift down to the entrance and couldn't believe I'd reached this stage, about to give birth to another human being under demanding circumstances. I was wrong about Mr Saunders and his sensitivity, and surprised and upset – he mentioned adoption several times. I would never give up a part of myself to someone else. I was tearful and depressed after the result and didn't feel any better after my appointment with the gynaecologist.

'I'll be here to help you, Julia.'

'Are you happy to stay in Sydney, Clare? I thought you were thinking of going back home.'

'Don't worry, I'm not going anywhere,' she said.

My two imminent tasks were to tell Austin and write home. It was ironic that Helen was happily married and had given birth to a beautiful boy, Laurence, and I was single and about to give birth out of wedlock. Was I the black sheep? I didn't know whether to write a letter to Mum or call her. Writing would be better, to avoid breaking down or crying over the phone.

SHE TAKES HER CHANCES

Sydney
March 1970

Dearest Mum

I am about to share some information and hope you will understand and sympathise. I am three months pregnant, which was a huge shock. The father is a man I have been seeing in Sydney, but it was unplanned. I am due in December, during my summer break. I intend to complete the degree course with a qualification in Psychology and French, so I am not giving up. Clare is a fantastic support and will stay here in Sydney with me. There is a crèche on the campus where I can leave the baby during lectures and tutorials. The doctor referred me to a gynaecologist who operates at a large hospital in Sydney, where I will go when I am due.

Dear Mummy, I miss you so much, but maybe you'll visit me (and your second grandchild) sometime, or I will travel to see you all in England.

Much love
Julia.

CHAPTER 28

Thornfield
Little Keeping

Dearest Julia

I was shocked to receive your letter, but now I am excited to have another grandchild. I also know that with your strength and resilience, you will succeed with your studies and manage the child. Ian was unsympathetic and rude when I told him, which resulted in an argument. He has no feelings whatsoever.

We all send lots of love to you and Clare.

As ever, Mum.

After Mum's letter, I received one from Ian.

I am very disappointed in you, Julia. First, it was the refusal to apply to Oxford or Cambridge and instead go to London and then to Australia. Now, it's the news of your pregnancy. How are you going to support it and study at the same time? How could you be so foolish to allow this to happen?

You should come home, have the baby, and accept Mother's help. You could resume your studies later. It would be a better solution than struggling on the other side of the world at a third-rate university.

Yours
Ian

The letter left me shocked and reeling. There was no sympathy but the proposition to return and be under Ian's control. I wondered if Mother knew of his letter, although she wrote about his lack of compassion. It made me more determined to stay and prove I could manage.

After the nausea had gone, I was always hungry and bought healthy food, grabbing a bag of peaches and nectarines or popping into a health food shop to buy packets of dried fruit and nuts that I took everywhere, even to lectures. I yearned for dates and cream cheese, together or separately, and couldn't get enough of them. I also loved Lamingtons, little cake squares covered in chocolate and rolled in coconut. But the smell of onions made me feel sick, and bananas gave me the shudders; how my taste buds had changed!

I always looked for Zoe in the lecture hall if we hadn't agreed to meet beforehand. One day, when I sat down, she said, "Do you mind if I ask you something?"

'Depends on what it is.'

'Are you pregnant? Your eyes glow, and your breasts look bigger.'

I was stunned she had noticed, as I thought I had covered it up successfully.

'You're very perceptive, Zoe. I was going to tell you, but it's been difficult to come to terms with.'

We had to stop talking as the lecture had started, and Zoe put her hand on my arm and mouthed, "I'm sorry." Despite my baggy trousers, I had fooled myself, although Clare said she couldn't tell, and I was sure most students didn't look twice at an "oldie" like me. They were too involved in their own lives.

CHAPTER 28

The following evening, Rich called me with their exciting news. Poppy had given birth to a girl, Verity Anne, and was doing well after a 48-hour labour. I arranged to send flowers to the hospital to congratulate them both, and on my card, I said I was sorry I couldn't visit. I still hadn't plucked up the courage to tell her, but when she called to ask me to be a godmother to Verity, I hesitated:

'I would be honoured, Poppy, and having been baptised and confirmed, the Church would accept me.'

'Is everything all right, Julia?'

'No, Poppy, it isn't. I have something to tell you.'

I started crying and couldn't finish the saga, but she got the gist. Finally, I had to end the call as my tears took over, and I couldn't speak. When I had calmed down, I was delighted to be Verity's godmother. Poppy was a good friend, and I would enjoy having contact with her daughter and watching her grow up. I took a long time to decide on a christening present and chose a silver box with her initials engraved on the lid, ideal for jewellery or other keepsakes. Verity was still a tiny baby, and they hadn't fixed a date for the christening. I would have to find a babysitter if the christening was after the birth, or maybe Clare would look after it. I imagined Poppy was dying to hear the circumstances of my pregnancy, but I had left the details up in the air and Poppy would have to wait.

CHAPTER 29

When Austin suggested a bush walk to get fresh air and exercise, I thought it would be an ideal opportunity to tell him about the pregnancy. We'd be on our own, on neutral ground and in quiet surroundings. The afternoon was unseasonably warm for late July, and I borrowed Clare's sunhat, although the walk was mainly in the shade. He had packed sweet and savoury biscuits for sustenance, bottled water, and fly spray in his backpack, and as he led along a rocky path bordered on both sides by gum trees, tall grasses and native plants, I took care not to stumble on the uneven ground. Sometimes he said, 'Left here' or 'Bear to the right' until I was mesmerised by the rhythm of our walking and the hiss and crackle of cicadas. We reached an inlet of green water and sat to rest and cool down on the nearby rocks.

'Did you go for walks in England, Julia?'

'Yes, I love walking, and we often took our dog on country walks through woods and open countryside.'

'One day Madeleine came home with a Spaniel puppy. I'm not too keen on dogs but didn't have the heart to send it back. We enjoyed our walks with the dog, but after Madeleine's miscarriage, we didn't walk so much.'

CHAPTER 29

When I heard the word miscarriage, I knew my opportunity to mention the pregnancy had passed, but I had to show sympathy towards Madeleine's tragedy.

'I'm sorry to hear you went through that, Austin.'

'It was very stressful for both of us. Madeleine was three months pregnant, and I had to leave work and rush home to be with her.'

I sat looking at the still water and didn't know what to say. Flies and other insects hovered around us where we sat, but when he puffed the fly spray, the flies kept coming, however much we flicked them away. He handed me water to drink and opened a tin of assorted biscuits. I finished most of the water from the bottle, but Austin was more careful and left some for later. We sat in the stillness, the only movement from a frog that leapt from one stone to another before it jumped into the reeds at the water's edge and disappeared. Austin got up and stretched.

'We'll make tracks back to the beginning and take the path we've been on,' he said, sounding confident. But after we'd walked for twenty minutes, the path narrowed with overgrown branches, and we had to push through bushes and spiky plants, and I was relieved I'd worn trousers. Austin stopped and turned.

'This isn't right, Julia.'

'No, I don't recognise it.'

We retraced our steps but couldn't see the stretch of water where we'd stopped to rest.

'Let me get my bearings. Where is the sun?' he said, but through the foliage, the sky had changed from blue to a yellowy grey.

'We'll try the path over there,' he said, pointing.

'Have you done this walk before, Austin?'

'Yes, but not for a while.'

We heard voices and saw two women with walking boots and poles as if they were about to climb Mount Everest. We stopped them to ask the way back to the car park, and they pointed to another stony path on the left from where we were standing.

'There's going to be a storm,' one of the women said.

My T-shirt stuck to my back in the humid air. I suggested we put markers down, which we should have done earlier, and he picked a yellow plant, and we placed the flowers at the base of tree trunks. When we came to a clearing where the trees had thinned out, I knew we were going the wrong way again. I sat on the ground, feeling dizzy, and finished my water.

'Come on, we need to find our way back to the car, or we'll be here forever,' he said, frowning.

We passed our yellow markers and looked at the oppressive sky between the trees. I followed Austin like an automaton, my headache throbbing over my right temple, and when I checked my watch, it was 6.30. We'd been walking for three hours, but when he quickened his pace, I ran to catch up and stumbled over my undone shoelaces. I sat on a rock to tie them up, and when I bent down, my stomach hurt, and I hoped I wouldn't be sick. I couldn't see Austin anywhere and shouted his name, but all I heard were buzzing insects and the screech of cicadas, loud in my ears. I walked quickly over the rocky path, tripped and put my hand out against a tree trunk. My ankle buckled, my hand started bleeding, and I fell onto the ground as he reappeared around the corner.

CHAPTER 29

'Julia, what's happened?'

'I think I've sprained or broken my ankle,' I screamed.

'Sit there, raise your leg and rest it on that rock. I brought paper towels, and I'll soak them in water from the inlet instead of ice cubes.'

'Are we nearing the water again? We must have gone round in a circle.'

I rested my back on a tree trunk and waited for him, and after what seemed like an eternity, he returned with the wet paper towel and wrapped it around my ankle, the sock keeping it in place. My hand had stopped bleeding, leaving a jagged-shaped cut, and although I wanted to stay there and rest, he hauled me onto my feet and said he knew the way. I tried not to put pressure on my ankle as I hobbled along, avoiding the jagged stones, but everything ached, my back, my head and my ankle, and I longed for a cool drink and a soft bed. It was hard going, but Austin was strong, and after an hour, we reached the car. I lay on the back seat with my foot raised, and we drove home so I could rest my ankle.

'I won't stay, Julia, but if it's not better in two or three days, my advice is, you should make a doctor's appointment.' But the following day, the ankle had improved, and the swelling had gone down.

After our walk, I felt dissatisfied and had to find an opportunity to tell him. The best place would be at his house, on his territory, if I could use an excuse to see him. I called him and arranged to return the book on sailing one evening after I'd been at lectures all day. When I arrived, the house was completely dark, with no lights on inside, and I thought he was out, although he'd parked his car outside the garage. He came to the door, told me a fuse had blown and asked me to wait while he fixed it. As soon as there was light, he offered me a drink.

'What would you like, Julia? Your favourite?'

'I'll have a small Campari and lots of soda. I'm driving.'

I knew I shouldn't have anything, but I needed Dutch courage. He handed me the drink diluted with soda, but enough to have the desired effect.

'How did you get on with the sailing book?' he said as I handed it to him.

'The instructions are complicated. I need to be on the boat, learning,' I said, hoping he'd invite me again.

'I agree. That is the only way.'

'How are the courses going? I hope you're finding them worthwhile.'

'Psychology is interesting and multi-layered. I love the French course.'

I was so nervous about telling him, but if the opportunity presented itself, I should grab it. I only needed a little more to drink to give me confidence.

'I expect you're fluent in French,' he said, sipping his whisky.

'It's easier when everyone is speaking French. Jim and I went to Southwest France, and the language came easily.'

He always talked about Madeleine, so I didn't feel guilty about mentioning Jim.

'When we visited Morocco, we spoke rather bad French, but we did try.'

'Did you find the antiquarian French poetry books you were looking for when you came to the bookshop?' I asked, remembering one of the first occasions I met him.

CHAPTER 29

'Someone gave me a contact in Melbourne, so I bought them from a bookshop there.'

'Do you have the books here?' I asked, interested to see them.

'No, they were for a friend.'

Austin got the Campari bottle and topped up my drink, which gave me a boost.

'I have something important to tell you.'

'Fire away.'

I hesitated and took a deep breath.

'I'm pregnant.'

He stared at me in silence, his eyes blank. I felt like running away until he spoke.

'Is it mine?'

'Yes, Austin.'

'I thought you were taking the pill.'

'I'm sorry, but I was so intent on finishing a paper that I forgot to take the pills for two days.'

'That's careless of you, or was it on purpose?'

'Of course it wasn't. Why would I do that?'

'Is it definite?'

'Yes, the doctor did a test and confirmed it.'

He was silent again and fiddled with his wristwatch.

'You don't seem very happy about it,' I said, my voice breaking.

'I'm sorry, Julia, it's a shock. I'll be travelling a lot more in future, but I'll give you money for the baby.'

There seemed to be no emotion, only a practical attitude.

'Did the doctor ask about the father?' he continued

'The GP thought I was married, as I wore a ring.'

'That will remain a thought only in the doctor's head,' he said, snarling.

My heart was sinking, and I felt angry with his negative attitude.

'How many months are you?'

'Five; it's due in December.'

He was silent again and had another gulp of whisky. I realised this wasn't going well, but I was rooted to the spot.

'When I had the appointment with the gynaecologist, I told him I wasn't married.'

'Why were you more honest with him?'

'I thought he'd be more sympathetic, but I was wrong. He talked about adoption, which upset me.'

'That's not such a bad idea. There must be many couples who'd be delighted to adopt a child and give it a good home.'

'How can you say that, Austin? I would never give up my child for adoption.'

I couldn't believe he was talking about adoption as well, especially about his child.

'How are you going to study and look after a baby? It's not going to work.'

'You sound like my stepfather now. The university crèche would have the baby while I was at lectures, and when I had a free day, it would be with me. Clare said she'd help.'

'You can't expect Clare to disrupt her life, and I have a company to run: Think about adoption.'

'That's not on the agenda. How can you be so thoughtless about your child?'

'If it is mine.'

'Of course it is. What sort of person do you think I am? I don't sleep around with different men.'

CHAPTER 29

We had raised our voices, and I hoped the neighbours couldn't hear, although his house was a fair distance from the houses next door, and all the windows were closed.

'How do I know you don't sleep around? You're flirtatious; the way you walk and the clothes you wear. You attract men, and men are weak.'

'Well, I'm not weak and easy prey.'

I was stunned and appalled at what he'd said. I glared at him and felt the pain again in my abdomen.

'How dare you say that about me, making out I am a promiscuous, immoral woman.'

'That's not so far from the truth. You come to my house, and then to my bed. You're here now, aching for it.'

I was horrified. What an arrogant man he was.

'I thought we cared for each other. Don't you have any feelings for me at all?'

I didn't wait for his reply, grabbed my things and slammed the front door. When I came out of the house, I was so angry I wanted to smash something of his. What better than his precious Ford Falcon parked outside in the driveway? Although it was dark, I found a stone on the path, threw it with all my strength at his car side window and shattered it. I had to drive off as fast as I could, or he'd come out and see what I'd done. My hand shook when I looked for my car key, but it was easy to find in the bottom of my bag. I turned the engine on, drove out of his drive, and as I turned left onto the road, I noticed him in my side mirror coming out of the house. He must have heard the window breaking, but I drove swiftly down the road and out of sight. My heart was beating too fast for comfort, and I felt the pain again.

I was furious, hated this egotistical man, and couldn't believe he had sucked me into his seduction. He seemed so understanding and kind, but how wrong I was. It was all a front to trap women, and basically, he was a bastard. I wondered if he was ever unfaithful to Madeleine or if her death had affected him so much he had turned into a nasty predator.

Perhaps he had lied about Madeleine's accident, and she was alive somewhere, and he was a fraudster. I vowed to have nothing to do with him from then on and would never allow him to see the baby. Not long after our dreadful conversation, I received a brief letter from him.

Hunter House
August 1970

Julia,

Please accept my apologies for the unforgivable and hurtful words. I have no excuse, but I'm sorry you found it necessary to break my car window. Please let me know when the child is born, and I will help with finances.

Austin

I read it twice, tore it into tiny pieces, and threw them in the bin.

CHAPTER 30

I had another cramp in a Psychology lecture that grew into a sharp pain, and I whispered to Zoe that I had a pain so harsh I had to go home. She offered to leave with me, but I told her I would be alright once I was resting in bed. I left the hall and almost ran to the car to get home quickly and lie down. The pain subsided once I had curled up like a foetus, and I fell asleep, but a bad dream about Austin didn't help and woke me up. He was throwing clods of mud at me, smashing into my face and shouting obscenities. The mud was wet, running into my eyes, down my face, and into my mouth. I couldn't see and tried to push the mud out of my eyes.

I awoke to Clare standing at the bedside, looking at me, concerned.

'You were groaning, Julia. Are you alright?'

'I was having a bad dream.'

I lay in a warm bath, rested my hand on my little mound and prayed all would be well. But it didn't turn out well. I slept until two in the morning when I awoke consumed by sharp pains making me cry out, and I knew I had to call an ambulance and have medical attention. I staggered into Clare's room but didn't have the heart to disturb her sleeping form, so I dialled the emergency services.

'Which emergency?' a woman said sharply. 'The wait will be 15 to 20 minutes. We're having a busy night,' she said.

The pain came on so severe that I sat on the stairs, feeling faint. I thought I might be bleeding, but when I looked, it was a colourless discharge.

'What are you doing, Julia?' Clare said, standing behind me in her nightgown.

'I've called an ambulance. The pains are so bad I must go to the hospital.'

'I'll cancel the ambulance and take you myself. An ambulance could take ages. I'll drive your car.'

I struggled to put on some clothes, and Clare helped me into the passenger seat while she took the driver's seat. She'd driven my car before when I was in bed with a bad cold, and we needed to do food shopping.

'Do you know the way to the hospital?' I gasped.

'I think so,' Clare said.

It was raining, and she had to ask me where the windscreen wipers were, but once she'd found them, she drove fast through the empty streets, bathed in reflected light on the wet roads from the streetlights. She had to keep stopping at red traffic lights in case the police caught us, and I sat doubled up in a haze of pain until we reached the outside of the large hospital. Clare helped me to the main entrance, ready to get assistance, but it was empty, with no one in sight.

'I'll find someone. Just sit there,' Clare said, and she helped me onto a small chair and disappeared down a corridor.

I stared at the floor to try and forget the pain and saw a brass button that must have come off someone's uniform, but I was too weak to pick it up. I watched it grow bigger,

CHAPTER 30

then smaller, the brass shining from an overhead light. I was relieved when Clare appeared with a nurse and a porter pushing a wheelchair to take me to the maternity wing. They wheeled me into a spacious lift, stopped at the first floor, and pushed me out and down a corridor to the ward to find a bed for me.

'How often are the pains coming?' the nurse asked when I was lying down.

'Every few seconds, and they are so painful,' I said, screwed up and wailing with the next one. The nurse said she'd give me an injection of pethidine to numb me, and after a few minutes, the pains subsided a little, although I could still feel them as if they weren't part of me.

'Which gynaecologist is treating you?' the nurse asked briskly.

'Mr Saunders.'

'He isn't in tonight, so someone else will attend to you.'

The pains came in bursts, seconds between them, and they wheeled me into the delivery room, where another gynaecologist, a woman, saw me and said I was going to give birth prematurely at 24 weeks.

'I am going to do an episiotomy to make the birth easier,' the doctor said.

Woozy from the pethidine, I didn't feel the cut, but a nurse held my hand and told me to push, and each time the pain came, I pushed again until I gave birth into the darkness, but all was deathly quiet, no baby cry, no one spoke, and I saw nothing.

'Where is my baby?' I shouted.

The midwife had taken a bundle away, and I shouted again, 'Where is my baby?'

'Mrs Langley, I am so sorry, but your baby, a little boy, was too small and couldn't live,' the midwife said close to my ear.

'Can I see him?'

The midwife returned with a tiny, still body, and I held him, perfect and small, his features closed and neat, who was not much bigger than the palm of my hand. I prayed for his soul and called him Troy.

It felt as though he moved, and I spoke to him quietly. I told him I loved him, would never forget him, and every year would think of him on this day, September 26th, his birthday. The midwife left me to hold him, but when she returned, I would have to give him up. She said I could arrange a proper burial for him in the next few days but would have to register his birth.

'You must stay in overnight so we can keep an eye on you. Mr Saunders will want to see you tomorrow.'

'Please tell my friend, Clare, who is waiting outside.'

The nurse went to find Clare and returned after a few minutes.

'Your friend said she'd call tomorrow to see how you are. Will your husband be visiting?' the nurse asked.

'No, he's away.'

'Get some rest now, Mrs Langley.'

I was given a sedative and lay on my back gazing into the semi-darkness, thinking about my dead son, whom I would never know. I was empty, and my sadness ran deep. I felt as if my heart had been ripped out, and there was nothing there except grief for my child. But I knew it was probably for the best. He wouldn't have had a loving father, and I would have struggled to care for

CHAPTER 30

him, but that didn't take away the deep longing I had for my little boy.

In the morning, a porter pushed my bed to a maternity ward, but watching the mothers in the other beds, breast or bottle feeding their babies, made my heart hurt, and I started crying under the bedclothes.

'What is the matter? Is your baby in the special baby unit?' asked the woman in the next bed. She was about my age, with short dark hair, almost like a boy, and was breastfeeding her tiny little girl.

'No, he died.'

'Oh, I'm so sorry, but they have put you on the wrong ward. Ask the ward sister to have you moved.'

When the ward sister walked by my bed, I called out 'Excuse me,' and she stopped by my bed.

'Could I please be moved to another ward, as my baby has died.'

'Yes, that is what we intend to do when a bed becomes available, which will be this morning. I'm sorry you had to be on this ward,' she said walking away rapidly to deal with another patient.

I was relieved when they moved me to the gynaecology ward. Observing the bonding of mothers with their babies was too much to bear, and as they wheeled me out, I could hear feeding and the comfort of food and warmth. I thought of Mummy and her miscarriage, uniting and bringing us together. I pictured Helen with her little boy, Laurence, who was healthy and strong and would enjoy his life with his loving parents. And my godchild, Verity Anne, whom I would get to know as she grew up. And lastly, Jim's little Elena, half English/Argentinian child, all gorgeous children, but no more beautiful than my little Troy. I knew that one day I would have a healthy child, another boy, who would be strong like Laurence. I had to write home and tell them the sad news, but there would be no letter to Austin. How could I have written when, as a father, he'd had no interest whatsoever in his unborn child? Why should he have known about the experience I had gone through and the way I had felt? He wouldn't have sympathised with my ordeal but instead, dwelt on his own baby loss with Madeleine.

They kept me in the hospital for three days and ran some tests but didn't have a definitive reason for the preterm death. When I told them about my degree course, they said stress can sometimes cause premature birth and death, but sometimes it's genetic or a medical health problem. I thought my stress with Austin was the more likely cause, rather than studying at a university.

As I lay there, I thought of Mummy's miscarriage when Helen had found her. One day, she had come in from a shift on a cancer ward and had called out for Mummy, but there was no response. Helen thought Mum could be out, but her car was outside the house, and Rex, their dog after Barny died, was in, following Helen from room to room, whining. Helen went upstairs, but when she pushed the bathroom door, it wouldn't open, until she realised Mum was lying against it.

'It's Helen. Can you hear me?' she said in a shrill voice.

Mummy didn't answer but stirred and tried to sit up. Helen stepped over her, felt her pulse, took off her blood-soaked dress, found a clean nightie in a drawer and helped her into bed. She called Dr Wainwright, who was about to leave the surgery, and said he would visit on his way home.

CHAPTER 30

He came in, carrying his doctor's bag, and examined her at the bedside.

'She's had a miscarriage,' he said after an examination. 'I'll make an appointment for her to see a gynaecologist at the hospital. Now she must rest.'

I didn't think she could get pregnant at age 44 but Helen said it was possible.

'Did you know she was?' I asked, thinking Mum might have confided in Helen.

'No, although she was quieter than usual.'

'Is a miscarriage painful?'

'Yes, it can be painful with a lot of blood loss.'

I started feeling faint and queasy and didn't want to hear any more medical details, although she told me Mum was eight weeks pregnant.

'Just think, Helen, we may have had a half-brother or sister. That would have changed the dynamics.'

I'd supposed Ian had never had any children unless he'd got some stashed away somewhere.

Helen had called Ian, who was away on business. When the receptionist dialled his hotel room, he didn't answer, so she left a message.

Later, he called back to say he would return on Sunday.

I caught a mid-morning train on the Saturday and a taxi from the station, and when I arrived at Thornfield, the house seemed quieter than usual, and even Rex looked at me with sad eyes. Helen was in the kitchen, and I stopped to talk to her.

'How is she today, Helen?'

'She is still weak but improving. She is eager to see you but might be asleep.'

I stepped into the room, which smelled musty and suffocating, with the curtains half drawn.

Mummy looked chalky but was sitting up in bed, a half-finished sandwich and a cold cup of tea on a tray, balanced on her knees. I took the tray and put it on the chest of drawers, sat on the bed while she held my hand and thanked me for coming.

'How are you feeling now, Mummy?'

'Weak, but better than yesterday.'

She had adjusted her position in the bed and pulled a light dressing gown around her shoulders. There were dark shadows under her eyes, and she had looked very pale.

'How is the art going?'

'I'm still managing to do that without Ian knowing, but this has set me back a little.'

'You'll recover, Mummy.'

Her eyelids had begun to close, and I rearranged the bedclothes.

While I was in the hospital, I had two visitors, Zoe and Clare. Zoe brought in a few pages of notes on grief and loss, which ironically was the current topic.

'Do you want me to leave these notes for you to read, or have you had enough grief for now?' Zoe asked, not sure how I would respond.

'Please leave them, Zoe. I might find them helpful. In a way, it will take my mind off being here. The last time was when I'd overdosed on LSD, although completely unintentional.'

'I don't think you've ever told me that story, Julia.'

'One day I'll enlighten you,' I grimaced.

CHAPTER 30

Mr Saunders advised me to rest over the following week and not to overload myself with work, but after the three days in the hospital, I felt a lot stronger and able to cope with some of the lectures and tutorials. I had to register Troy's birth and death, and afterwards, I arranged for his funeral service to be held in the hospital chapel, attended by Clare and me. Poppy said she would be there in spirit. The tears came again when I saw his tiny coffin, and the priest gave comforting words about his soul. His grave was in the churchyard near the church where Poppy and Rich had had the christening, although I had to get permission and pay for the burial plot.

When I got home from the hospital, I took an airmail sheet and wrote to Mummy.

September 1970

Dearest Mummy

I have some devastating news. My baby boy, Troy, was stillborn on September 26th. The doctors were unsure of the cause but said it may have been stress, although there could be other reasons. None of the tests were conclusive. It was a very traumatic experience, but I suppose it was for the best.

Love Julia

Her reply took a week to arrive.

SHE TAKES HER CHANCES

Thornfield
October 1970

Dearest Julia

We are all deeply saddened to hear your news about Troy. As you say, it was probably for the best, but one day, dear Julia, you will have a lovely, healthy baby, and I will be a Granny for the second time. You are in our thoughts, and we hope you'll grow stronger to finish your degree.

Helen and I plan to come to Sydney to attend your graduation ceremony at the end of next year.

Much love
Mummy

There was nothing from Ian and no mention of him. He was probably relieved, in case I had followed his advice and lumbered him with a child born out of wedlock.

CHAPTER 31

One afternoon, before my final exams, I drove to a beach, wandered to a grassy area and found a shady spot. I leant against a tree trunk and read an unusual case study of a woman who was abusive towards her husband and made a note to do more research on the subject. I finished the chapter, packed the book away and walked down to the beach but in the distance, I saw a man who looked like Austin, walking along the edge of the water, holding his shoes. But when the man called to a large, brown dog, I knew it wasn't Austin. He wouldn't have a dog, although he did with Madeleine, and anyway I thought they weren't allowed on beaches. But oddly, when I returned to the grassy bank, I saw him walking towards me, his arm round the shoulders of a woman with a mane of dark, wavy hair. I shivered, although the day was hot and had to keep walking towards them with no idea what to say. They were animated, chatting together but when they drew level, he looked at me with no recognition. I was about to greet them, but his face was blank, and he resumed his conversation with the woman. When they had passed on their way to the beach, I sat in the shade to recover from the shock. 'What an actor!' I said out loud; to pretend I was a stranger, and be so rude, but that closed the Austin chapter for good.

SHE TAKES HER CHANCES

My car was like an oven. The steering wheel was too hot to touch, and the afternoon glare made my eyes water. I sat with the driver's door open, waiting for the slight breeze to cool the interior, and the wheel was safe to touch, but before I drove, I felt in my bag for a 20-cent coin for the bridge toll. I was always careful to stop the car at the right spot, as I'd seen drivers stay too far away, forcing the attendant to leave the booth, spewing out ugly words. The roads were busy and sitting in traffic with the sun on my face, I longed for an English downpour. I parked outside our house, under the shade of a tree, and blessed the thick walls and the coolness inside.

On the morning of the first final psychology exam paper, I woke up early, my stomach churning. I lay there, my mind blank, and couldn't believe how quickly the time had gone, and I'd reached the end of my degree course. The day's temperature was in the mid-30s, and I was beginning to get a headache. I could hardly eat breakfast, so I had to survive on a bowl of cereal.

I joined the queue of students, talking non-stop or pale and baggy-eyed, and hoped my brain would work once I'd sat down and read the questions. Zoe and I walked in together, but her desk was a few rows from mine, and we wished each other good luck. I sat on the hard seat, took out my pens, and when we had the command to start, I found there were subjects I could write about. After I'd finished a few minutes before the end, I looked at Zoe's head still bent, scribbling away, and the others, some gazing at the ceiling, fiddling with their hair or writing as if their lives depended on it. When the invigilator told us to stop writing, my neck ached, and I couldn't wait to get

CHAPTER 31

out of the hall to follow the mass of students and catch up with Zoe.

When we found a spot outside to analyse the paper, we decided it was not a good idea and agreed "What's done cannot be undone". Zoe went to find refreshments and I looked around at the crowd sitting or lying on the grass and knew I wouldn't miss this segment of my life. It was an experience, but I'd always been on the sidelines and not immersed in student life, except when a young psychology student had invited me to a party at a house she shared with three others. I often sat with her in tutorial groups and liked her friendly and open-minded nature. I hesitated, but when she said, 'You're welcome to bring someone,' I tried Zoe, but unsurprisingly she wasn't free. The little house was heaving with guests knocking back cans of lager and talking at the tops of their voices. One of the psychology boys got me a beer, and I leaned against the wall and pretended I was 18, in my flares, but we couldn't hold a sensible conversation as the noise level was too high.

'How are you liking the course?' he shouted.

'It's interesting.'

'Testing?'

'Challenging.'

'Scavenging?'

I gave up.

'Is there anything to eat? E- A -T?'

He returned with a bowl of crisps, and we crunched our way through them. I was about to go when he dragged me to a room at the back, and we jigged up and down to the Beatles, but when he disappeared to the men's and didn't return, I grabbed the opportunity to leave the party and pushed my way through the crowd to find the girl who'd invited me, but no one had seen her. I looked at my watch. It was eleven-thirty, and I'd be home by midnight, but halfway across the bridge, the car spluttered and died. I turned the key in the ignition, but it only made a clicking noise. I sat there woozy with lager and pondered what to do when flashing lights from a police car blinded me, and an officer approached, rotating his fist to wind down the window.

'What's the trouble, Miss?' he said with a loud drawl.

'My engine has died.'

'Can you open the bonnet?'

Without waiting for a reply, he leaned in and pressed a switch under the dashboard, exuding the smell of sweat and greasy chips and went to fetch the jump leads, but when I turned the key, there was a dull thud. I tried again, and the same thing happened, but on the third turn, the engine came alive.

'You'll need a new battery, but it'll get you home. Don't stop the car,' were his last words as he lumbered away.

I prayed the car would keep going, and I kept revving the engine when I stopped at traffic lights, but when I arrived home, Clare was about to call the police.

'What are you smiling about?' Zoe asked, walking towards me with two cans of fruit drink and sandwiches.

'Thinking about that student party.'

'What, when you broke down on the bridge?'

We moved into the shade to eat lunch and stretched out on the grass.

'One down, two more to go,' Zoe said, rolling onto her stomach.

CHAPTER 31

The following week, we had two more psychology exams with time to do more revision, but if we weren't up to speed then, we'd never be.

'How was the French exam?'

'No problem with the literature and oral, but the grammar was a struggle.'

'You don't need to worry, Julia. You'll do well.'

At least Zoe was positive, but she did well, particularly with a family to look after.

As we walked to the carpark, I was sad I wouldn't see so much of Zoe, but we vowed to keep in touch. I looked back at the library building bathed in the purple light from the Jacaranda trees, that spread their branches nearby. I recalled the number of times I'd sat there in silence to absorb the many fascinating strands of psychology. The two other psychology papers turned out to be hard-going, and I didn't want to see another exam paper for a long time. When I received my results, my fingers shook, and I stared at the envelope, daring myself to open it with a knife from the kitchen, I slowly slit it open, took out a sheet of paper and digested my results. My psychology marks were good enough to do an honours year, and I'd got a First in French. I put my head in my hands and sighed with relief.

Mum, Helen, and Ian had booked flights to Sydney for my graduation, although, according to Mum, Ian had another appointment and wouldn't attend the ceremony. But as far as I was concerned, he had planned to do something else on purpose because, on no account would he lower himself and be seen in a "third-rate university". Ian had booked a hotel in the centre of Sydney near the harbour, but Mummy and Helen were to share a room, while Ian had booked a separate room for himself. It sounded an odd arrangement, but perhaps they had a good reason for the decision. When I asked them later, Mum said Ian had some late business appointments and didn't want to disturb her when he returned. It seemed like an excuse to me, but Mum didn't seem to mind and was probably relieved.

Graduation day was long and hot. The graduates had to arrive early to rehearse and choose a gown and mortarboard. I tried on three before I found one that fitted. The first two were too big and swamped me, and when the fitter said I had it on back to front, I had to say it felt better the right way around. I wore a cream-coloured dress, visible under my gown, with cream shoes to match, and Zoe commented how learned I looked. She had also received good results, and we congratulated ourselves and nervously looked forward to collecting our certificates. Martin was my third guest who brought Mum and Helen to the ceremony in good time.

They were excited and chatted non-stop, but I couldn't see them in the packed hall. When I heard my name called to collect my certificates, I prayed I wouldn't trip or do anything silly, but I managed to walk the distance without stumbling or falling on my knees. After the speeches, we gathered outside and met Zoe, her husband, Clive, and their two boys. Zoe's parents had travelled from Brisbane, looking pleased and proud. Zoe's friend from Anthropology was also there with her husband and their 14-year-old daughter and we all enjoyed glasses of champagne and couldn't stop grinning at each other.

'I'm having a celebratory party for Julia and her friends, and you're all invited,' Martin said to the assembled group.

CHAPTER 31

'Do you intend to use your degrees?' Clive asked.

'I am hoping to be a psychotherapist, so the answer is yes,' I said.

'I'm proud of my daughters,' Mum said softly, and Helen touched her hand.

They stood together in summer suits and hats: Mum in pink and orange, and Helen in yellow, and they looked across at me, chatting with Zoe, and smiled. I was delighted that my family had made the journey, and their presence helped me forget the painful experience of last year's baby loss.

Everyone we expected came to Martin and Sasha's party, except Ian, who was invited but had another engagement. I suggested Mum and Helen take their swimming gear if they felt like going in the pool, although Mum was shy about showing her white, waxy legs to the crowd. Martin came out to set up the barbecue and looked expectantly at the men.

'Want any help, mate?' Kes called out to him.

'Thanks, Kes, come and set it alight.'

'Sorry, I'm late,' Dresden called, rushing to assist with the food.

'Hi Dresden, your help is very welcome,' Martin said.

I hadn't seen Dresden recently and thought he'd lost weight.

'How are you?' I asked when he put a piece of sizzling steak on my plate.

'Bearing up, Julia. Having diabetes keeps me on my toes.'

But later, after we'd eaten, he walked around looking disorientated and flopped onto a chair, his head resting on his chest.

'Dresden's having a hypo,' Dora said, and went to the kitchen for honey and a spoon.

'Sasha, where do you keep the honey?' she shouted.

'In the middle cupboard and spoons are in the drawer underneath,' she called to Dora. She gently raised Dresden's head and spooned the sweetness into his mouth until he sat upright to see Dora bending over him with a sticky spoon.

'What's going on?' he said.

'You were having a hypo,' Dora said.

'I feel fine,' he replied.

Some of us took our plates of food to a shaded area, but the Australians sat in the sun. Dora and Pam were under a parasol of pink and red stripes and sipped their glasses of punch, filled with summer fruits. Zoe's older boy was shy about getting his plate of food from the barbecue, unlike his younger brother, who didn't hesitate. Zoe went with him and returned with a plate of sausages, steak, a tossed green salad, and a glass of lemonade. Briony and Molly sat with Martin and Sasha and eyed the boys shyly while long-legged Leanne, who picked at a sausage, ignored them.

'What are your favourite subjects at school?' Helen asked Leanne, hoping she'd respond.

'Science and Maths. I want to do something in medicine.'

'Same as your dad. I'm a sister at a children's hospital,' Helen said, pleased they had a topic in common.

'Dad works at St Mary's Hospital,' Leanne said proudly.

'Anyone want a swim?' Sasha called, looking at the children, while she held a pile of towels for the pool house.

But in a moment of madness, Mother, Zoe, Helen, and I stripped off our outer layers, jumped in the pool, and moved through the water in a circle, singing Cliff Richard's song,

CHAPTER 31

"Congratulations and Celebrations". Sasha rushed inside and put on the record, and because the words weren't right, we made up our own. At the other end of the pool, the girls and boys were playing a team game with a ball, and we heard shouts of 'Your point' or 'No, that's ours', and the parents relaxed, glad they were getting on. Mum, Helen and I took off our wet bathers, wrapped towels around our shoulders and sat in the sun.

'That was fun,' Sasha said, referring to our dance in the pool.

'We're all on a high,' I said.

'How is your little boy, Helen,' Sasha asked, smiling at Helen.

'Laurence is two now and a treasure,' Helen said, looking the proud mother.

I was delighted for her and not at all resentful. Laurence was my nephew, after all, and I longed to meet him.

Helen wanted to see the unfinished Opera House so she could tell Steve about it, being an engineer. We booked our tour for eleven the following morning and wore comfortable shoes as there were 200 steps to climb overall. Our group consisted of ten people, including us, so it was easy to hear the guide as we toured the building. He showed us the concert hall, with its impressive, vaulted ceiling and cathedral-like ambience, the smaller playhouse and the drama theatre for opera, ballet and plays. However, the main stage was not big enough for a grand opera, although later it was to be modified and enlarged and I looked forward to attending a performance in any of the theatres when it was open. We wandered outside along the spacious walkways and passed the theatre entrances, the water always in our sights.

'It's impressive, but don't you get tired of the bright light and sharp colours?' Mummy said.

'Where are your sunglasses, Mum? You need to wear them all the time when it's sunny.'

'I dropped them, and the lens cracked.'

'I'll buy you another pair,' I said. We found a shop near the opera house, and she tried on good quality sunglasses that fitted her petite face perfectly. She wore them for the rest of the time in Australia, and they lasted for years afterwards.

Mum and Helen's winter blues changed into summer tans after spending time on different beaches. They preferred the ocean with the high waves but were happy to go to the smaller, more crowded harbour beaches. Helen loved swimming in the sea until her head was a blob on the horizon, while Mum sat on the sand and brought the scene alive with her paints.

'Come on in for a swim, Mum. Julia will look after our things,' said Helen, pulling Mum to her feet.

I watched them run together into the water and heard Mum's small scream when they jumped the waves and swam out into the deeper water. I had just picked up her half-finished picture, the sky a solid blue and the water turquoise in contrast to the yellow sand when Mum shrieked. I jumped up, dropped her pad and went to the water's edge.

'Something's bitten me,' she shouted.

'Maybe a jellyfish,' I said.

'Are they poisonous?' Mum screamed.

'Some are, but others are harmless and only sting.'

She sat on the sand and showed us a small mark on the ball of her foot, but I didn't think it looked serious. She said

CHAPTER 31

the heat was getting too much for her and looked forward to cooler temperatures.

'I love this weather,' Helen said, stretching out on the sand.

'Will you come back home to live?' Mother asked, peering at her foot.

'Who knows about the future? I'm here for a while.'

'Do you miss anything, apart from us?'

'Australia is a harsh country: the climate, landscape and the people. We're gentler, mostly, and I miss that. And the sense of history.'

I looked around at the tanned bodies lying on the sand and had a picture again of the children's peeling backs from sunburn, but this was the 1970s and the attitude to sun damage has changed since then. I got up, stripped off my sundress, and ran into the water, but when I looked towards the beach, Mum and Helen were talking, heads together. It was so wonderful they were able to be at my graduation even though Ian had decided not to attend, which was probably a good thing.

After we'd been to the beach, Ian invited us to have dinner with him at the hotel.

'Hello, ladies,' he said, greeting us in the large hotel foyer, busy with guests checking in and out. We followed him into the restaurant, and sat at a table with a white tablecloth, shiny cutlery, and empty wine glasses waiting to be filled.

'I apologise for not attending your graduation ceremony, Julia,' he said, after we'd ordered. 'I hope it was a success,' he added, with a smirk.

'She behaved impeccably, and we congratulated her on her excellent results,' Mum said.

'Here here,' Helen added, raising her glass.

Ian made a point of not replying and neatly cut a piece off his medium-rare steak and popped it into his mouth.

'Did you read in the paper about a painting stolen from a small gallery in the Eastern Suburbs?' Helen asked.

'No, I didn't. Was it by a well-known artist?' I replied.

'I can't remember the artist's name, but it was a serious theft.'

'When was it stolen? Didn't anyone see them?' Mum asked.

'Apparently, it was in the middle of the night. Somehow, the thieves gained access, but no one was there when it happened,' Ian contributed.

'I hope they find the thieves,' Mum said.

I changed the subject and asked Helen how Steve and Laurence were getting on.

'They are having a ball. It snowed overnight, and they managed to build a snowman, but it didn't last long and melted into a large puddle,' Helen said, making the shape with her hands.

After dinner, they went to their rooms while I caught a taxi home, although the driver had no idea where to go and kept looking at the map.

The evening before Mum and Helen's departure, Dora set up her projector to look through Helen's photos of us bulging out of bikinis, faces in mid-chat at Martin and Sasha's party, and ones of the graduation ceremony. There were a few slides of Zoe and me standing swamped in our robes and a blurred one of me collecting the certificates. I had taken some of Mum and Helen on a ferry, their hair blowing across their faces, and outside the opera house on the steps, with the sails in the background, and I would always treasure the memory of their Sydney visit.

CHAPTER 32

After the excitement of my graduation and the family visit, I had to find a job. A psychology lecturer rang me about a sub-editor's position in a psychology magazine. He gave the editor my details, and we arranged a day and time for an interview. The magazine office was on the second floor of a building on a busy street, and it took me a while to find the address. But when I did, I had to climb a flight of dark wooden stairs to a door that opened into an open-plan office, with three desks piled high with papers. The editor, Patrick, greeted me and shook my hand.

'Welcome, Miss Langley,' he said, showing me his office and pulling up a chair.

He had studied my curriculum vitae and congratulated me on my academic achievement.

'How did you get on with the copywriting job at Pericles Publishing?' he said, taking off his glasses.

'I enjoyed it. It was my only job while I lived in London, apart from sorting out files when the company first hired me.'

'Are you good with detail and have a keen eye for mistakes, Miss Langley?' he asked, putting on his glasses again.

'I pick out errors and anomalies without difficulty,' I replied.

I had also sent him Susan's reference and one from the lecturer who had told me about the job. After we had discussed pay and conditions of the job, he looked and smiled.

'Your references are excellent, and I would like to offer you the position. Do you want to go away and think about it?'

'No, I accept your offer,' I said, relieved.

'Would you like tea or coffee?'

My choice was black coffee and no sugar to make it simple. He gave our order to his secretary and continued the interview.

'Did you know Russell Bankes, who worked at Pericles for a while?'

I could feel a hot flush creeping up my face when I heard his name and remembered the beaded girl at the LSD party who mentioned him. I was on edge waiting to hear what Patrick had to say.

'We went out together for a while. How is Russell?'

'He's back in London as editor of a science magazine.'

'Does he live in London? When I knew Russell, he lived in Ealing.'

'I think he lives near Baker Street.'

'Is he married?' I asked, my voice sounding different and too loud.

'I don't think he's married. He has a partner, and Sammy, who is about ten or eleven. He went through an unsettled period after his father died, but he's more stable now.'

'I met Sammy when he was four,' I said, wanting the conversation to continue.

'Well, we have a mutual friend,' Patrick said, removing his glasses again.

CHAPTER 32

'Please give him my best wishes when you next have contact,' I said, feeling more relaxed.

It was nice we had a connection, but what a coincidence. People say it's a small world.

'So, Miss Langley, when can you start?'

On my first day, it was like déjà vu. My office was a small room overlooking a yard at the back and next door to Patrick's. I had to tidy the office as the previous employee had left a jumble of files in an untidy pile and as I sorted the mess into a coherent order, I remembered my first day at Pericles and the dusty, broken files and wondered if history was repeating itself. I was relieved to have found a job after graduation, as I had heard young graduates found it hard to get work.

One evening, a few weeks after starting work, I had a call late in the evening. I answered with a terse "Hello", hoping it was the wrong number, but when I heard Austin's voice, I stiffened, and when he suggested meeting, I made a firm excuse and said I was busy. He adopted his sexy voice and persisted with other suggestions, until finally, I agreed to meet him at the beach where I had seen him with the dark-haired woman. I didn't fancy dredging up the trauma I had suffered over a year ago, but if I saw him, he might let it rest. I recognised his back, sitting on a bench staring at two surfers riding the high rollers and skimming over the water with grace. I walked over to the seat and sat a few feet from him. He put out his hand to hold mine, but I took my hand away before he had a chance and when he tried again to take my hand, I picked up my bag and placed it on my lap.

'Julia, I was very sorry to receive your note about the stillbirth, and wished I could have been more support.'

I didn't look at him but straight ahead at the sunbathers and surfers and was sure he didn't mean a word of it.

'You weren't interested, Austin, when I first told you. You were extremely insulting, which was very upsetting.'

'I truly regret those words I said to you, Julia. It was insensitive of me, and I'm sorry.'

'I was very unwell in the hospital, and only Clare came to see me, and she was the one who took me there in the first place.'

I looked at him and realised I felt nothing, only a weariness and a desire to forget the whole experience.

'And thanks for being rude and ignoring me when I saw you here before, with the dark-haired woman. Who was she?' I had to ask.

'A friend of Madeleine's I have known for many years. And I'm sorry, Julia, I agree it was very rude, and I have no excuse. I'd like to take you out again, for dinner...' but before he'd finished the sentence, I stood, picked up my bag and walked quickly away, as I couldn't stand any more of him. He tried to catch up with me, but I managed to drive off, and chose the long way home, one he wouldn't expect me to use, and was relieved I didn't see him. It was all too late. I had worked through the trauma and put it to bed as far as I was able, and it had to stay that way.

More importantly, I wanted to concentrate on counselling. I stood in the room tucked away at the back of the house, and envisaged how it would look like a consulting room. It would be calm and relaxing for my clients and I would always have a vase of flowers on my desk, a jug of water and glasses on the coffee table. I bought a small sofa, and an easy chair for me, both in a beige fabric with

CHAPTER 32

a golden thread. I hung three of Mother's landscapes in a group on the wall behind the sofa, their vibrant colours brightening the room, reminding me of waves of pink and mauve that were spread over a pebbled beach we used to visit when I was a child. When I wasn't counselling, Clare and I could always use the room for relaxation. Clare was agreeable with my plan, and if she wanted to sit outside in the courtyard, while I had a client, she could use the side gate.

My first booking was on a Saturday afternoon, and I was apprehensive.

A woman in her early 40s knocked gently on the front door. She was well-built but not fat, with thick-lensed glasses and short, mid-brown, wavy hair. She followed me to the sunroom, and when we had settled, she coughed, and I smelt cigarette smoke. Her name was Hazel, born in the Isle of Man but had lived in Australia since she was a small child and was married with two young children, aged five and three. Her husband was a salesman for a Whole Foods Company and away most of the week, but when at home for the evening meal, nothing was right with Hazel. The vegetables were overcooked, the casserole was too dry, and once, he threw a bowl of ice cream across the kitchen, and it smashed into a globby mess, missing her head by inches. And as a child, she had had low self-esteem.

'Mum, I'll come with you when you take Benji for a walk,' Hazel said unexpectedly.

'Don't you have any friends to meet on a Saturday?' her mother replied.

'They're busy this weekend.'

'Come on, you need the exercise, Hazel, you're getting too fat.'

They met a passing acquaintance, and she stopped to talk to them.

'Hazel is growing into a nice-looking young lady,' the woman said kindly.

'Hmm, but she wears glasses,' her mother muttered.

'That doesn't matter,' the woman said, and walked on.

Hazel had joined a book club, and every month, each member chose a title to discuss when they met. When it was her turn, Hazel picked Diary of a Mad Housewife by Sue Kaufman, and it was a big hit among the group. Everyone enjoyed the banter and came up with their points of view, giving Hazel confidence she'd made a good choice until one picky woman interrupted her mid-sentence; 'You've missed the point there, Hazel.'

Hazel's face had turned red and mottled, and she couldn't wait to go home, but when she'd got in, she had an asthmatic attack, although as an adult, the attacks had been less frequent. She opened the front door and leaned against the wall, fighting for breath, until she got a glass of water from the kitchen and went upstairs to the bedroom. She checked on the sleeping children and lay on the bed while her husband was so engrossed in a television programme, he barely knew she had come in. We worked through her feelings of low self-esteem, and I booked her in for four weeks.

In a roundabout way, I had gleaned that she attended a pottery class, and some of her work was good enough to be shown in an exhibition.

'I suggest you continue with the book club, Hazel, as you seem to enjoy it despite the critical woman,

CHAPTER 32

whom you should ignore. You are skilled at pottery, so concentrate on that.'

I heard the phone ringing in the kitchen, but I wanted to finish the session before I answered it. Clare was out, so I had to let it ring, but it finally stopped. I made another appointment for Hazel the following week and looked forward to continuing her treatment.

The phone started ringing again, and I thought it must be urgent. My hand shook when I picked it up. It was Helen.

'Julia, I have some shocking news,' she said, her voice shaking.

My heart went cold thinking of all the things it could be, hoping someone close hadn't died or a tragic accident.

'What is it, Helen?'

'The police have arrested Ian.'

'Arrested? Where, at Thornfield?'

'No, in a hotel in London with two other men.'

'What's he done?'

He wasn't particularly appealing, but I wouldn't classify him as a criminal. I hoped he hadn't murdered or badly injured someone.

'Allegedly, he was part of a syndicate who stole valuable artworks.'

I wondered if he was connected to the art theft in Sydney when they came for my graduation.

'Oh my God, Helen. How is Mum coping?'

'She's very shocked as you can imagine but being very strong in the circumstances. Steve and I are staying at Thornfield with Laurence, and of course Grandpa is here now.'

'And the Matisse painting upstairs; was that stolen?'

'The police took it away, and the Jaguar.'

I thought the Jaguar was an extravagance as there was nothing wrong with his previous car.

It all went quiet, and I wondered if Helen was still on the line. I thought of all those alleged business meetings, Ian in Sydney, and the note Mum had found about the gallery.

'Are you still there, Helen?'

'Julia, could you get a few weeks' leave and come home? You do, in fact, owe us a visit.'

'I'll ask my boss and let you know.'

I put the phone down and sat stunned, hardly taking it in. I thought of the nagging doubts I'd had, and the suspicion about so many different things. I presumed it would be a prison sentence if he was found guilty. Poor Mummy, she must be shattered and what an idiot to get mixed up in art theft. He must earn a good salary – unless the company had fired him, and he pretended he was still working. I prepared what I would say to Patrick and hoped he'd allow me to take two weeks' leave. It wasn't long enough but it would be awkward to ask for more; but Patrick was understanding and said that, in the circumstances, he'd permit me, especially as I hadn't been home since living in Sydney.

Clare was as shocked as I was, especially as she'd met him and thought he was pleasant and friendly. Well, he would have been with her, a visitor to his house. She agreed I should go and be with my family during such a traumatic time, and she'd hold the fort and look after Lottie, our adopted cat that had belonged to Dora's disabled neighbour. At first, she was very nervous and wouldn't come out of the cat basket. But when we ignored her, she emerged, had a

CHAPTER 32

few bites of food, and soon became part of the household. We couldn't imagine life without her.

When I saw Dora in the local greengrocer buying nectarines and peaches, it was a good opportunity to tell her about Ian.

'I've had some bad news, Dora, about my stepfather, and I am going to England for two weeks.'

'I'm sorry to hear that, Julia,' but when I told her the reason, she was shocked and held my hand. Zoe was also horrified and sad that I'd had so much to contend with recently. I also had to tell Poppy, who recalled how suspicious we were seeing him in the Sydney gallery. Rich and Poppy were soon to leave Australia for New Mexico, where Rich was posted, but Poppy suggested we travel together to London and she could see her family, before their move to America.

CHAPTER 33

Our flight had landed late, at six in the morning, and Steve and Poppy's family must have got up in the middle of the night to meet us. On the journey to Thornfield, the countryside looked too neat and cultivated. The weak sun cast a blue shadow over the frosty farmland, and the fields, divided by hedgerows, looked like a patchwork quilt. The green of the new Spring leaves seemed too bright, and our brick houses were sturdy, in contrast to the sprawling Australian timber ones on bigger plots of land.

Steve had filled me in with as much detail as possible about the arrest. Ian had been walking through the hotel foyer, where they were staying, on his way to join two other men from the art theft syndicate for dinner. He was about to enter the restaurant when two police constables apprehended him and took him to a local police station. A business colleague had tempted him to join the syndicate with the ease of theft and the promise of wealth from the stolen paintings. As far as we knew, he had been a member for about three years. I listened in amazement.

'Will he get bail?' I asked, thinking he'd be home within the week.

CHAPTER 33

'No, apparently not. Ian will probably end up in prison, but the sentence will be shorter than for a crime like murder or armed robbery.'

'Heavens, Steve, what do you think? Are you surprised?'

'Although I didn't know him well, I am surprised. An architect would have a good salary, so perhaps the thrill of danger attracted him. It is ironic his wife's an artist.'

'In retrospect, I'm not surprised. On several occasions, I was suspicious of my stepfather, not that he was specifically involved with art theft, but that he was up to something dubious.'

'Such as?' Steve said as we neared Thornfield.

'It was seeing him in the Sydney gallery that made me suspicious. Although he had an explanation, it didn't seem authentic.'

'Of course, all that was after the event,' Steve said, which was partly true.

When Steve stopped outside Thornfield, I looked at the old, weathered stone walls and the ivy growing over one of the windows, too thick and overgrown, and had a flood of emotions I could hardly contain. It was like turning the clock back to a previous life and seeing everything with fresh eyes.

The house looked older, more rambling and unkempt than I remembered and needed a coat of paint. The cold air cut like a knife, a temperature you never had in Sydney. The frost was still on the ground, and two birds were pecking at a layer of ice in a stone birdbath. I wanted to give them some water, but my main objective was to go inside and warm up. I stood in the hall and smelled the remains of breakfast, heard the murmur of voices coming from the kitchen, and couldn't wait to see them all.

'How wonderful you're here, Julia,' Helen said, coming out of the kitchen and giving me a firm hug. 'How was the flight?'

'Long.'

'Are you hungry?'

'I could eat a little. We were delayed in Bangkok and herded into a small, crowded airport building, and they took away our passports.'

'You must be tired,' Helen said. She made me toast and homemade marmalade, Mum's creation. The marmalade tasted comforting and sweet, with pieces of peel to give it a homemade texture.

'How is Mum?'

'She's still in bed but dying to see you.'

We were interrupted by a little voice and running feet into the kitchen.

'Mummy, where are you?'

Laurence trotted in holding a toy London bus that he pushed along the floor, making engine noises.

'Here I am, darling, and this is Aunty Julia,' Helen said, pulling Laurie onto her lap.

'Aunty Woolia,' he said.

'It's Julia.'

'Woolia.'

We all laughed at the little boy with fair wavy hair.

'I am Aunty Woolia from now on,' I said.

Grandpa appeared in a tartan dressing gown, ready to have his breakfast of porridge and toast. His hair was still thick, with grey streaks intermingled with his brown hair. He looked young, in his mid-70s and stood tall and upright. I thanked him for supporting me during my university years and gave him a granddaughter's kiss.

CHAPTER 33

'Congratulations, Julia, on your achievement. It was money well spent.'

I climbed the stairs, passed the space where the Matisse painting had been, and wondered what had possessed this controlling man, who was influenced by a work colleague, to steal paintings.

Mummy looked as if she was about to get out of bed, but she settled down again when I went in.

'How are you, dear Mummy, after this huge shock?'

'It's like a bad dream and feels unreal. Everyone's support is helpful, and I'm taking it one day at a time.'

'We'll do everything we can to make it easier.'

Her skin was pale, and her eyes looked tired, surrounded by dark shadows. I offered to bring her breakfast, but Helen came in with her breakfast tray of a bowl of cereal and a large cup of coffee with hot milk.

'Do you think Ian will end up in prison?' Mummy asked, her mouth in a stern line.

'It's highly possible, Mum,' I said, thinking of Ian sharing a cell with a tattooed thug.

'If he is guilty of theft, he should receive a punishment,' Mummy said.

'Will you visit him if he goes to prison?'

'Yes, Julia, I will. I'm his wife, and I won't abandon him.'

I admired her strength and loyalty. Helen would offer to go with her, but she was strong enough to go alone.

'I knew you were suspicious of the note you found. Did you question Ian about the numerous meetings in London or his trip to Australia?' I asked, intrigued by her response.

'I tried to show an interest in his work, but when he never responded, I gave up and assumed he wanted to keep his home life separate.'

'What about Australia? Were you surprised he was travelling so far for just a week?'

'When I questioned it, he agreed it was a long way, but because it was necessary for business, he travelled the distance. If he doesn't want to elaborate, he won't.'

He could shut down like a clam, and any further discussion was impossible, and I sympathised with Mum's frustration. He was an aggravating man, stubborn and set in his ideas, and nothing would change him.

I went to my room to unpack and passed our portraits on the landing, hanging in the same place, and felt the eyes watching me as I walked past. I stood in my room, neat and unslept-in, and recalled lying there with flu before my move to London. Mum's paintings were still under the bed, but now that Ian wasn't there, they could emerge from their hiding place. I opened the wardrobe door, and one of Mummy's paintings fell out, an oil of a busy street in the snow, the road disturbed by walkers into grooves and troughs, the different colours reflected on the white ground. I picked up the picture and leaned it on an empty shelf to give the room more life. From the bedroom window, I watched a trio of blackbirds on the grass foraging for food, pecking at the hard ground to extract a worm for breakfast. The end of the garden merged with the empty farmland shrouded in the morning mist, and without anyone in sight, I could have been in a deserted land far from anywhere.

Helen and Steve had arranged Laurence's christening to coincide with my arrival. The short ceremony was at the

CHAPTER 33

end of the morning service at the local church. Chloe had agreed to be his godmother and Alex, a godfather, but the other godfather, Steve's friend, was unwell and unable to attend. I looked forward to seeing Alex again after many years, and there was much catching up to do. Helen had invited Babs, mainly for my benefit, and she had accepted, much to my delight. Ian's brother and wife, Nadine, were too appalled and shocked to venture anywhere.

We found seats at the back of the church near the font and Laurence sat quietly between Helen and Steve, not sure what was happening. When it was the sermon, the vicar's voice boomed around the church as he talked about the sanctity of marriage and how the influence of parenthood was of uppermost importance. At the end of the service, most of the congregation left the church except our small group, who gathered around the font. The vicar stood Laurence on a chair, and when Laurence felt the water on his forehead, he laughed with surprise; he thought it was a game and said, 'Do it again.' The vicar smiled and continued with the godparents' vows while I studied a stained-glass window of an angel praying, the hands pale and gentle in contrast to the deep blue background.

Mrs Tidey had Thornfield looking cosy with a roaring fire and a spread to die for. Laurence was excited and listened with big eyes when everyone talked about his funny comment in the church. It was wonderful to see Babs again, who was still in the Holland Park flat but had a different flatmate from the one who had taken my place. Her American boyfriend was still on the scene, and Babs had settled on even ground, which was a change for her.

Alex hugged me lovingly, and I was pleased to see him again. He said he was sorry and shocked about Ian's arrest. I asked him about New York.

'I still love it there, but it's always full-on. The city never sleeps.'

'So, you're there for a while, then?'

'Looks like it.'

He was silent for a few seconds and sipped his wine. I wanted to find out about his girlfriends, but he told me before I could ask.

'Not long ago, I split up from a girlfriend, but she was moving to California anyway, so in a way, it worked out.'

'What was she like?' I asked, intrigued.

'I think I have a photo in my wallet.' He went through a few sections until he pulled out a picture of a slim girl with long brown hair, laughing, standing on a bridge.

'She looks fun. Which bridge is she standing on?'

'Brooklyn Bridge. She had an apartment in Brooklyn, although I lived in Manhattan.'

I wondered why he kept her photo in his wallet, but maybe he hadn't found the time to take it out.

'What about you, Julia? Any men, or shouldn't I ask!'

I debated who to choose but opted for Jim and told him the story of his crash and how I wasn't ready for marriage. Austin was at the bottom of the list.

'Yeah, I understand. I'm not either, and this girlfriend was going down the marriage route.'

I was comforted that I wasn't the only one who thought like that.

'I'm sorry I didn't contact you again after we saw that film. I haven't an excuse but regretted it,' Alex said suddenly.

CHAPTER 33

'Don't worry, Alex, it was ages ago. I was also sorry, but I went to London afterwards, and my life changed.'

'What about you and Sydney? Are you settled there?' Alex asked, his dark eyebrows raised.

'I am fairly settled, Alex. I am setting up a counselling business and already have one client. One day, I might return for good.'

'Perhaps I'll give Sydney a go if I get fed up with New York.'

'You'll always be welcome,' I replied, wondering if it would ever happen.

I looked around the room, hoping everyone was happy and getting on. Mum and Dot were sitting together deep in conversation, Steve was chatting to Grandpa, and Helen had taken Laurence upstairs for a nap as he was getting fractious. Chloe, who had known Alex from way back, came to talk to us. She was a ward sister and nursed in a large London hospital, and had a long-term boyfriend who was a doctor, but they preferred their independent lives. Babs and I discussed the evening we had followed Ian and agreed we were suspicious back then, although it must have been his early days of art theft unless he'd been doing it for longer than we thought. Before everyone was about to leave, Helen came down the stairs with Laurence, rubbing his eyes, and he waved to the assembled group and said, 'Bye-bye,' and everyone laughed and waved at him.

On some nights, I read to Laurence before he went to sleep, but he always asked me to read his favourite book, The Very Hungry Caterpillar.

'Sit here, Aunty Woolia,' he said, patting the bed beside him.

I sat there, my legs under the blanket, and he'd open the book at his favourite page where the caterpillar had made a hole in the apple.

'Look, Aunty Woolia. My finger goes in the hole.'

He wiggled his finger, and I hoped it wouldn't get stuck. But after the christening, Laurence wanted his mother to read his bedside story, not Aunty Woolia, so I gracefully gave my Aunty hat to my sister for her Mummy hat.

Towards the end of my stay, Clare rang one morning, which was her evening, and I hoped she wasn't the bearer of bad news. But no, everything was going well, and a work colleague had asked her if she knew a good counsellor, and she'd recommended me.

'I'll contact the person when I return,' I said, pleased I had a prospective client. 'How's everything else, and Kes?'

'Kes is the best. All is going well there.'

I thought it would be ironic if she married him after all her critical comments about Australians, the country, and her plans to return home. Clare and Kes complemented each other, and you could see he was besotted with her, so I prepared myself for a wedding after I returned.

Ian was sentenced to five years in prison, although some of the thieves involved were incarcerated for longer. When Mother sat opposite Ian in the prison visitors' room, she took his hand and said he must live through the prison sentence to atone for his crime. He had lost weight, his face was grey with more lines, and his hair was lank and lifeless. He had lost a tooth, and the gap made him look dishevelled as if he had been sleeping rough. Sometimes Helen accompanied Mum to the prison, but she usually went alone. Ian was repentant, and whenever she visited,

CHAPTER 33

he asked for her forgiveness and said how stupid he was to get involved in such a hair-brained activity. I hoped these were not empty words, and once released, he'd return to his old ways.

I pushed two pairs of shoes into my suitcase, folded the thick dressing gown on top, and pressed hard to lock the case. It was starting to sleet, the small snowy drops intermingled with the rain and once again, I watched the blackbirds forage for their morning food. I straightened Mother's snow picture and visualised the contrasting beauty of the English and Australian scenes that hung in my internal gallery. I closed the bedroom door, picked up my case and slowly descended the stairs to go and find my waiting family.

Printed in Great Britain
by Amazon